Books by Rita Mae Brown & Sneaky Pie Brown

WISH YOU WERE HERE • REST IN PIECES • MURDER AT MONTICELLO
PAY DIRT • MURDER, SHE MEOWED • MURDER ON THE PROWL
CAT ON THE SCENT • SNEAKY PIE'S COOKBOOK FOR MYSTERY LOVERS
PAWING THROUGH THE PAST • CLAWS AND EFFECT • CATCH AS CAT CAN
THE TAIL OF THE TIP-OFF • WHISKER OF EVIL • CAT'S EYEWITNESS • SOUR PUSS
PUSS 'N CAHOOTS • THE PURRFECT MURDER • SANTA CLAWED
CAT OF THE CENTURY • HISS OF DEATH • THE BIG CAT NAP
SNEAKY PIE FOR PRESIDENT • THE LITTER OF THE LAW
NINE LIVES TO DIE • TAIL GAIT • TALL TAIL • A HISS BEFORE DYING
PROBABLE CLAWS • WHISKERS IN THE DARK • FURMIDABLE FOES
CLAWS FOR ALARM

Books by Rita Mae Brown featuring "Sister" Jane Arnold

OUTFOXED • HOTSPUR • FULL CRY • THE HUNT BALL
THE HOUNDS AND THE FURY • THE TELL-TALE HORSE • HOUNDED TO DEATH
FOX TRACKS • LET SLEEPING DOGS LIE • CRAZY LIKE A FOX • HOMEWARD HOUND
SCARLET FEVER • OUT OF HOUNDS

The Mags Rogers Books

MURDER UNLEASHED • A NOSE FOR JUSTICE

Books by Rita Mae Brown

ANIMAL MAGNETISM: MY LIFE WITH CREATURES GREAT AND SMALL
THE HAND THAT CRADLES THE ROCK • SONGS TO A HANDSOME WOMAN
THE PLAIN BROWN RAPPER • RUBYFRUIT JUNGLE • IN HER DAY
SIX OF ONE • SOUTHERN DISCOMFORT • SUDDEN DEATH • HIGH HEARTS
STARTED FROM SCRATCH: A DIFFERENT KIND OF WRITER'S MANUAL
BINGO • VENUS ENVY • DOLLEY: A NOVEL OF DOLLEY MADISON IN LOVE AND WAR
RIDING SHOTGUN • RITA WILL: MEMOIR OF A LITERARY RABBLE-ROUSER

Claws for Alarm

Claws for Alarm

RITA MAE BROWN &
SNEAKY PIE BROWN

Illustrated by Michael Gellatly

BANTAM BOOKS
NEW YORK

Claws for Alarm is a work of fiction. Names, characters, places, and incidents are the products of the author's imagination or are used fictitiously. Any resemblance to actual events, locales, or persons, living or dead, is entirely coincidental.

Published in the United States by Bantam Books, an imprint of Random House, a division of Penguin Random House LLC, New York.

BANTAM BOOKS and the HOUSE colophon are registered trademarks of Penguin Random House LLC.

LIBRARY OF CONGRESS CATALOGING-IN-PUBLICATION DATA
Names: Brown, Rita Mae, author. | Brown, Sneaky Pie, author. | Gellatly, Michael, illustrator.
Title: Claws for alarm / Rita Mae Brown, Sneaky Pie Brown; illustrated by Michael Gellatly.
Description: First edition. | New York: Bantam Dell, [2021] | Series: Mrs. Murphy mystery; 30.
Identifiers: LCCN 2021016177 (print) | LCCN 2021016178 (ebook) | ISBN 9780593130094 (hardcover) | ISBN 9780593130100 (ebook)
Subjects: GSAFD: Mystery fiction.
Classification: LCC PS3552.R698 C59 2021 (print) | LCC PS3552.R698 (ebook) | DDC 813/.54—dc23
LC record available at https://lccn.loc.gov/2021016177
LC ebook record available at https://lccn.loc.gov/2021016178

Printed in the United States of America on acid-free paper

randomhousebooks.com

2 4 6 8 9 7 5 3 1

First Edition

Book design by Diane Hobbing

With remembered laughter
for
Anne Seaton
June 14, 1971–April 23, 2021

CAST OF CHARACTERS

THE PRESENT

Mary Minor Haristeen, "Harry" was the postmistress of Crozet right out of Smith College. As times changed and a big new post office was built, new rules came, too, such as she couldn't bring her animals to work, so she retreated to the farm she inherited from her parents. Born and raised in Crozet, she knows everyone and vice versa. She is now forty-five, although one could argue whether maturity has caught up with her.

Pharamond Haristeen, DVM, "Fair" is an equine vet specializing in reproduction. He and Harry have known each other all their lives. They married shortly after she graduated from Smith and he was in vet school at Auburn. He generally understands his wife better than she understands herself.

Susan Tucker is Harry's best friend from cradle days. They might as well be sisters and can sometimes pluck each other's last nerve as only a sister can. Susan bred Harry's adored corgi. Her husband, Ned, is the district's delegate to the General Assembly's House of Delegates, the lower house.

Nancy Parsons owns Country House Antiques in the Keswick/Cismont area of Albemarle County. Formerly president and CEO of the National Sporting Library, her management skills are formidable. Now, years later, her aesthetic abilities shine at the antiques store, a magnet for buyers looking for unique items at reasonable prices.

Candida Ballard Perez possesses buoyant energy and an interest in people. The only reason people know she is ninety is that most residents of Albemarle County grew up with her. Lone Pine, her lush estate, founded in the mid-seventeenth century, reflects her exquisite taste, her passion for protecting the family papers, almost four hundred years of same.

Constance O'Donnell is Candida's daughter. In her early sixties she, too, possesses quiet taste. Jealous of her brother, she is generally liked by others but is in her mother's shadow. Then again, everyone is in her mother's shadow.

Ballard Perez at sixty-four is a few years older than his sister and a beloved son to a doting mother. Most people who imbibed as much alcohol or drugs as he did have been rock stars. Ballard was notorious yet basically a decent, nice man. Five stays in hideously expensive rehab clinics finally took hold. He has been clean for seven years.

Jerry Showalter, years back, held a high position at the University of Virginia library, back when John Casteen was an enlightened president of same. As the university changed bit by bit, Jerry struck out on his own to locate and sell valuable old books. Few are as well qualified as he, partly because along with his background he is alert, hardworking, and sparkling company.

Deputy Cynthia Cooper is Harry's neighbor, as she rents the adjoining farm. Law enforcement is a career she is made for, being meticulous, shrewd, and highly observant. She works closely with the sheriff, Rick Shaw, adores Harry, and all too often has to extricate her neighbor out of scrapes. Harry returns the favor by helping Coop with her garden. It probably isn't an equal exchange but they are fine with it.

Tazio Chappers is an architect in her late thirties, born and raised in St. Louis. Being educated at Washington University, she received an excellent education, winding up in Crozet on a fluke. Just one of those things, as Cole Porter's song lets us know. Warned off a job at an architectural firm by many people back in Missouri, due to her being half black and half Italian, she came to Virginia, anyway. No one can accuse her of being a chicken. Now owner of her own firm, getting big jobs, she is happy, married for two years, and part of the community. She is also terrifically good-looking, which never hurts.

Big Mim Sanburne, an outstanding horsewoman born to an avalanche of money, has Tazio's husband, Paul, running her stables. She is called the Queen of Crozet and while not much in evidence in this book, she'll be a bigger part of others. Sooner or later, Big Mim (who is tiny) gets her way.

THE EIGHTEENTH CENTURY

Cloverfields

Ewing Garth owns this vast estate on the north side of the old road to Wayland's Crossing (later named Crozet). Worldly, intelligent, he has the courage of his convictions, risking everything he owned during the Revolutionary War.

Catherine Schuyler is Ewing's oldest daughter at twenty-five. She married a hero of Yorktown, John Schuyler. He is modest, reliable, not well educated, but he can think quickly during a crisis. He was born for battle, having natural leadership abilities. He worships his gorgeous wife and she has helped him modify his hardscrabble Massachusetts ways to Virginia's sometimes comical sense of elegance. Virginia is as close to the Cotswolds as an American can come. A terrific horsewoman, Catherine works with her father, soaking up much of what he knows about business, people, life.

John Schuyler has been put in charge of developing the Virginia militia, as we still don't have a standing army but we do have enemies.

Rachel, younger than Catherine by two years, is also beautiful but it's a warm, very womanly beauty. Catherine focuses on facts, profit, getting the job done. Rachel focuses on easing people's way, caring for them, and struggling with the injustices of the day. She has taken in as her own a little girl, now six, Marcia, who is the product of a brutal neighbor's inflicting himself on the best-looking slave woman on his plantation. He was killed. The unwilling paramour and her true love blamed. Ultimately she died in hiding, with Rachel having full knowledge of all this, desperately trying to save the woman. Bettina and Bumbee really covered the escaped slave's tracks. She and Catherine concocted a story about Marcia's beginnings that used one whopping lie to cover another. She is years ahead of her time in many ways, although accepting of a woman's place.

Charles West is Rachel's husband. John Schuyler captured him at the Battle of Saratoga and Charles was marched to the prisoner-of-war camp on land now abutting Cloverfields. When the war finally ended, Ewing managed to buy much of the POW camp as well as other farms. Having marched through the new land from New York State down to Virginia he realized how rich the land was, how mighty the rivers, and how many. Although the younger son of a baron he had no desire to go back to that life, providing he lived. He did. He stayed and fell in love with Rachel. Following his heart he also became an architect. He is a supremely happy man and a terrifically well-educated one.

Yancy Grant, like Ewing, risked his goods to help finance Virginia's part of the war. His knee was shattered in a duel. He limps, needs a cane, but manages. He, like Garth, is in his middle fifties. He never married, whereas Ewing did, losing his wife ten years back. Yancy, like Catherine, loves horses but, now living in reduced circumstances, he has given her his best horse, Black Knight. He had to stop drinking because it was affecting him in bad ways. He did it and has earned back much of the respect he lost thanks to the bottle.

THE SLAVES

Bettina is the head cook, a woman so creative with dishes that she is known throughout the former colony. She takes no guff from anyone. She was close to Isabelle, Ewing's wife, nursing the woman on her deathbed. Isabelle asked Bettina to look after her two girls, which Bettina did. Now that the girls are grown, have families of their own, she is making a new life for herself emotionally. Bettina misses nothing.

Bumbee runs the weaving cabin. She works at a huge loom and there is a smaller one for her assistants. All intensely creative like her, slave or free. She has a wonderful way about her, plus the patterns she creates, the clothing, dazzles the women. The men are happy with their shirts, no surprise. Her husband, Mr. Percy, is flagrantly unfaithful, bringing her misery, anger, confusion, for she still has a strong draw to him. She's taken to living in the large weaving cabin, while he lives in their cabin. She is approaching middle age, feeling old, but some of that is due to heartache, a heartache women have known for centuries.

Jeddie works with Catherine at the stable. A natural rider with a good eye, he works horses daily and Catherine is teaching him about bloodlines, as horses are being imported from England, a new type called blooded horses (today's Thoroughbreds). He is ambitious, decent, and loves horses more than people. He is nineteen.

Barker O drives the carriage horses as well as being in charge of all carriages. There are different types of conveyances for different jobs, the most splendid being the coach-in-four. He handles it with such ease it looks as though he is doing nothing. He is in hot competition with DoRe at Big Rawly; it's a good competition, as each brings out the best in the other.

Tulli is eleven, Jeddie's shadow. He is such a small fellow. Jeddie gives him jobs, as does Catherine. Tulli often rides with Catherine's son, about four, on Sweet Potato, JohnJohn's pony. Tulli is pretty good and will do anything to shine. His father died in a farm accident when Tulli was five. His mother, Georgia, has ever since been distracted and sad, so everyone takes Tulli under their wing. He is an uncommonly sweet child.

Serena helps Bettina in the kitchen. She does good work, likes to cook, but lacks the creativity of Bettina. Then again, most do.

Mr. Percy, good-looking, smooth-talking, has a way with plants. He oversees the Cloverfields gardens and Ewing allows him to take commissions to design other people's gardens, plant them. So Mr. Percy gets to move around a bit and he has a wandering eye. His body wanders with it.

BIG RAWLY

Maureen Selisse Holloway has a refined cruelty toward anyone who crosses her. Born in the Caribbean to a banker father and educated in France, she has no time for ideas of modern government. She is fine living in the New World but she thinks the politicians naïve. Money talks always and ever. In Maureen's case it whispers, but everyone knows she is one of the richest women in this new nation. And she wants more. She believes in a strict caste system. As far as she's concerned, the Bible countenances slavery and so will she.

Jeffrey Holloway is Maureen's much younger second husband; an Apollo, he is so handsome. The son of a cabinetmaker and that was his profession when he met the new widow. She took one look at this divine creature and determined to have him. Strange as it may sound, he did learn to love her, being dazzled by her education, her worldliness. She built him an enormous work shed where he could design and build coach-in-fours. The results are slowly being seen as far north as rich, rich Philadelphia. He is now swamped with orders and happy, although he tries to mollify Maureen's more savage impulses.

DoRe is the coachman, Barker O's rival. He limps from a long-ago horse accident, tries out each new carriage Jeffrey builds, and is invaluable to the operation. He has found love, being widowed years back, with Bettina, herself having lost a husband. Maureen has agreed to the marriage but she will get her pound of flesh. Jeffrey is doing his best to protect DoRe.

Sulli ran off with William, a self-centered young man who promised wealth, freedom, fabulous clothing. He beat her but did manage to make it to Royal Oak, a large farm in Maryland. So they were free, but they were caught. No one on Royal Oak was part of this, but caught they were, and stolen back, delivered to Maureen, where life is hell. Sulli just turned seventeen.

William, hamstrung during the drive back as he tried to escape, is a beaten creature. He is chained every night and will stay chained until Maureen's revenge is satisfied or she's distracted by something else. He lied, he cheated, he stole, he jeopardized every slave at Big Rawly. He has not one friend but many enemies, including Sulli, who has sworn to herself to kill him someday. William may or may not have learned from what he did to Sulli and how he made life even worse for those at Big Rawly after he ran away. There's no arrogance left and no hope.

Toby Tips works with Jeffrey as his second-in-command. He knows this business. Most importantly he stays clear of the Missus. She'll have people flogged for the slightest offense. Jeffrey has stopped that, he thinks, but if he goes off the farm she has someone battered who she feels is no good.

Martin was a slave catcher but he and his partner have good work now delivering the sturdy work wagons that Jeffrey is building. They deliver goods for other people, too. The money is pretty good, with much less risk.

Shank is Martin's partner. They do their job, are happy to take a bit of money or goods under the table. Neither man has much fear. Violence is part of life and they have little regard for life other than their own.

Elizabetta is Maureen's lady's maid. She paid dearly when William and Sulli ran off, for she was in charge that day. She hates those two with a white hot passion. However, she hates Maureen even more. She covers it well.

THE ANIMALS

The Present

Mrs. Murphy is Harry's tiger cat. She is bright, does her chores, keeps the mice at bay when need be. Harry talks to her but not baby talk. Mrs. Murphy just won't have it.

Pewter is fat, gray, and vain, oh so vain. She irritates Tucker, the corgi. She takes credit for everyone else's work. However, in a pinch the naughty girl does come through. She's also quite bright.

Tucker, the corgi bred by Susan Tucker, runs around everyone. She's fast, loves to greet every person once she has checked them out, and particularly likes to herd the horses. The horses are good sports about it, which is a good thing. Tucker is brave and she loves Harry totally.

Pirate is a not-yet-fully-grown Irish wolfhound who landed in Harry's lap as a puppy when his owner died. Huge, able to cover so much ground, he can be dominated by Pewter sometimes. Tucker has to give him pep talks. Like Tucker, Pirate has great courage, loves being part of the family. He is trying to understand people. The others help. A sweet, sweet animal.

The horses, the big owl in the barn, and the possum aren't in the forefront in this book but they are around and will be their usual selves in future. This also applies to the barn mice, who have a really good deal at the farm.

THE ANIMALS

The Past

Piglet, a corgi, traveled through the war and the POW camp with Charles. He's slowing down, sleeps most of the time.

Reynaldo is a blooded stallion who is proving himself in the breeding shed, along with his half brother, Crown Prince. Other than Catherine, only Jeddie can ride these two.

Black Knight is Yancy Grant's horse, stolen by William. After an arduous experience and injury, he was found and brought back to Yancy, who asked Catherine to care for him. She has and he, too, is proving himself in the breeding shed. He'll never run again, of course, but he gets around pretty good.

Penny is a kind mare that Catherine bought from Maureen for her father. Maureen felt Penny not fancy enough for her. She lost a really good horse thanks to her vanity.

Miss Renata is John's horse. She's 17 hands. He is a tall, powerfully built man and she can carry him. She's a good girl. John can ride but he's not really a horseman. Catherine takes care of all of that.

Sweet Potato is a bullheaded pony. Tulli is in charge of him. He's learning, but then so is Sweet Potato.

Claws for Alarm

1

September 20, 2019

Friday

Fairy skirts twirled through the air. Glossy white, tiny seeds dispersed into seven-mile-per-hour winds. Milkweed balls, equally as glossy, floated along with the fairy skirts, which some people call Devil's dandruff. All living creatures—whether two-legged, four-legged, or plant—were responding to the loss of light, the cooler night temperatures.

Pharamond Haristeen, DVM, all six feet four inches of him, stood in the aisle of Big Mim Sanburne's perfect brick stable. He looked out the opened doors to watch the parade of skirts, the tiny ballerinas filling the air. The walkway to the stable gleamed white from all the fairies that had fallen.

Returning to Loulou, a large gray mare, now in her late teens, he knelt down, ran his hands over her swollen hind leg.

Big Mim, standing behind him as Paul, her stable manager, held her halter, mentioned, "Those fang marks are so noticeable."

"Gray horses are harder to keep clean but it is easier to see in a situation like this." He gingerly, gently touched her. "Good girl."

"Is she drugged?" asked Tucker, Fair's corgi, sitting properly to the side of the aisle.

Fair took his two dogs with him today, figuring it was like take-your-daughter-to-work day. Tucker was the female; the Irish wolfhound, Pirate, just turning one year old, was male. Pirate sat watching everything. He was trying to learn the business.

"Paul, you found her?"

The young man, married to Tazio Chappers, one of Fair's wife's best friends, nodded. "She wasn't moving well so I walked out and saw the swollen leg plus the marks. Had that snake struck a dog, the animal would be dead."

"What an awful thing to say," the corgi grumbled, then peered more closely at Loulou. *"She's not drugged."*

"How can you tell?" The young wolfhound was curious.

"A horse hangs her head. Nods off. I should have noticed right away." Tucker puffed out her chest. *"I've been working with Daddy for years. You wouldn't believe what I've seen."*

Fair had put his bag on a tack trunk. His dually truck was outfitted with everything. Truly a moving equine hospital, it included the latest high-tech equipment and rows of meds costing as much money as human medication, and for some, even more. He reached for bandages, set them on the tack trunk. Pulled out a needle, a small bottle of Gentocin, another one of Excede antibiotic/MI, and also dexamethasone.

Patting Loulou's neck, he then pinched some skin and injected the Gentocin. "One down."

He filled the Excede and repeated the process. "Two down!"

One more needle. "Okay, girl, good girl."

In went the dexamethasone.

"How long before the swelling subsides?" Big Mim spoke again.

"You should notice tomorrow. Given her excellent state of health,

I think the leg will be normal size in three or four days but it might still be ouchy. Those fangs bit deep."

"Betadine?" Paul asked about an antiseptic.

"Yeah. We cleaned her up pretty good but I'd unwrap her, wash it each day, then wrap up again. I'm leaving you some chlorhexidine wipes, too." Fair knelt down to wrap her leg, not tight but not loose, either.

The last thing one wants is for a wrap to unravel.

Uncrossing her arms, Big Mim, now in her early eighties, stepped up to the beloved mare and ran her hand over a well-muscled hip. "Best hunt horse I ever had."

"Icecapade blood." Fair knowingly cited her illustrious bloodline. "So many went to the track. She was lucky to come here and enjoy a different kind of life."

"Jump the moon." Big Mim smiled broadly.

Fair handed Paul a bottle of Excede, an antibiotic, quick working. "Put her in her stall. Keep her quiet. No point in helping the poison spread, but I think you got her in time. It had to be a copperhead. They're everywhere right now. Getting ready for winter."

Paul slid the stall door closed, as Big Mim had replaced the old Dutch doors with one-piece doors looking almost like chain link. This allowed good airflow, vital in summers. In winter you closed up the barn and perhaps threw an extra blanket on. It was summers that wore you and the horses out. He walked back to Fair, who was writing in his notebook.

Tearing the page off he handed it to Paul. "Okay. In four days give one dose of the Excede and then four days later another. Fifteen milliliters. Do you have enough needles?"

"We're good," Paul replied.

"Hand walk her in the barn. When the swelling is completely down, turn her out in a small paddock. My caveat is, if she stocks up, turn her out sooner but keep an eye on her. No equine hijinks." He laughed. "My memory of Loulou is she expressed a lot of personality."

The three of them laughed, for the mare, a happy creature, knew how to untie her lead rope if not tied tightly. She would visit other horse trailers if at a hunt meet. Should the food look better than what she was eating, she'd try to stick her head in that bucket. Loulou was not above stealing another horse's blanket if folded or on the wheel well. Cowboy hats were a big favorite, too. Big Mim forked over cash for many a new cowboy hat.

"Thank you for getting here so quickly. I know how busy you can be." Big Mim smiled at Fair, whom she had known all his life.

Teased as the Queen of Crozet, Big Mim automatically took charge. Her husband had been elected mayor of the tiny town so often, he had the office for life. Their daughter, Little Mim, languished in the wings, but now she had a child soon ready for kindergarten so she discovered the labor of parenting. If nothing else, she had never answered so many "Why?" questions in her life, nor had her husband.

"So far it's been a light Friday. Anyone else need a look?"

"No. Thank heaven." Paul smiled.

Fair glanced out the open barn doors. "Have you ever seen so many milkweeds? It's a blizzard."

"Good for the monarch butterflies." Big Mim cared about butterflies and much else.

"That it is. Well, let me be on my way. Loulou should be fine. If not, you know where I am. Got to keep the old girl going."

Picking up his bag, he walked into the "snow"storm, head soon white from the fallout.

"*Tickles.*" Pirate sneezed.

"*Does.*" Tucker agreed as a milkweed landed on her black wet nose.

Opening the passenger door, Fair slid his bag onto the floor then opened the back door for Pirate while he lifted up Tucker. He loathed the size of the double-door truck but he could stash more in it, plus he had a built-in box covering most of the bed, which he could lock. That contained the X-ray machine, the ultrasound equipment, rows of drugs, whatever he needed.

"Good kids." He shut the doors, climbing in front.

Driving down Big Mim's long driveway, he marveled as he always did at the beauty of her estate. Stopping at the end he picked up his cell.

"Hey."

"Hey back at you. How was Loulou?" his wife, Harriet Haristeen, called "Harry," asked.

"Same as always but that copperhead nailed her. She'll be fine. Big Mim watched. She loves that horse. The girls there yet?"

He referred to Harry's best friends, Susan Tucker, who had bred Tucker, the corgi, and Tazio Chappers, an architect who had married Paul two years ago. The restoration of the old so-called colored schoolhouse from the late nineteenth century onward was an important project for all of them. The term *colored* causing no end of trouble, which lasted to this day. "The girls," as they thought of themselves, were determined to use the school to help schoolchildren learn about the old days by spending time in the old space.

"Coming down the driveway now."

"If I don't get an emergency call, I should be home by three."

"That would be a miracle."

"On my way to Ben Wagner. He's finally set up his clinic and wants me to make suggestions. I give any young vet credit who goes out on his or her own. The cost alone could give you a heart attack."

"How old do you think he is?"

"Ben? Oh, maybe late thirties, mid-thirties. About the same age as Tazio and Paul. Well, see you in a few hours, I hope. How about we both clean up and go out to dinner?"

"Sounds wonderful." She paused. "Susan, come on in. What have you got?"

"A disgustingly rich apple pie," Susan answered as she walked through the door followed by Tazio.

"See you later, honey."

"Bye." He clicked off, turned right, drove through Crozet toward White Hall, and then turned left next to a vineyard where fences

gleamed, for Ben had them newly painted; his new buildings and barn, also freshly painted, maybe a quarter of a mile away, looked terrific.

Tucker, face pressed to the window, observed every single thing. Pirate, on the other side, also watched.

"Keeping fences painted is a full-time job." The corgi admired the work.

"It's pretty." Pirate saw an osprey fly overhead, so some form of water had to be nearby. *"Why aren't there more stone fences?"*

"Cost. New England, poor soil, had stones, so they made fences out of them. Virginia had better soil, according to Mom, so wooden fences or snake fences."

"What are snake fences?"

"Like split rails but they're resting on one another at a running angle, so snake fencing. It's pretty." Tucker sniffed the air. *"And you don't have to paint them."*

"Why do humans paint stuff, anyway?" the giant dog wondered.

"Pirate, they even paint their faces."

"No." Pirate was shocked.

"No kidding. When you see a woman with red lips or super-smooth skin all the same shade. Paint. They dye their eyelashes. You wouldn't believe it."

"Not Mom."

Tucker scratched her large ear. *"Well, if she's going out, she whips on mascara, she throws on a little lipstick. She fusses over her hair. She's not crazy about it, but still."*

"Do men do that?"

A long pause followed that, then Tucker answered diplomatically. *"Some do, but you can usually tell."*

"This is confusing." The Irish wolfhound knew he had a lot to learn.

Fair parked in the driveway, cut the motor. Looking around for a moment he thought Ben's layout sensible, especially considering how winter some years can be snowy. The young vet could walk from the office to the layup barn without getting blown to bits, for he had built a covered walkway. Not cheap. A good farm road behind the layup barn ran over a low ridge to a state tertiary road, rarely used.

Getting out, he opened the back door and the two dogs jumped out. Even Tucker, who could get out a lot easier than she could get in.

"Manners." Fair sternly spoke to his two friends.

"Yes, Sir." Tucker looked up with large brown eyes brimming with the promise of good manners.

"I mean it." Fair opened the door. "Yo."

No answer.

The two dogs stood transfixed.

"Blood," Tucker announced.

"Hey, hey, you two, where are you going?" Fair called as they scooted away from him down the super-clean hallway.

Tucker found the source of the smell first, Pirate bumping into her behind. *"Dad! Dad!"*

Irritated as he might be, Fair recognized the universal distress bark. He hurried down the hall to an open door. Ben Wagner, faceup, lay on the floor.

Fair knelt down, took his pulse. There was none.

He was careful not to touch the body except for taking the pulse. "My God."

"Fresh blood," Pirate noted.

Tucker stuck her nose on Ben's outstretched hand. *"Still warm."*

Fair rose, ran back down the hall to the front receiving desk. Ben had not had time to hire a secretary/receptionist yet, nor to furnish his receiving room. He picked up the phone, dialed 911. Given he had the receiver to his ear, his back to the windows, he did not hear a car drive away from the layup barn in the back. The dogs did. They knew someone drove over the ridge away from the main road. It could only be someone who knew the farm road.

The 911 operator picked up the phone.

"Get Sheriff Shaw down here to Ben Wagner's new clinic immediately. He's been shot. I'll wait, of course."

Fair hung up the phone then walked to a chair, where he sank down. The dogs sat with him, on the floor.

Tucker leaned into Pirate. *"He couldn't hear the tires."*

Within fifteen minutes the siren screamed out on the road. The sheriff's office and county jail were maybe twelve miles away.

Sheriff Shaw, first through the door, looked at Fair, whom he had known for years. Fair got up, walked down the hall. Said not a word.

The ambulance team followed.

Sheriff Shaw had seen his share of corpses.

"No pulse," Fair simply said.

Shaw studied the bullet wound, a clean shot right through the heart. He motioned for his investigative unit then turned to Fair.

"This place is immaculate."

"It is. The dogs found him."

Sheriff Shaw glanced down at the two solemn animals.

"Fair, walk through the back rooms with me." The sheriff pulled out his pistol to lead the way.

Fair tried to open one of the hall doors. "Locked."

A smudge mark was on the bottom as though someone had kicked it.

"Darrel, go up front and see if you can find keys anywhere," the sheriff ordered a young officer.

Darrel returned in a few minutes with a fistful of keys. Sheriff Shaw started trying them, was finally rewarded with a satisfying click.

Pulling on plastic gloves, he turned on the lights. "Should have thought of that when I put the key in the lock."

Fair walked in slowly, examining each shelf. "Someone will have to go through his inventory on his computer. All is neat. Vet drugs can be as desirable as human drugs. Without his inventory, we don't know if drugs have been taken."

Sheriff Shaw nodded in agreement. The team scoured Ben's truck; the X-ray equipment was there, his computer was untouched. An expensive pair of Leica binoculars rested next to the driver's seat.

Using the keys, they unlocked the door across the hall, which also had a kick mark. Clean lab coats hung on hangers, along with one winter jacket. Frames with prints leaned against the wall, under the coats.

Fair waited, then Sheriff Shaw told him to go on. He'd find him if he needed him.

The sheriff did say, "If this is a robbery, they knew exactly what they wanted and where to look."

"The X-ray machine alone could bring five digits if new." Fair found it odd that such expensive equipment was left untouched.

"Any thoughts on who could have done this?"

Fair sighed. "No. He was a young man, ambitious, on the way up."

2

September 21, 2019

Saturday

"Would any of these drugs bring a price on the black market?" Deputy Cynthia Cooper, the Haristeens' neighbor, asked.

Fair, standing in the unlocked medical supply room, replied, "Sure, but not to the financial level of ketamine. ACE, used all the time in barns, can zone you out. Would it do the same to a human? It would, but ketamine caught on. In a sense ACE is more diffuse."

Harry popped her head into the supply room, for she had been going through the tack room at Ben's layup stable. "Not much there. New blankets." She looked at the rows of carefully rolled bandages, some in plastic wraps.

A row of medicines, a low strip of wood facing the shelf so bottles could not easily be knocked over, seemed to be precisely organized.

A small section of the large room was used for office supplies: papers, ink cartridges, envelopes.

"Honey, Coop was curious why these other drugs were not stolen. They can all affect human behavior."

She stepped inside while the two cats and two dogs wandered into the main building from the layup barn, where all had searched for mice. Not a one. The place was too new for mice families.

"Why are you asking me?" She looked up at her husband.

"Because I'm a vet and I'll get technical. You can explain this in plain English."

Harry looked over at Cooper. "Well, I can try. Any drug that's a depressant can be used for date rape, I guess, but Special K can work in five to fifteen minutes if it's snorted."

Cooper ran her forefinger over her lips. "The girl, I'm assuming it's a young woman, would think it was cocaine? Would be in a party mood to begin with?"

"More or less, if the drug was snorted. If it had been slipped in a drink, it might take a half hour to work. She wouldn't know, of course. If the drug was slipped into her drink, she was blindsided."

Cooper noticed bright eyes looking into the supply room. "Your posse is here."

"You all stay outside," Harry ordered.

No one moved but the animals were interested.

"Are there antidotes?" the tall deputy asked.

"For Special K, no." Fair shook his head. "The strongest effects will usually wear off in one to two hours but a person's judgment can be compromised for twenty-four. It's a tricky drug. No antidote. No antidote at all. Some of the other horse-calming drugs may have one, but not ketamine. The speed with which it can work and then the shortness of the effect make it popular. The big rage seems to be over but it's still in use."

"There must be equine drugs that speed up a system, literally," Cooper asked.

"Oh, there are plenty of drugs for horses whose use will give the animal an advantage in racing or running through injury and pain. They are supposedly controlled." He exhaled loudly. "And, of course, they are not. The most difficult drugs are steroids. Many horses are put on them before fully mature. It's a miserable combination. Often the animal is harmed for life. Then there's what steroids can do to the mind. If I get a horse off a track that's been juiced, I tell whoever has given this animal a home to turn it out to pasture and let it crash, so to speak. After a year that stuff is out of the system. They remain muscled up but the side effects are over."

"Some are still crazy," Harry added.

"She's right, but most do recover. It's one thing, Coop, if we as humans willingly take drugs. It's another thing if an animal is loaded with them . . . or again, say a student, snorting Special K, who has no idea. If people choose to harm themselves, what can we do? If they choose to harm others, we can do a lot if we catch them."

"Well, Fair, you hit the nail on the head." Cooper cast her eyes over the shelves again. "Anything else jump out at you?"

"No."

"Would a large farm find it worthwhile to steal all kinds of drugs? I know Harry knows a lot because I've seen her go over your horses, and of course, you would have given her what the horse needed. What if you weren't a vet?"

"Would I know how to use various drugs? Yes. Most horse owners have a rudimentary knowledge but would it be worthwhile to get equine drugs on a black market? Not really. Drugs for human use or abuse is where the money is."

"Why don't they use catnip?" Pewter prudently suggested.

"Doesn't work for them," Tucker answered. *"Liquor works and drugs."*

"The issue is what is legal and what's illegal," Mrs. Murphy added.

Pirate wondered, *"How can you tell?"*

"Old white men sit around and make rules. This doesn't mean they don't use the illegal stuff themselves." Pewter huffed. *"I know that because of when Mother read the book about FDR, well, it was Prohibition but he drank."*

Pirate's long eyebrows turned inward for a moment. *"How could he get the illegal liquor?"*

"Same way everybody else did back then. Buy it from a bootlegger, a person who

sells illegal booze." Tucker accepted such hypocrisy, seemed natural to humans.

"*Well, President Roosevelt was so rich, he probably bought up an ocean's worth of liquor before the Prohibition laws went into effect. Money solves these problems. After all, President Kennedy had a huge stash of Cuban cigars once trade with Cuba was stopped.*" Pewter had been reading over Harry's shoulder and felt she was now an expert on many subjects.

Then again, Pewter felt that way whether she had read something or not.

"*Cohiba, Diplomáticos, Montecristo, oh Daddy loves his Cuban cigars.*" Tucker smiled.

"*He does?*" Pirate was shocked.

"*He has a few patients who keep humidors. They give him the good stuff as a thank, you,*" Mrs. Murphy told the Irish wolfhound.

Tucker couldn't help herself as she turned her head up to Pirate. "*You know, Pewter can't really read. Notice when a piece of paper falls to the floor, even a stamp. She sits on it. She thinks she can absorb the letters.*"

"*Poopface!*" Pewter jumped on the corgi's back.

"*Lardass,*" Tucker shouted as she ran down the hall with an irate cat on her back.

"I could kill them." Harry complained then quickly said, "Sorry."

Tucker slammed into a closed door. Pewter now hung on the dog's side, so Tucker slammed again. The door opened, popped.

Harry, hurrying down the hallway to separate the two, stopped at the door, clicked on the lights.

Pewter hopped off, sauntering into the closet.

"*I dare you to follow me, especially now that Mother is here.*"

Tucker, knowing at that moment she was not high on Harry's happiness list, sat down to glare at the gray cat.

Mrs. Murphy and Pirate sat outside as Fair and Cooper walked to the closet.

"He was neat." The blonde deputy noticed the hanging lab coats, work boots lined against the wall.

Everything had been left untouched from when Sheriff Shaw and Fair unlocked the door.

"Look . . . oh, these are beautiful." Harry knelt down to flip over the framed flower drawings lined up, backs facing the viewer. "Hand painted. Or should I say the colors are done with pastels." She handed up one, nine inches by twelve inches, to Fair.

"Vivid. Can't be pastels. Maybe watercolor?"

Cooper now examined the print. "You can get bright colors without oil paint. And the frames are thin gold. How old are these?"

Harry flipped over another one. "Doesn't say. They seem old. You know who would know, Nancy Parsons."

"Right. I'll see if I can get her to come out here. We can't move anything yet. Not till our team has gone over everything. Put it all back." Cooper admired the lily drawing, white with a deep pink throat.

"Who gets this stuff?" Harry asked.

"His sister is next of kin. I expect she'll make decisions after the worst of the shock wears off. She lives in Flagstaff, Arizona." Coop handed the drawing back to Harry, who replaced it exactly where she'd found it.

"It's sad he didn't even get to hang these." Harry stood up. "I would think everything can be sold as is to another vet, all the meds, the lab coats. Just seems logical to me."

"Does," Fair agreed.

Tucker, now inside the big closet, ignored Pewter. Pirate was too big to step in without moving the humans. Mrs. Murphy slid between Fair's legs.

The three examined the work boots then the flower artwork.

"*Odd.*" Mrs. Murphy sniffed a pink tea rose drawing.

"*What do you mean?*" Pewter now stuck her nose almost on the glass.

"*Old. An old smell.*" The tiger cat sniffed again.

"*Well, of course it's an old smell. Didn't our mom say these were old?*" Pewter stated the obvious.

Tucker, possessed of her long snout and canine abilities, inhaled deeply once, then again. She sat down, puzzled. *"She didn't say. They look old."*

"Well?" Pewter was about to start another fight.

"Kind of smells like an old skin." The corgi said the only thing that came to mind.

Mrs. Murphy again sniffed the framed print, the glass wasn't helpful to scent. *"Could be. I don't know. It's faint."*

"Doesn't matter. Let's provoke Harry to take us home. I'm hungry." Pewter called her human by name.

As the three left the closet, Tucker paused, returned to take another deep breath, then she ran to catch up to the others while Cooper shut the door.

They walked into Ben's small, organized office. A new, large computer sat on his L-shaped desk. In front of his chair, heavy pottery cups were filled with pens, all various nibs. Above that, different inks rested in a cubbyhole, envelopes in another, and stacks of good paper in yet another.

Cooper, thin gloves on, inspected the pens. "These nibs are gold."

Harry peered at them. "Flexible. A gold nib is the best, I think. And the ones in the jar with the leaping fox, pick one up."

Cooper did, turning it over for Harry, who shouldn't touch anything.

"Italic nibs," Harry noted.

Then Cooper pulled out a neat stack of envelopes, next to another stack. "Pretty."

The heavy paper of each envelope was addressed in italic script.

"Clients. Maybe to alert them to his new address. He probably emailed people, too, but this helps. I expect whatever the card was supposed to be, it's pretty." Harry looked over Cooper's shoulder.

Cooper didn't find cards. "Had an artistic streak."

"Did. Had an eye for good work, too. Those flower drawings are so detailed."

Cooper nodded. "Let's go back to the reception room."

Standing in it for a moment, the deputy looked around. "Fair, do you think Ben took drugs or sold them?"

"I never saw anything that would lead me to that conclusion. Were he selling drugs, why be killed for them?"

"Yes." Cooper nodded. "Unless the killer was a rival of some sort or an addict."

"It would have to be someone close to him. Someone who knew what he carried in his truck, what drugs a vet usually had on hand." Harry noticed the late afternoon sun, the long rays sliding over the still green grass outside.

"Well, thank you. Sheriff Shaw wanted me to go over everything with you. He's determined to solve this, as am I. Right now it's lots of questions. Not many answers."

As they walked outside, the door shut and locked behind them. Tucker whispered to Mrs. Murphy, *"Plant prints with a faint animal smell."*

"Maybe whatever the long-ago artist used to color the drawings has an odor."

Tucker walked close to her friend, saying nothing. That scent bothered her . . . then again, it could be the coloring scent. Who knows?

3

March 6, 1789

Friday

Four broodmares grazed in a pasture, struggling to shake off winter. Hay ricks had been created so the mares could pull off what they wanted. Each, owned by a different owner hoping to improve his bloodstock, had been bred to one of Catherine Schuyler's three stallions. Good food was essential.

A breeze brushed by, soft, perhaps four miles an hour from the west, where the Blue Ridge Mountains glowed in the late afternoon sun.

Ewing Garth, owner of Cloverfields, said, "Success." He paused then smiled slightly. "We hope."

Beautiful as a goddess, Catherine, now twenty-five, turned to her father. "Takes years but if the foals are well made, that truly is a beginning. All horsemen live off hope."

He nodded, his black curly hair now half gray, which added to his gravitas, for Ewing was an important man in Virginia, having helped finance the Virginia troops when all appeared lost. "Given our continuing losses in France, I keep thinking I should build my own sawmill. People need good lumber."

He thought, then shook his head. "One man in the pit, one above sawing endlessly. However, one can make money with planed lumber. Just stay out of the pit." He grinned.

"If one has men who know how to do it." She folded her hands together. "You've thought of everything, Father."

He sighed. "There is that."

"France has a weak king. A weak king is worse than a bad king." She shrewdly observed the world.

"We can thank the Lord an ocean lies between us and the troubles of Europe. Putting one's faith in a king or a queen seems foolish to me. Then I think of someone like Catherine of Russia and I realize not all kings are useless if you get a great one. Then they die." He grimaced.

Catherine followed his thought. "It's quite rare that one great king or queen follows another. Then again, what might happen when President Washington retires?"

Ewing laughed at his daughter. "Well, we may be fine for some time. You will see more than I, my dear. One can only hope good sense prevails."

She breathed in. "It will take us years to make up what we've lost, but we can. So long as we are careful."

"That is my prayer. Ah, Jeddie."

The young man, nineteen, number two at the stable, Jeddie Rice, walked toward them from the second barn. "Master. Miss Catherine."

"How many horses did you ride today?" Catherine, who ran the stables and had a gift for it, asked.

"Four. Started with Crown Prince. He was a good boy. Do you think Mrs. Selisse will send us another mare?"

"Given that we have to breed for free, no doubt. Remember to call her Holloway." Catherine smiled. "She makes money even when she sleeps."

"Well, when you've inherited as much as she has, she would have to be severely mentally compromised to lose it." Ewing tightened his scarf. The temperature hung in the mid-forties.

A cloud passed over the lowering sun, which dropped the temperature.

Catherine pulled her shawl around her shoulders. "The wind bites."

"I'm glad for all our firewood. Had a feeling this spring would drag her feet."

"You're good at looking ahead, Father." She changed the subject. "I'd better go to John." She named her husband. "He'll need help packing."

"Your husband does seem to forget things when he packs." Ewing smiled. "I wonder how he made it through the war."

"Wore the clothes on his back and had one bag back at camp. He told me he had one change of shirt, two extra socks, and one pair of breeches, one pair of boots. Left to himself, that would be his wardrobe today."

Jeddie smiled as Tulli, his small barn helper at eleven years old, walked in Penny, a sweet new mare.

Tulli put the good girl in her stall.

"Check the water," Jeddie ordered him.

Tulli called back, "Full."

"Who do you think filled the bucket?"

Closing the door again, the little fellow looked up at Jeddie, almost twenty. "You did."

"I did. Now go fetch some oats." Jeddie liked the boy, as did everyone.

Tulli nodded then addressed Ewing and Catherine. "Is it true we're going to set up a steeplechase course?" he breathlessly asked.

Jeddie chided him. "That's none of your business."

Catherine smiled at the child. "We are talking about it. They're running in Ireland. We ought to try it here."

"I can ride in it," the little fellow boasted.

"Tulli, go get crimped oats. Now." Jeddie tried to sound commanding.

As the boy skipped away Jeddie smiled. One couldn't help it.

Catherine said half-jokingly, "If it weren't for Tulli, I don't know what I'd do. He's a better mother than I am."

"Miss Catherine . . ." Jeddie thought a moment. "You have great patience."

"Ha." She laughed and her father laughed with her.

"Well, I'm going back up to that pile of mail." Ewing sighed.

When he was out of earshot, Catherine told Jeddie, whom she trusted completely with horses as well as for his discretion, "I don't know if we could organize a race but if I can goad Maureen into it, maybe. Then others will want to compete because the purse will be high."

"She doesn't have any good riders. Good horses though." Jeddie waited a beat. "Thanks to you."

"You're kind, Jeddie, but I give her credit. She brought her good mares to me and has bought fine ones out of Pennsylvania. She has all those rich friends in Philadelphia."

"Yes, Ma'am. Will you ride tomorrow?"

"I will. Morning. We can ride over to the Barracks." She named the remains of the prisoner of war camp.

"Good." He loved riding with Catherine because he could learn, for she would talk to him about horses, bloodlines, conditioning.

The other thing was she allowed him to ride the best blooded horses at Cloverfields. Jeddie, naturally talented, improved constantly.

4

March 8, 1789

Sunday

John Schuyler, Catherine's husband, sat with eight other men—all of whom had fought in the War of Independence—at Hawk's Nest, which overlooked the James River.

It took a day to reach Hawk's Nest if one used the river. Two days if by horse or coach. John chose to ride with Percy Ballard, with whom he had served in Lafayette's regiment. John, not a talkative man nor a well-educated one, relaxed with former comrades. As a young major he breached the redoubts at Yorktown. He dismounted, gave his horse to a private, to lead his men right into the thick of it. No officer riding around for John. His example, crazed bravery, sent a surge over those well-built British fortifications on October 14 and the Americans won the day. The battle ended on October 19, thanks to a combination of factors, the French Navy certainly being one, but also because of young men like John who were willing to die to be free of King George. Lafayette was deeply impressed with Schuyler and kept him close thereafter. Hailed as a hero of Yorktown, John, tall, powerfully built, handsome, never spoke of it. If anyone asked, he gave his men the credit. His attitude reached the commanding officer, General George Washington, who developed an interest in the taciturn Massachusetts man.

Colonel Ulrich, papers in his lap, sat by the fireplace, smoke wafting up a well-built chimney. The room was most pleasant, and Colonel Ulrich's wife had attended to everyone's needs, including a welcome midday meal.

Marrying the right woman was a path to success. With the exception of two fellows in the room whose wives had died in childbirth, every man there had found a true helpmate. If the women resented it, they were wise enough not to show it. To marry a man with a future, to be part of building a new country, offered perhaps more enticement than what their mothers faced before the war.

John listened intently to the colonel and the other men in the room, all of whom had proven themselves during the war. Brigadier General Daniel Slipka, a quartermaster, was as respected as the men who faced the guns. Without the Slipkas, the Colonials wouldn't have prevailed. As it was, quartermasters had to beg for muskets, clothing, food, and hay.

The former colonies were digging themselves out of war debt, and not very successfully. The tensions between Hamilton and Madison, considered Jefferson's creature, already bubbled up. Jefferson tried to appear above it all. Hamilton wanted a strong central financial system, Jefferson felt the states should control all.

John knew this most especially because his father-in-law, who had fronted thousands for the cause, kept him apprised. His wife worked with her father. Few knew just how much Catherine knew of money and politics but John knew she understood far more than he did. He was a man of action, not thought.

Percy shifted in his seat. "So we have a small army approved by Congress but we have no funds?"

Brigadier General Slipka cleared his throat. "Captain, it is a thorny problem which we, as military men, can't resolve. The resolution must come from Congress."

"Whatever happened to a paymaster general?" Former Major Horace Moses had little patience for the politics of this.

The colonel, a high political man, nodded. "Approved as a rank June 3, 1775. However, a paymaster general without funds or clear direction cannot work a miracle. My reason for bringing you gentlemen here is twofold. I know you. We have served together. You are men who if you say you will do something, you do it. Believe me, in some ways war is easier than peace. The bickering, the unwillingness to accept responsibility." He took a deep breath. "Forgive me. This has been going on since Thucydides, who wrote of it in excruciating detail in the fifth century B.C. I don't mean to stray from the true issue, which is that we must keep our Virginia militia and expand it. And we must find a way to train our young men in military service. Should the British return, we will be prepared. Gentlemen, this country must never find itself in the situation we did when the war began."

All agreed.

"Has our governor been sounded on this?" Slipka asked the obvious question.

"Yes." A wry smile crossed the colonel's lips. "He will not oppose our efforts. He prefers to observe and offer assistance unnoticed."

"Oh, balls!" Horace, never known for restraint, lived up to his reputation.

"The Randolphs are uncommonly shrewd," Percy observed. "I expect they will still be running this state in years to come."

Horace shifted in his chair, a wing chair covered in an expensive brocade. The colonel's wife displayed fine taste. Fortunately he had the money to support this, thanks to his hemp and tobacco holdings.

"Whether they do or don't, we've got to deal with them now. Beverley Randolph is a cautious man. In the long run we may be grateful for this," Percy commented.

"Perhaps," the colonel agreed. "Gentlemen, the reason you are here is known to you. Virginia cannot rely on Congress for protection. I am not pointing fingers. How our new government will pay our war debt and raise money, I don't know, but I do know if we don't do this, we will not be taken seriously by any merchant in Europe . . . or Russia, for that matter."

Daniel Slipka nodded. "As our people move west, over the mountains and into the new Ohio Territory, we must protect them. New people mean new business, new farms, more crops going down our great rivers, Virginia is extremely fortunate in our rivers, we can get goods to the seas easier than some of our brethren."

"Well, I see only one answer." The colonel stood, walked to his burnished walnut secretary, slid out an envelope from one of the cubbyholes, then returned to his seat. "We must expand our militia, expand it greatly."

"In contradiction of the army?" Horace wondered.

"I prefer to think of our militia as an augmentation to the army, which is frightfully small. Seven hundred eighteen men."

"As our navy started with two ships, I expect we must consider growth there, too. Think of our coastline." Daniel, as a quartermaster, thought in hard facts.

"England boasts of the mightiest navy in the world." Percy had visited England, sent overseas by his father before the war. When it appeared imminent, he was recalled home.

"So they do. And they prey upon us and will continue to do so. When they closed West Indies' ports to us, our trade plummeted. It was a petty act of revenge for being defeated by people they considered barbarians. However, greed being what it is, they found they need our products more than they needed revenge, but we are vulnerable, gentlemen, vulnerable." The colonel studied history. "Think of Salamis. What would have happened if the Persians had won that sea battle when they outnumbered the Greek navy three to one? We must think boldly like Themistocles. Boldly. We need a strong army and a fearsome navy. If Themistocles could redirect the Athenian military planning, so can we. If nothing else, our New England states have begged for a navy since the beginning of the war in 1775. If we develop and maintain a large militia, we can at least defend our coastline from invasion. We can't stop our enemies from disembarking but we can give fire to send them back to their ships. We must have a large militia." The colonel's voice rang with conviction.

"Colonel." Horace's voice remained even. "Are you suggesting we will be invaded?"

A long silence followed this, then the middle-aged, impressive man cleared his throat, fingered the envelope. "We contain riches beyond imagining. The French have seen this, here and north of us. The English have seen our lands, our rivers, our lakes, those huge lakes. The officers along for observation from Spain, Poland, Austria; they, too, have seen our natural wealth. We have an ocean to offer some protection from their incessant wars." He paused. "Before our great conflict and during it, what did the English do? Make treaties with the tribes to turn against us. Many did. Others did not. I have no doubt, no doubt, gentlemen, that in time Europe will be back to meddle in our affairs and to do their best to stop our westward movement and claim those lands for their own. We must be strong enough, young though we are and frightening as we are to kings, to dissuade them from any form of attack or stabbing us in the back through tribal hostilities."

A very long silence followed this.

Then Daniel murmured, "One doesn't like to consider this, Colonel. Those nations have large navies and huge standing armies."

"Which is why we must prepare and hope it doesn't come to that," Horace chipped in. "If nothing else, England would like to wipe out her humiliation. At least Lord North is destroyed." He named the prime minister who took a hard line and swayed King George.

"Those countries have their navies and their armies but can they afford a war across the Atlantic?" Percy stated the obvious. "When the English sent their commercial ships to the Caribbean ports, did the navy help them? They may have protected their merchants but did it not mean less ships to fight in Europe? Thank God, there is an ocean between us. Those people have been killing one another for thousands of years. We can't afford to be drawn in, no matter what.

"Well, you know Mr. Jefferson is thrilled that the people of France . . . not the aristocrats, but those deemed the people . . . are restive. Cites our example. We can't take sides even though they helped us in our great cause." Percy cleared his throat.

"But why did they help us?" The colonel quietly spoke. "Because they wished to weaken the English. Captain Ballard is right. We can't afford to be drawn into whatever conflicts occur there. The Russians will always want Constantinople. The Austrians will wish to control those states around them, and Spain, still rich beyond belief, has no sense of how much power it has lost. That makes them dangerous. We must look to ourselves, which brings me to this letter." Colonel Ulrich handed it to John.

John read it, his face registering mixed emotions. "Colonel, this is a great honor. One I do not deserve."

Percy leaned over but John handed the letter back to the colonel.

"Each of you will recognize the signature." He handed the letter first to Daniel, from whence it made the rounds, returning to the colonel.

All the men looked at John.

"You have our complete confidence, as you have the confidence of our great commander." He smiled slightly. "Our president. I must become accustomed to General Washington's new title."

Face blushing, John, not an articulate man but an intelligent one, struggled to form his thoughts. Few could think as quickly as he in battle, which is why the Marquise de Lafayette recommended him to Washington, who knew of John's extraordinary bravery at Yorktown. Washington loved Lafayette like a son.

"I will do as General Washington asks. I will expand our small militia." He swallowed then continued. "I am a soldier. I do not know if I have the skills to form and train a large state militia, but I will do my best."

The colonel smiled broadly. "I think I can speak for every man in the room. We will fill the line."

They all smiled at the military reference.

Percy, thrilled for his friend, piped up. "A boy born in 1781 is eight now. A fellow who was fifteen is now twenty-three. They know nothing of war even though they lived through it. You, John, are a hero. With you at our head I believe the young will want to play their part."

"Well." John didn't know what to say.

"Young men need an example. Think if those leaders of France had truly led, had cared for those not as fortunate as themselves, who respected their men in battle if they fought, their veterans, if that had happened I think there would not be a financial crisis and now a leadership contest. How can anyone from the Third Estate, the people, understand the king? How can the king understand his people? We each must teach our young. The time will come when we lay down life's burdens. They must pick them up."

An appreciative murmur followed this.

The comrades talked for another hour. The world was changing at lightning speed. While a few felt France could learn from our more open society, others did not. France would always need a king. But each was far more concerned with the survival of the great experiment, as they thought of it, and each man accepted mistakes would be made but with hard thought and continued sacrifice perhaps not so many.

Colonel Ulrich and his lady had prepared rooms for the visitors, set a marvelous table that evening, then sent them off with a grand breakfast. All the house servants, slaves in expensive livery, danced attendance on the former soldiers.

As they rode off to their various directions, John and Percy rode together. They would separate the next day. John would take Three Notch'd Road to the west and Percy would ride north of Charlottesville.

That night they stayed at an Ordinary.

"Percy, I'm not a learned man. I can't speak as you, the colonel, and Horace can, or Daniel Slipka. You are educated men with educated language."

"All you need to do is walk among the men. John, you have a leader's bearing. Your height alone means we all have to look up at you. Perhaps not the general, but you tower above us and you are as strong as a bull. You and I can sit down once the fields are planted. The last frost is nearing. We have to figure out how to train those who have no training. Some may not even know how to load a musket."

"How will we pay for firearms?" John asked.

"We'll let the money boys figure that out, as Colonel Ulrich said."

"So you think, Percy, we start with drills?" John asked.

"Yes. But short drills. We had to learn how to fight the British way. The squares, the incredible discipline, but I think, I truly think, the more we use our land, the more we slip through the forests, the more successful we will be. Let Europeans fight their way. Think of how you captured Charles West at Saratoga. How is he, by the way?" Percy answered.

"He's become a builder. He can draw anything. The Lutheran church he built at Wayland's Crossing is beautiful."

"Ah. He is a good man, even if he is English." Percy grinned, for it was impossible not to like Charles, who had married Catherine's younger sister, Rachel.

"You and I both had the great good fortune to marry extraordinary women," John added. "My wife is far more intelligent than I and," he paused and gave Percy a light punch, "so is your fine lady."

"Of course she's more intelligent than you," Percy bedeviled him, punching back.

They laughed, men who had faced death together and were happy to be alive, to be able to think of a future, to have love and to have children, which both thought of as the future.

Percy then added, "John, you are the right man for this command. You are too humble. Don't worry about book learning. Some of the dumbest people I know are the most educated."

John blinked a moment. "Remember Zachery Thigpen? No matter how many times you showed him how to load his musket, how to ram down the powder, he couldn't do it. It's a miracle he lived through the war." He stopped a moment. "Had courage. No matter what, he tried, but he couldn't remember, especially under fire."

"The good Lord protects drunks and idiots. And do you know, he has made a fortune in Leesburg?" Percy laughed.

"Zachery?"

"He started a stagecoach line to Philadelphia, Richmond, Baltimore. Zachery Thigpen, of all people."

"Rich?"

"Pots of money."

"Well, Percy, I believe we will have to visit Zachery soon. We need muskets and perhaps some of those new rifles. And I suppose we will need shoes."

"Shoes?"

"If we are lucky, if young men agree to serve, we must take care of them, and many of our poor boys have no good shoes."

Percy stared at John for a moment then said with admiration, "You will be a strong leader, Colonel Schuyler."

"Ah." John had paid little attention to his jump in rank thanks to President Washington.

As they sat there, a newly kindled fire warming them since the night had turned frosty, the proprietress brought a complimentary decanter of whiskey, for she knew of John's actions at Yorktown, as did most people.

Each man prayed Europe's problems would stay in Europe, they prayed we would try to solve our difficulties without violence, but they would work tirelessly in case Europe's problems sailed over the Atlantic.

5

September 29, 2019

Sunday

Large windows allowed natural light to bathe the enticing items throughout Country House Antiques, which anchored the intersection of Routes 231 and 600 in Albemarle County. Nancy Parsons, sitting at her desk at the back of the main room, studied her computer as she glanced up from time to time to see if a customer needed assistance. Country House usually hosted two or three people at a time, rarely empty but rarely jammed with people. The space would have felt crowded with fifteen people in the main room and the side room.

Prints hung on the walls, some colored, some true paintings, some etchings. The variety in the smallish shop would provoke customers to ask questions. The furniture, special things like old rocking horses, also tweaked people's imagination. Where did she find these things?

As if to answer that, for an early-middle-aged lady had fallen in love with an ancient baby cradle, in walked Candida Perez, accompanied by her sixty-four-year-old son, Ballard Perez, and her few years younger daughter, Constance Perez O'Donnell.

"Mrs. Perez," Nancy stood up and motioned toward the attractive lady hovering over the cradle, "this lady would like to know the history of the cradle." Nancy turned to the customer. "Allow me to introduce you to Candida Perez, who brought the cradle to me."

The woman with the honey-colored hair reached out her hand to shake Mrs. Perez's. "Jillian Howard. What good fortune to meet you."

Candida Perez, now in her element, which is to say she was the center of attention, began the story of the hand-carved and painted cradle. The violets on the cradle were in honor of her great-grandmother, who rocked her progeny in this cradle. She loved violets.

Both Ballard and Constance, having heard this story for decades, easily slipped away separately while their mother expanded.

Nancy smiled as the two came to her desk. "Sunday drive?"

Ballard, low voice, replied, "Yes. We've called on Kenny Wheeler, we stopped by Andy Lynn. Then Meredith McLaughlin. We just had to drop in on Kenny Jr. and Ceil. Then as we thought we could get to the Grill at the club, who should come down the driveway but Lizzie Beer? You all knew Lizzie's mother, so our mother had a gallop down memory lane until Lizzie's eyes glazed over."

Before more details could be forthcoming, the front door opened and in scooted Tucker followed by Pirate.

"Pirate, sit down by the door. Good boy."

The giant dog did as he was told, sitting like a statue, watching everybody, but he didn't move a muscle. Tucker, on the other hand, sped through the store straight to Nancy.

"Are you glad to see me?" The extroverted corgi stood on her hind legs, putting her front paws on the edge of the chair.

Nancy reached down. "You're here for the dog print. I just know it."

Harry followed. "I can take these two out."

"No. They're better behaved than some people."

Harry overheard "Oh those dark blue eyes and that black curly hair—"

Candida Perez had just got to the point where she first saw her husband. Jillian appeared enraptured. Candida had blown through three generations in swift order but now would be lingering over Bernardo, "Nardo," Perez.

Constance shook her head. "I swear she relives that moment each time she tells the story."

Harry smiled. "And here you are. The result of the story. Haven't seen you and Ballard for months. Either we are all living dull lives or we're too busy for fun."

Ballard sighed. "Too busy. I shouldn't complain when business is good."

Constance tilted her head. "Rocks. Hard to believe."

Ballard sheepishly grinned. "You want every garden to look like Sissinghurst." He named Vita Sackville-West's famous garden in England.

"Well," Constance drawled out. "Rocks. Hardscaping."

Ballard changed the subject to whisper, "Perhaps I should rescue Mrs. Howard?"

"How do you know she's married?" his sister asked.

"The ring on her left hand." He smirked at his sister, who usually noticed such things first.

Constance immediately swiveled. Sure enough, an enormous diamond sparkled. Well, one best take Mrs. Howard seriously.

Ballard walked over, slipped an arm around his mother's still small waist. "Mother, Mrs. Howard probably would like to look at other wondrous things in the store."

A slight blush crossed Jillian Howard's face. "I was enraptured. Just enraptured."

"Mrs. Howard."

"Oh, do call me Jillian." The attractive woman beamed at Candida.

"Jillian, this is my son, Ballard. He likes to give orders now that I am The Ancient of Days and I like to ignore them."

Ballard kissed his mother on the cheek and they both laughed.

"My mother is one of a kind."

"Yes, but you didn't say what kind," Candida fired back in good humor. "Jillian, allow me to give you this cradle. Nancy, don't take a penny from this engaging soul." She then gave Jillian a stern look. "Ballard will carry this out to your car." She paused, looking up at the taller woman. "You may kiss me on the cheek."

Mrs. Howard bent over, leaned forward, and kissed Candida on the cheek. "Thank you for your generosity."

"Enjoy the cradle." Candida was tempted to say "and fill it." But one didn't say those things these days.

Ballard lifted up the heavy cradle, for it was solid wood, carrying it to Jillian Howard's new Mercedes station wagon, one of the really fast ones.

Constance beamed. "Thank God she didn't make us take it home. We are having a terrible time getting Mother to organize her things. She can't pick up an object without a half hour or hour declamation of its history, her history, the family's history." Sighing, Constance, flecks of well-groomed gray in her deep chestnut hair, continued, "God bless her. She won't part with one paper, one letter, one ancient postcard, something from Paris in the 1920s. And I don't think she should. The papers are priceless and important. But things like the now-given-away cradle, not so much."

"Objects like cradles, old prints, old quilts have devotees." Nancy knew what was out there, more to the point, the kind of people who were out there, who became obsessed with something, a time, a color, who knows?

"I suppose. Ballard has more sensitivity to things than I do. I focus on handwritten letters from Woodrow Wilson to my grandfather, stuff like that. You, Constance, never cared," Candida called, as she had heard some of the discussion.

"Ah." Ballard joined them. "Jillian Howard and her husband, Kenneth, have bought the old Pemberton estate."

"Well, they will have a lot to fill." Harry thought of the old painted-brick home, lovely.

"Where did you get this jewelry box?" Candida called again from the front of the store.

"Wheatlands." Nancy called the name of the estate.

"Old Frolic Ulrich?" Candida thought of the deceased owner as old, which she was when Candida was middle-aged.

"Odds and ends wind up here. I hear the closets were stuffed full." Nancy knew more about the treasures of old places than most people.

Many stories were sad. Others simply reflected a change in the taste, the times, and others sprang from that reliable seventh deadly sin: greed.

"Mother, let's go to lunch. I'm famished." Constance nudged her mother.

Tucker had wandered into the smaller second room, where an old ragdoll—old as in a century old—sat on a ladderback chair. The corgi sniffed, a faint, so faint scent lingered on the doll's little shoes. Another dog had slept with the doll. And the doll probably rested under a little girl's arm. A little girl long gone.

"I'll be back," Candida promised Nancy.

"I count on it," Nancy called to her then sat back down at her desk. "Here's what I was doing. Come round."

"I see." Harry beheld the drawings, photographs of those men who had been U.S. president when the school they were restoring had been in operation. "A lot."

"What I'm looking for is the official presidential photograph. Those that might have hung in the schoolhouse."

"*Can I get up now?*" Pirate quietly asked.

Harry looked up, hearing the deep voice. "Pirate, your tail is lethal."

"I will just come sit by you," the youngster promised.

"All right, big boy. Come here. Down the middle. Good boy. Now sit next to Nancy."

Nancy reached over to pet the head, at desk level. "Pirate, you are a good boy."

"Thank you."

Tucker ambled in from the next room. While it's reassuring to be petted, she wanted to smell everything. Something like a shawl draped over a chest of drawers, a low chest, might carry a message from the past.

"So we need the official photographs?" Harry inquired.

"Yes. I'm learning a lot. Each picture I find has a little bit about that president."

"Speaking of presidents. Do you think Candida has letters from presidents and famous people?"

"Harry, I expect Candida has all kinds of things. She was a Ballard before she married Bernardo. That's an old Virginia family."

"Right." Harry nodded. "All that weight to carry."

Nancy smiled. "Oh, some carry it better than others."

"True. Ballard maybe has found his way. He has to carry the family name as his first name, speaking of weight. He'd start a business, find a new passion, run through his money. Candida would bail him out, after Nardo was dead, of course. As long as Nardo lived, he was tough on his son."

Nancy reached over to pet Pirate again. "It's an old story, isn't it? The struggle of a son who has inherited money yet can't get his hands on it or make his way?"

"Struggle for a woman, too."

"It is, but it's different. Well, you and I aren't going to change how people look at those with money, but come look at the presidents again."

Good-naturedly, Harry returned to the images. "What awful beards."

"Were."

They laughed, they liked each other and the dogs did behave.

Later that night, Candida Perez got to thinking about the letter to her grandfather from Woodrow Wilson. She wanted to read it. Knew right where it was.

6

September 30, 2019

Monday

Constance O'Donnell, peeved that her mother had not answered her text, called Ballard.

"Mother's supposed to go to her eye doctor appointment today. Aren't you picking her up?"

"I thought you were. She always goes to doctors' appointments with you."

"Dammit, Ballard, I told you I have a foundation meeting at eleven."

"No, you didn't," he insisted.

"What are you doing?"

"I'm at Zion Crossroads on my way to Richmond."

"Dammit."

"You already said that, Constance. I have a meeting in Richmond at the Hodges Group. Then I'm meeting Bill Yancy for dinner. I won't be home until late."

"You owe me one. I'll cancel my meeting and pick her up. But I know we discussed this."

Trying to keep his eyes on the road, he simply agreed. "I guess I forgot. Slammed with business right now."

"Then why are you driving to Richmond?"

"Well, as you know, the Hodges Partnership specializes in public relations. I would like to talk to them to see if I can afford a statewide campaign. There are a lot more landscape architects than hardscape architects."

"Really?" Her voice took on an acidic tone. "You can blow money faster than anyone I ever met. All you are is a jumped-up stone mason."

"I'll talk to you tomorrow." He clicked off and said loudly, as he was alone in his Ram 2500 truck, "Bitch!"

Driving too fast on Route 22, Constance hung a hard left at Turkey Sag Road, pulling into the circular driveway of the old, large-frame farmhouse built in 1834.

Cutting the motor on her Lexus, a car she loved, she walked around to the back door, opened it.

"Mother," she called.

No response. Usually Margaret, the maid of four decades, would be there but Monday was her day off, with a half day on Wednesday. Even in her nineties, Candida hosted many a small tea on the weekends. Given all the money she had paid Margaret to polish the silver over the years, Candida would giggle and swear she had to use it.

"Mother, let's go! We'll be late."

No response.

"I'll kill her," Constance muttered under her breath then laughed as she strode into the living room. Her mother wasn't there. She walked into the next room, the library overflowing with books. Candida couldn't bring herself to throw out a book.

"Mother!"

Candida Perez, slumped over her library desk, two Moroccan leather boxes on the floor, papers scattered, didn't move.

Constance hurried over, felt her mother's pulse. With great composure she called 911.

"Hello, this is Constance O'Donnell at Lone Pine on Turkey Sag Road off Route 22. I'd like to report a death. My mother has passed."

Then Constance called Margaret. "Margaret, did you talk to Mother last night or this morning?"

"No, Ma'am. I left at seven. Your mother wanted to look over some old letters and papers. Said her curiosity was plucked."

"She's dead."

"No!" Margaret screamed. "I'll be right there."

"I wanted you to know. Stay where you are, there's nothing you can do. Heart attack, I'd say. You can come tomorrow. It might be a little calmer, as it's about to be chaos." Constance heard Margaret sniffle. "You were dear to her and served her well."

"I loved her. I know she's ninety. But she never seemed old. I thought she would live forever."

"Apparently not, but I thought so, too. I hear the ambulance. Bye."

The ambulance stopped at the front door. Constance walked through the long hall filled with paintings and prints, to the front door, which she opened. She saw a sheriff's car pull in behind it.

Constance waited, as she recognized Deputy Cooper, Harry's neighbor. A neighbor in these parts was anyone within half a mile, and Harry and Cynthia, given that definition, lived next to each other on the western side of the county.

Cooper walked up the steps. "Mrs. O'Donnell, I am so sorry. I've come to see if you need anything. Otherwise I'll go with the ambulance team."

"Well, I suppose you should examine her. I took a pulse. I was too shocked to do more."

"Of course." Cynthia did not state or ask if Constance thought there was something irregular about her mother's death.

Standing in the library, a large marble fireplace in the center of the north wall, Cooper spoke low to one of the ambulance crew. "Anything," she lowered her voice, "unusual?"

Jacob, the registered nurse, shook his head. "No."

"Take her away, then." Cynthia turned to Constance but before she could speak, Constance said, "Hill and Wood."

She'd named a funeral home in Charlottesville.

She decided not to call her worthless brother, whom she considered a first-class loser. She thought with delicious malice that someone would call Bill Yancy. Word of Candida's passing would not be kept quiet for long. Wouldn't it be funny if Ballard heard of Mother's death from Bill, a compassionate and kind man? Well, she'd call Ballard later, telling him she hadn't wanted to ruin his dinner.

Let someone else ruin it.

Jacob nodded and the other three men picked up Candida, now on a gurney, covered. She couldn't have weighed more than one hundred pounds, having lost a great deal of fatty tissue with age. Candida was never fat, but each year there seemed to be less of her.

"If you need me or Sheriff Shaw, we would be happy to post an officer outside. I'm certain people will respect your privacy but your mother was one of the great characters of the county."

"That she was. I think people will be respectful." Constance smiled then looked at the papers and old envelopes. "I'll call Jerry Showalter to put all this back in order. She saved everything. It has historical interest."

Jerry Showalter was an expert on old books and historical papers.

"I would think it would." Cooper nodded slightly then left, wondering how Jerry would sort through what looked like a big mess.

Constance walked to the front door to watch her mother be driven to Hill and Wood, then she called the funeral home.

Once that was accomplished she sat down. Were her husband, Kevin, still alive she would have called him, but he died at fifty-six of a massive stroke, a terrible shock to her and everyone. He was a robust man, a stockbroker sought out by many. Well, too many of the female gender, but Constance had put those peccadillos behind her. She missed him at times like this.

She knew she would miss her mother even though Ballard was the adored child. Not calling him felt delicious. Revenge was sweet.

7

March 8, 1789

Sunday

Two huge fireplaces at either end of the large workshop roared. The night proved bitterly cold and the day promised a snowstorm. If Jeffrey Holloway stepped outside his shop at Big Rawly, a large estate, and looked west, he would see the clouds piling up behind the Blue Ridge Mountains. As it was, he stayed inside, where he and his crew carefully attached a door to the four-in-hand coach he was building.

A perfectionist, Jeffrey wiggled the handle, which eventually would be gilded. "Toby, my ruler."

His head man, a slave, Toby Tips, handed Jeffrey a six-inch thin ruler, used for tight spaces. Both men peered at the slight gap between the door's edge and the coach body.

"Ah." Toby exhaled through his nose.

"I say an eighth of an inch." Jeffrey held the ruler firmly in place so Toby could look closer.

"You're right."

Jeffrey ordered the young men in the huge shop, "Take the door off, boys."

As the young men pulled over two short ladders, one on each side of the door, two stepped up to the top rung, while two held the door in place as they began to lift it off its hinges.

"You're the only man I know who would build a new door for an eighth of an inch. Someone else would have wedged felt on the coach body side or whatever else they thought would close the gap." Toby thought a moment. "Which it would for a time, you know."

"Mmm." Jeffrey stepped back as the door slowly was lowered to the shop floor, which was composed of large planed boards fitted together, tongue and groove.

Hollowing out that long groove then cutting the fitting board so it would slide in took patience and precision. When Jeffrey built the building, a newlywed and new to Big Rawly, the estate of Maureen Selisse, now Maureen Holloway, the men chosen to work with Jeffrey soon realized he was adamant. Do it right or don't do it. He'd find another man. Given that building coaches brought anyone working on them an enhanced reputation as well as tips from the individuals picking up the coaches, everyone in that building wanted to keep working.

In fact, that's how Toby came to be known as Toby Tips. He usually stood next to Jeffrey, handed up the new driver to the top of the coach or held his hand to help up a passenger. Each coach would be painted in colors the buyer chose, colors that gleamed like jewelry.

Big Rawly's coachman, DoRe, would sit next to the buyer's coachman, and tell him the details of the coach as the driver tested it on the estate roads, turnabouts, hills, and declines. DoRe, a fierce competitor with Barker O, Cloverfields' coachman, could make any team of horses look good but in this case it really was the coach that mattered.

Jeffrey's father, a carpenter, had taught his fabulously handsome son all he knew. Jeffrey, happy to be a skilled laborer, wanted to build coaches not furniture, but he worked with his father until he caught the newly widowed Maureen's eye. The widow, one of the richest women not only in Virginia but in the former colonies, could buy what she wanted. Men flocked to her, eager to present themselves as the ideal second husband. Few women would deny such attention. She allowed them all to swirl about her. Jeffrey didn't court her but as her attentions moved in his direction, he would deliver a piece of furniture, stay for a repast or a walk along the carefully laid-out grounds. Maureen wondered where was she going to put all this furniture she was ordering from Jeffrey's father, so she could see his son.

Aphrodite can't be denied and Maureen possessed more allure than simply money. A fine-looking woman with adipose tissue where men most liked it, she was not averse to wearing low-cut dresses, a light shawl wrapped around her shoulders. If the day proved cool, the shawl would be of heavier material and a gentleman might pull it tighter for her comfort. Some said Maureen was twenty years older than Jeffrey, a man in his mid-twenties. Others declared no, she was only fifteen years older. Maureen felt no compulsion to reveal her age. But as they conversed, Jeffrey discovered he could talk to her. She was born in the Caribbean, educated in France, and as the daughter of a powerful banker in a clearinghouse for New World money, she had a formidable intelligence that leaked out even when she tried to hide it. Here he was, a cabinetmaker, listening to a woman who had seen Versailles, danced at huge balls in London, beheld the beauties of Barcelona. He fell in love with her.

Once married she spoiled him. His dream was to build coaches. She built him a seventy-foot by forty-foot shop. Any tool he needed was there. She built a forge outside the woodworking building. Jeffrey could make his own axles. Any metal could be made into exactly what was wanted or needed. Each coach took six months to create. A coach could be made in less time than that but Jeffrey insisted on perfection. The other distinguishing feature of his work was the balance of the coaches. The minute the horses began walking, a passenger could feel the difference. The driver, his job made easier, was grateful.

Business boomed. While those of her class laughed behind their gloved hands that she had married a mere cabinetmaker, they soon stopped laughing. Of course, he was beautiful beyond handsome but he had the respect of other men, as well as their jealousy. All that money. All that adipose tissue.

Toby motioned for the men to lean the door against the back wall. "We might be able to use it in the future. You know, sort of build a coach around it."

Jeffrey, on the other side of the large vehicle, double-checked that door, ruler in hand. "This one's tight."

"Yes, it is." Toby walked over to him after making sure the rejected door was secure against the wall.

"This is where people cheapen their work. You wouldn't think such a small disparity between the right door and the left could make a difference but it can. That eighth of an inch would mean the door would be imperceptibly lighter than the left door. In time that weight contrast would affect balance. Again, Toby, those are big doors that need to swing easily. The windows, the hinges, exactly the same."

Toby, having heard it all before, nodded. Jeffrey would almost pulsate with excitement the first time DoRe drove a new coach. He'd sit up next to DoRe and give orders regarding speed, turning radius, whatever popped into his head. Jeffrey also had the sense to listen to DoRe.

"Starting to snow." Caleb looked out the window of the huge double doors.

"Can't do close work in lantern light. I am determined to . . ." His voice trailed off as William, twenty now, pulled open a door and limped in. "Yes."

"Mason wants to know what the Poulsons want on the wagon seat." He named the man who ran the wagon building.

A second workshop for work wagons rested about thirty yards away.

Jeffrey looked up at William. "Cowhide. You can start tomorrow. The light is fading fast. Soon be dark."

"Yes, Master." William limped back outside.

"I've told him not to call me master." Jeffrey walked along the row of carriages in various stages of construction.

"He'll never listen. If one person told Mrs. Holloway he did not call you master, she'd have him beaten. It's a rare hatred she has for William," Toby remarked.

"Yes." Jeffrey agreed.

William had run to freedom but not before breaking the shoulder of Jeddie Rice during a horse race, stealing Yancy Grant's horse, Black Knight, and disappearing. The horse was eventually found. William, arrogant fool that he was, months later snuck back to Big Rawly to entice Sulli to run away with him. He said he loved her and would she show him where Maureen kept her jewelry? She couldn't but she showed him where the "pin money" was, those dollars kept for unexpected household expenses. She also showed him where some inexpensive jewelry was. Off they ran in the dead of night, accompanied by Ralston, who had run away from Cloverfields, and who loathed Jeddie Rice, a more talented rider than himself.

Eventually William and Sulli were caught, but not before William sexually abused her, proving his declarations of love were worthless. He and Sulli were captured by bounty hunters, William tried to run away but was caught, his hamstring slit so he could never run again. Once returned to Big Rawly the two young people, despised by the others, all of whom were jeopardized by their theft and escape, realized they would live years in misery because Maureen would see to it. Each night, William was chained to a bearing beam in the middle of the wagon shop. He had a blanket. That was it. As for Sulli, she was given a job tending to the simpleminded. She barely spoke and when she did, half the people she tended to didn't understand what she was saying. But a tiny blind baby had been dumped in her care. Olivia, mid-sixties, was in charge of the people born with problems and in need of care. She noted that whatever tenderness was left in Sulli's heart was touched by the blind baby girl.

Running outside to bring in a load of wood before the storm hit, the sky nearly black now, Sulli saw William limping back to the wagon building. She hoped the cold increased his pain tenfold. She also vowed to kill him one day.

In time, she knew she would get her chance.

In time, she would learn the gods use us for sport.

8

October 1, 2019

Tuesday

Three students, spaced apart, trotted in the large sand ring at Brook Hill Farm. The owner, Lynne Beegle Gebhard, gave a lesson while her husband, Mark, cleaned up trees downed thanks to high winds. A lieutenant colonel, now retired from the Air Force, any job calling for a power tool was one he wanted to do.

The roar of the chainsaw buzzed far enough away that it didn't override Lynne's voice. These three students, talented, hoped to make their way on the show circuit.

Fair Haristeen drove into the farm, turned right across from the ring, and parked by the barn. Another vet and terrific rider, as was Lynne, waved to him as he climbed out of his truck cab. Tiffany Snell, DVM, usually rode with Lynne as well as hunted with Farmington Hunt Club. Everybody knew everybody.

Fair walked up, the horse in question was tied on the crossties, standing calmly.

"What have we here?"

Tiffany answered. "A splint. Not bad. Here, I can show you." She clicked on her computer, as she had the X-rays. The technology was now so advanced a vet could show X-rays as taken. Equipment that used to be ungainly, heavy, could now be carried as could a portable computer.

Fair studied them. "That will reattach."

"I know. My problem is the owner thinks a two-month turnout way too long. Another instant vet, thanks to the Internet."

"Ah." There was nothing else for Fair to say.

The Internet caused unnecessary complication for anyone in the medical profession, be it dentistry, human medicine, or veterinary medicine. Someone surfed the Internet, read articles, and suddenly they knew more than the medical person who has spent years studying and then years practicing. If there's one thing anyone in any kind of medicine learns, it is that humans and animals don't always follow the textbook. A heart can be on the right side of the body. A hormone balance in one horse could send another through the roof. No matter how advanced the technology or pharmaceuticals, a professional needed to study the whole organism.

In this case the organism was a calm older Thoroughbred. He'd served his time on the track and fortunately found a good home afterward. He was turned into a foxhunter and that person sold Winston to his current owner. The lady, fiftyish, new to horses, showered affection on the good fellow as well as needless anxiety.

If Winston coughed, Tiffany was instantly called, regardless of the hour. Tiffany, like every vet, needed to earn a living but this was ridiculous. The lady was throwing money away.

"It's already beginning to heal." Tiffany pointed to the X-ray, then clicked on one from two weeks prior.

Fair looked, stood up, patted Winston's nose. "You're a healthy fellow, Winston. How old is he?"

"Winnie is now fifteen." Tiffany also stood up.

Fair smiled at the 16.1 hand fellow, a light bay with such a kind eye.

One had to like him.

Three young ladies, leading their horses, stopped at the opened barn doors.

Tiffany unhooked one side of Winston's cross ties. "Come on, ladies."

Fair listened to the clop as three horses walked by, each one stopping before his stall, where the young woman removed tack.

"What can I do for Winston and you?"

"Write a letter as a collaborating vet saying he is healing quickly but turnout will guarantee the process."

"Of course."

"She wants me to stuff him with drugs. There has to be some form of calcium booster. Fair, the last thing this fellow needs is drugs. He's fine. I am pretty opposed to fooling around with anything that can alter an animal's natural balance if the animal is healthy."

Fair pulled up Winston's top lip. "Must have just had his teeth floated. His gums look good. Let me borrow your stethoscope."

Tiffany, her scope around her neck, handed it to Fair.

His listened to Winston's heart, to his breathing, carefully repeating the process. Fair was a thorough veterinarian.

"Sounds fine."

"He's a good athlete, too."

Fair handed her back her scope. "Bloodwork?"

"Yes." She walked to her bag, pulled out a file, handed it over.

He leafed through it. "Up-to-date on all his shots. His Coggins." Fair mentioned a mandatory test for all competitive horses.

"She wants me to jam him full of vitamins. He is just fine and he eats good hay. Two scoops of grain a day. Winston is an easy keeper."

"I'll make note of that. I'm not saying there isn't a time when an older citizen doesn't need vitamins, but he's a long way from that." Fair took a pen out of his short beat-up work jacket, a small notebook followed and he wrote down the lady's name and address. "Give me two days. I'm jammed."

"That time of year. Hunting is picking up, a bit cooler, the runs are longer and faster. I haven't had many injuries, though I have had more colic than usual."

"We usually get that in the winter. Well, who knows? I remember one month about three years ago when I had four eye injuries. I hadn't had an eye injury to that day and I haven't had one since. Odd stuff."

"It is."

"Hey, Fair. Good to see you." Lynne, big smile and a happy voice, came over, rubbed Winston's nose. "Best horse in the barn. Aren't you, Winnie?"

Tiffany replaced her file folder. "I was sorry to hear about Ben Wagner and sorrier that you found him. Has made me lock my truck."

Lynne remarked, "People on drugs do crazy things."

"Yes, they do, but I don't think whoever killed him was on drugs," Fair evenly replied. "They certainly stole all his ketamine but I figure this was motivated by profit. That stuff will bring money. The sheriff's department studied his inventory on his computer."

"You think Ben got in the way?" Tiffany, like everyone who knew Ben, was curious.

"I don't know," Fair honestly answered. "The clinic was spotless. All the doors were locked except the room where he was killed. Nothing was damaged or touched and whoever did this could have walked off with his brand-new X-ray machine. My old X-ray machine cost $30,000. I don't want to know what a new one costs."

"I guess they knew what they wanted," Tiffany said. "But just to be on the safe side, I'm locking my truck."

"Heard Candida Perez passed away. She had good long innings. Ben, not so much," Fair remarked.

"Should be in tonight's paper," Tiffany said.

"Harry had just seen her at Nancy Parson's store where, she said, Candida corralled a customer with stories of her romance with Nardo and who knows what else." Fair smiled as he thought of the exuberant Candida. "I expect she had a heart attack. At least she went fast."

"Neither of her children has her personality. Not that they are unpleasant but she lit up a room." Lynne, who had joined them, spoke forthrightly, as she was among friends.

"Well, Ballard's long battle with drugs didn't help him." Tiffany felt badly for him.

"He cleaned up but how many trips to rehab did that take?" Fair wondered.

"A couple of hundred thousand a pop, I bet. He would only have been sent to the most exclusive." Lynne knew Candida would pull out the stops for her only son, who greatly resembled his father.

"Constance, at least, avoided that," Tiffany concurred.

At that moment Constance and Ballard, in the library at Lone Pine, papers picked up and in boxes, fought with thinly disguised viciousness.

"No autopsy!" Constance snapped at her brother.

"We ought to know how she died. Just in case it's hereditary, you know." He stood his ground.

"For Christ's sake, Ballard. She was ninety. It doesn't matter how she died. You aren't going to live that long, anyway."

He stopped for a moment. "And why not?"

"All those drugs you crammed down your gullet have to have weakened your system. I always thought that was the real reason you were so happy to go back to St. Paul's every fall as opposed to switching to St. Christopher's. Better drugs."

She cited two private boys' schools.

"Bitch. Well, you don't have to live to be one hundred, Constance. You already look seventy. Those California plastic surgeons will get you every time."

St. Paul's, an expensive prep school in Concord, New Hampshire, affiliated with the Episcopal Church, was unfortunately where Ballard had found drugs. He had teachers who cared for him, counselors who watched over him. He more or less kept on the rails, with weekend blowouts. It wasn't until he matriculated at Yale that he dove deep into the drug scene, easy to do in New Haven, or unfortunately most any university.

St. Christopher's, on the other hand, was a boys' prep school in Richmond, Virginia. A fine school, not without kids peddling drugs and taking same, it didn't suit Ballard. It was too close to home. There wasn't a school anywhere free of drugs, but why let Mother hover over him?

Constance attended Miss Porter's, thence Mount Holyoke. A good student, she majored in political science then did nothing with it. But she married seemingly well so no one much cared. If she did, she kept it to herself.

Neither sibling was cut out for the rock and roll of employment in the non-rarified world.

"I'm going to get a lawyer to stop you from ordering an autopsy. Just leave her alone." Constance folded her arms across her chest. "It's so disrespectful."

"You probably killed her." He curled his upper lip.

"Oh, Ballard, grow up. If anyone were going to kill Mother, it would be you. I doubt your hardscape business is making any more money than all the other businesses you've tried. Maybe she died of exhaustion; she tried everything with you."

Face crimson, he shouted, "I am doing very well. What the hell are you doing?"

"Well enough. And don't say you never wished Mother dead."

"I never did. Not once. Not even when I hit the bottom at the third rehab joint. Would I have been rich? Yes. Could I have bought any drug I wanted? Yes. I thank God she threw me in those places and wouldn't give in to my whining."

A long pause followed this. "That surprised me. You, the adored son. She paid for those clinics but she didn't bail you out."

"I feel so guilty about the things I said to her when I was high on whatever." He peered at her intently. "I doubt you've ever felt guilty in your life."

Constance shrugged. "Well, once or twice, but I wasn't lying in gutters in New York, either."

"Musical beds." Ballard nearly licked his lips.

"And so what? When I found the right man, and Kevin was the right man, I stopped all that. I often thought Mother was glad you were gay, then no other woman would have you. She'd be the center of your life."

"Bullshit."

"Back to the autopsy. No. Ballard, just let her go in peace."

He said nothing. "Grace Episcopal Church. On Saturday."

"We've got so much to do. Where do you want the celebration? I mean after the service. No one says funeral anymore. I say here at the house."

"She would have wanted that." A look of loss crossed his face.

"She promised she divided all her assets in half with strict instructions about what would go to the foundations she supported. It's the house I wonder about." Constance looked around at the subdued, handsome room.

"We'll cross that bridge when we come to it."

She sighed deeply. "Yes. I'm not worried about it, I just don't want the house sold. There's nothing like it in this county."

"Mmm."

"You're already counting your profit, aren't you?" She glared at him.

"No. But I don't want it. So if you take it, given its historical value and its worth, we'll have to balance out finances."

She interrupted him. "I am willing to bet you one thousand dollars Mother thought of all that. In the meantime, we have a funeral to plan and it better be worthy of her."

"It will cost a fortune."

"Ballard, Mother had a fortune."

9

October 5, 2019

Saturday

Grace Episcopal in Keswick, a stone church of great charm, looked like the scene for a rock concert. Six sheriff's cars routed traffic for the parking lot, which had been filled an hour and a half before the morning service. Constance, expecting this, hired school buses and limos to drive mourners from designated spots along Route 22. Many homes along that twisty road allowed people to park in their fields. Everyone, close here, intended to do what they could to honor Candida Perez.

Ballard, never the best planner, went along with Constance. He would sneak out of the reserved space for family to check outside.

"You can't believe it. Half the county is here and the other half is looking for parking."

Constance glanced up as he shut the door behind him. "Everyone in the church or outside has known Mother all their lives. Who can imagine life without her? I think only Ellie Wood Baxter was here before Mother, and she, by the way, is in the first row, along with Chuck Beegle."

"The governor is here, too. Guess he didn't have any trouble finding a parking place." Ballard sank down in the chair, already overwhelmed.

Before the pulpit, in the fourth row, sat Nancy Parsons, Harry and Fair, Susan and Ned back from Richmond, and Susan's mother and grandmother.

A choir, specifically flown down from Washington, D.C., sang as people waited for the service to begin.

Deputy Cooper, beholding more school buses disgorging people, said to the sheriff, "We're out of chairs."

"They'll have to stand." Sheriff Shaw looked up, grateful the sky was sunny, the temperature in the mid-sixties. If one was going to have a funeral, these proved perfect conditions.

Another fifteen minutes passed. The Episcopal priest checked her watch. Candida much liked having a female priest, finding she could more readily unburden her woes to another woman. On one hand, she thought any priest was helpful but there were sorrows one need never explain to another woman, or so Candida believed. The abiding tension in her life was the relationship between Constance and Ballard. The siblings fought relentlessly even as toddlers. The grand lady felt powerless to create peace.

Finally the reverend stood up, walked to the center of the raised altar floor. She held out both her hands. "Please rise."

A good audio system allowed the two hundred people near the church to hear. Those out almost on the road just imitated everyone else. All stood, and the service for the dead began.

Later, the masses gathered at Lone Pine. The caterer and staff wore themselves out tending to the mourners. Sunlight filtered through the trees, centuries old. People, especially those up in years, drew together. Funerals, often seen as a burden when young, become a fitting tribute when older, a way to reconnect with friends old and new.

"Remember when Candida had a horse running at Foxfield? Oh, back in 1997?" Ballard spoke to Fair.

"Good horse. Bosun's Mate." Fair remembered horses he had seen in childhood. "A bay."

"Well, here was Mother, not quite seventy, and the fellow with a horse running thought she was this sweet little thing. She was standing near the finish line and he was bragging about how his horse would tear up the turf. You know the type."

"Only too well." Fair grimaced.

"So Mother said, 'I'll bet you two thousand dollars that Bosun's Mate will come in first.'

"'Well now, little lady,' said the stranger. 'I'll take that bet,'" Ballard repeated the dialogue.

"Sure enough, Bosun's Mate won and the blowhard wrote a check on the spot, as everyone was watching. When Bosun's Mate was officially announced winner, Mother took the check and walked into the winner's circle. Ha. He about died."

"Well, she had an eye for a horse." Fair smiled. "And an eye for so much. She gravitated toward beauty. Lone Pine testifies to that."

As they talked, Constance circulated, thanking people for coming. Nancy Parsons pitched in, bringing drinks to some of the elderly, as did Susan's mother, in her seventies, a snap still in her step.

Harry wandered into the library, the room was open. Jerry Showalter stood there, hand under his chin, thinking.

Looking up when Harry entered, he gestured to the boxes. "She was going through them. That's what Constance thinks. Papers scattered on the floor. This library is filled with treasures." Jerry cast his eyes around the shelves, leather bindings almost glowing, the gold leaf and gold printing on the spines brighter in the light pouring through the windows.

"All this is worth quite a bit, isn't it?"

Jerry nodded. "You know, this is my business. Buying libraries, selling them to institutions or individuals, but I truly hope Constance and Ballard keep this intact. It is so beautiful and I think," he emphasized *think*, "this library should be made available to library science students. There are books and letters dating back to the mid-seventeenth century. Let them come here and study. How many young people will ever get the chance to see a great library owned by an individual? Institutional libraries are wonderful, of course, but it's not the same."

Harry walked over, slipping a midnight-blue bound book off a shelf.

"'Every man is, no doubt, by nature, first and principally recommended to his own care; and as he is fitter to take care of himself than any other person, it is fit and right that it should be so.'" She closed the beautiful book. "*Theory of Moral Sentiments*, 1759. A first edition, Adam Smith."

"Most every book in here is a first edition. This library is worth millions, but I truly believe it should be left intact. These books reflect the curiosity, the thoughts, the struggles to learn and live expansively, of generations of Ballards. Candida Ballard Perez was true to her roots." Jerry smiled. "She loved Adam Smith, by the way." He paused, sighed deeply, then looked at Harry, whom he had known for years. "You know today in The Service for the Dead, the *Domine, refugium*. 'Lord, thou hast been our refuge, from one generation to another.' Well, that's what this library is and I am in need of refuge. Ballard has contacted me. He wants all his mother's papers sold and the library, too. He suggested Emory University. You know Constance will hit the roof."

"You're in the middle," Harry acknowledged.

"I could walk away but then someone might come in who has no loyalty to Candida, and will be enticed by the large commission. Ballard as well, Ballard always needs money."

"He's been clean for years now." Harry liked Ballard despite his drug days.

"Oh, Harry, I don't think either of Candida's children is good with money. They know how to spend it, they don't know how to make it. Although they try. At least Constance married a businessman, but at the end Kevin was faltering. Ballard was always faltering. Constance tried to hide her reduced circumstances. Her mother did not bail out Kevin but she always bailed out Ballard. That only intensified the anger."

"Ah." Harry thought, then offhandedly advised, "You'd better go to your lawyer. First you have to protect yourself then you have to protect Candida, if possible."

"I know. I know. Well, the one thing I can do is organize all those papers found on the floor. Both Constance and Ballard would like them back in order. I wonder what she was looking for?"

"When we were all at Country House Antiques, Candida, a new victim in hand, mentioned the family letters from the centuries and she named Woodrow Wilson. Maybe she wanted to be reminded of what was in his letter."

"Could be."

"Well, let me go back outside. You know we both have to pass and repass."

He smiled. "I do."

She paused. "Jerry, don't tell anyone else about the impasse between brother and sister. With your permission I'll tell Fair. He has great good sense."

"Indeed, he does. He married you." Jerry kissed her on the cheek and they both walked out into the celebration, the mob, the early afternoon sun.

10

April 2, 1789

Thursday

Tricorn hats shed rain. A good thing because John Schuyler stood in a flattish field, rain pouring down. Next to him, Zachery Thigpen swept his hand outward.

"Ten miles to the Potomac. This is flat. Would work."

"Yes. It's Virginia's good fortune that you own all this."

"A man can never own enough land," the dark-haired fellow solemnly intoned. Then he laughed. "If there's another war, I can fill in the potholes."

John laughed with him. "Never thought of that."

Zachery turned and they sloshed their way to one of his coaches. The driver, already on the ground, opened the door. A small foot heater, warm charcoals in a metal box, rested on the floor.

Zachery put his wet boots on this. "Might be April but it's raw. Put your feet up. Helps."

John lifted his feet, gingerly placing them on the charcoal. "Commodious, as my father-in-law would say."

"Your father-in-law is a farsighted man. Well, look at it this way. Travel is tiring. Roads are rutted. Rain like today changes everything and if a driver isn't careful or lucky, stuck. So then someone has to come pull the coach out and the passengers must stand outside in the rain. This does not sit well with the ladies."

John took his hat off, a bit of water still dripping through the three corners. "You've done so well. It's good to see your success."

Pleased that his former officer complimented him, Zachery replied, "Ah well. If a man can't make something of himself now that the British are out, he's either lazy or simpleminded."

"No doubt, but to determine what you need to operate a stagecoach line, I can't begin to figure it out. You need sturdy carriages, good drivers, good horses and teams of horses throughout your routes. The cost of feeding and shoeing them has got to be," he said thoughtfully, "a huge expense."

"The horses are easier than the people. You try finding a driver who doesn't keep himself warm with copious sips of the bottle. Between drunkenness and tolls, well, every line of work has its problems. I'm getting better at weeding out drunkenness."

"How so?" John was interested, as alcohol plagued the military as well.

"If a man comes to you for a job and he's married, try to meet his wife and children. If the children are thin; the clothing a bit worn; the wife very worn, no matter her years; you've got a drunk. Don't hire him."

"This feels good." John pointed to his feet.

"When we get back to the house, I'll give you a change of clothes. No point sitting around wet." Zachery looked outside the window. "Think it will rain all day."

"Yes." John looked out, too.

The brick house in Leesburg, on the main street, provided warmth as well as good company. Zachery had invited some of his neighbors and friends to meet Colonel John Schuyler. John found himself the center of attention. Although a little shy, he was fine; Catherine had helped him master social settings.

As the men left, each shook John's hand and promised the colonel could call on him.

John sat in a chair next to the fire, it was still raining and raw, as servants brought more drinks.

"You never were a drinker." Zachery lifted a glass of whiskey.

"A sip. That's it for me. You know those men. Are they as good as their word?"

"They are. When I received your letter I was proud that you have been selected to train our young men. And I know the state of Virginia will not be very helpful."

"I fear not."

"Money. It always reduces to money and our elected fellows don't have the head for it. The new money isn't going to be tobacco, hemp, apples, and so forth. Will those crops make money? Yes. Will pine be a good source of income? Yes. But when Mother Nature is your business partner a lot can go wrong. Two years of drought. We have to develop other types of business, of producing goods. Perhaps we can even learn to create investment funds. Our former enemies have a genius for managing money. This doesn't include King George, of course. Look what the weather has done to France. If they'd had good harvest years, I don't think Louis XVI would have ever called the Estates General. We, like France, are dependent on the weather."

It didn't occur to John to ask how invested money could be made and by what kind of people.

"My father-in-law keeps up with countries across the ocean. He does business, or did business, with France but now he focuses on England. Odd, I think, after a war, to more or less pick up where we left off."

"Way of the world." Zachery put down his glass. "Which is why we need our shores protected. I will raise one hundred men, pay for their equipment. You, of course, will have to train them but I can suggest some good junior officers up here in northern Virginia so training can continue consistently even when you are home or traveling."

"That is very generous, Zachery. I don't know how I can ever repay you."

With a wave of the hand, Zachery tilted his head to the left. "Well, John, if men like ourselves don't think about the future, who will? I begin to think that peace is harder than war."

"Yes. When we served we acted as one. Now it's not at all that way."

Taking a deep breath, Zachery said, "I suppose that has always been true. But if we do now fund a standing army and a true navy, perhaps the English won't be back but someone else will. The Atlantic Ocean can only protect us for a time and any nation with a good navy is a danger to us."

"Colonel Ulrich said as much."

"And how is he?"

"Well, I think he has been eating his wife's good food."

They both laughed.

"What are your plans?"

"First, we need to concentrate on infantry. We need a reliable force in each county who can hold off enemies until the rest of us can get there. Look at our coastline, Zachery. Troops can land anywhere along Virginia's shores. The mountains protect us to the west but if our enemies who have been turning the tribes against us manage to create solid alliances, those tribes will know the ground better than anyone. I fear them more than I fear an invasion. Having fought the English I have great respect for them." Zachery murmured in agreement. "But I fear the tribes more." He half smiled. "No infantry squares."

Zachery nodded. "I've always thought fighting with the British during the French and Indian War prepared Washington for what we would face here. Our terrain alone demands careful study."

"That it does." John leaned forward. "Zachery, I hope to create militias in each county. Leesburg has been the county seat for Loudoun since 1757. What you do, others will follow."

"I'd like to think you're right but having the Potomac as our northern boundary in some ways has forced us to be ready. At any time the British could have sailed up to us on small ships. Well, look what they did on the James."

He cited the depredations of farms along the James River during the war.

"What I hope to do is bring every county along on the militia and then start artillery training. Percy Ballard will focus on what artillery we have."

"Aha." Zachery liked Percy.

"I believe artillery is the key. Think of the rows of guns on those ships at Yorktown. We don't have enough cannon. We've got to have artillery from larger guns to small, highly mobile ones. If anyone is foolish enough to invade us, we need to give them a bellyful of shot."

This made Zachery laugh. "I don't think anyone will ever accuse you of not taking the fight to the enemy."

"Ah." John shrugged. "We only know what we have experienced. The next war, if there is one, will be somewhat different. I don't want to get stuck like a stagecoach sunk in the mud."

"Yes. Yes." Zachery's mind was whirring; though not a natural soldier, he had a good mind and could appreciate John's military prowess. "We have no foundry."

"No. Nothing that can produce cannon. Nor do we have caissons, no ammunition wagons. There is a small forge near Cloverfields. It's too small to forge cannon but I think the fellow who owns it, Jeffrey Holloway, might be able to help in some fashion. As to ammunition wagons, they need to be sturdy. I don't know if we can impound farm wagons, should the need ever arise."

"Yes. Let me think. There's a fellow over in Maryland who has been building sturdy wagons and those are based on wagons from York, Pennsylvania. Studebaker is the York fellow's name. A cut above the rest."

"I would like to meet him."

"Let me give this my attention."

A discussion among comrades, one that would bear unintended consequences for John Schuyler and those at Cloverfields.

Perhaps there are no accidents.

11

October 7, 2019

Monday

Picking up a stiff envelope, Harry wrote down the date the letter had been sent, January 19, 1901, put down her pen, carefully opened the letter to scan it.

Jerry Showalter had set up a table, courtesy of Constance O'Donnell, wherein all the papers once scattered on Candida's library floor were piled. The two friends sat on two library chairs, each making notes. Jerry tidied up the piles but figured as they picked up each letter it would be placed in a year, so all the 1901s would wind up in the 1901 pile.

The two boxes had been hastily filled to protect the letters scattered on the floor. The first leather box contained the correspondence from 1900 to 1915. It was overflowing already.

On the wall the gilded banjo clock with a pastoral scene painted on the face displayed 10:20 A.M. They'd started at 9:00 A.M.

Harry wrote down, "Charles Augustus Peabody, Jr. New York, New

York. May 2, 1901." "I am trying not to read the letters but it's hard," she admitted.

Jerry, folding back the letter he held after checking the name, said, "You get better at scanning them as you go along. Most are full of domestic detail, whereas others, the business ones, are strictly business. What I find interesting when I do read a letter throughout is how the men were expressive, not effusive but expressive."

"Right. This one, really, I only scanned it, is from Charles Augustus Peabody, Jr., to Senesh Ballard, describing his father, whose health was failing. Charles Jr. thanks Senesh for his kind sentiments."

"Sitting down and writing organizes one's thoughts. Of course, that was the only way to communicate then. Yes, one could make a phone call but to call from New York to Virginia was prohibitive in 1901."

"How did you know where Jr. lived?"

"A famous banker. Made pots of money. And the father, the one failing, did well in life, too. Then again, the Ballards did well, too. Everyone knew everyone."

"You must know everything," Harry complimented him.

"No, but given my years at the University of Virginia I gathered who was important here, who their contacts were, especially in New York City, Boston, and Philadelphia. Then again, so many also had foreign contacts. Just think of Thomas Fortune Ryan, the second richest man in America. Born in Fortune's Cove in Nelson County. From here to New York City. He died in 1928, worth $200 million. Can you imagine what that would be worth today? Billions. Tobacco and transportation." Jerry carefully laid the letter he had scanned onto a pile rapidly growing.

"It's a born talent, making money." Harry selected a pale blue envelope.

"Yes, well, I missed it." Jerry laughed.

"I've been in your house. It's lovely."

"You are too kind. But one doesn't make a lot of money being a librarian. Once I left library service and struck out as an antiquarian dealer I began to see big or bigger money, if you will."

"How so?"

"At the university I would procure items of special interest for special collections or book collections. So I met those with resources or someone with an interest, say, in some form of Virginiana, like foxhunting. But that's not the same as mingling with the active collectors, some of whom own libraries worth millions of dollars, the rooms are temperature controlled. The door opens when one of them dies. Very often the children have no interest in a first edition of Thomas Hobbes. So the entire library can go on the market or more often be subdivided into special interests."

"Why do that?" Harry wondered.

"Because a dot-com whiz might not want the library of a railroad giant in toto but would be interested in anything, say, of the sciences. Or a book by or about Babbage, the inventor of the computer."

"I would guess they'd pay a fortune."

"Fascinating man, Babbage, and to think he understood the principles of computing in 1821."

"We're stuck with it now." Harry laughed.

Constance walked into the room. "Shall I have Margaret bring you anything?"

"Oh, no, thank you," Jerry responded.

"Looks like you're making progress," she rejoined.

"Well, we have only two boxes to sort, what your mother was sorting through. If I were to go through and write down everything in this family's correspondence, I'd be here for a year."

"You would be delightful company." She looked at Harry. "How did he woo you into this?"

Harry raised her eyebrows. "He swore he could find the Duke of Portland's equine breeding papers." Harry loved studying Thoroughbred bloodlines.

"Ah, but which duke?" Constance also knew a bit about bloodlines.

"The sixth. The one who imported Carbine from Australia."

"Very good." Constance smiled. "But don't overlook the fourth duke. Good horseman."

The Ballards had been prominent in American racing in the 1920s and '30s along with Candida, who as a child had met some of these legendary people then she, herself, became one, more for her effervescence than horses, but she had good horses.

"I'll start studying all the Bentincks." The Bentincks inherited the title Duke of Portland, the first title being created in 1633, reissued in 1689.

The family in subsequent generations produced a few eccentrics; but then, any long-lived family will do that.

"Jerry, shall I assume the correspondence has great value? I know the library does."

"Yes." Jerry faced the imposing Constance although he was seated and she standing. "Again, one would need to go through the entire collection."

"What about, say, a decade or simply a century?"

"Yes, that would have value, you could take a specific time frame, like the 1930s, or you could single out correspondence from a famous individual; say, letters from a president or a prime minister or an artist. Those always bring money because there is a university somewhere trying to corner all that material."

Constance crossed her arms above her waist. "Yes, I was afraid of that."

Neither Jerry nor Harry said anything and Constance continued. "Ballard wants to break down the papers and sell by writer or subject, depending. I utterly refuse."

"Ah." Jerry was thinking fast. "It may be that your mother has attended to this in her will, which would certainly lay the matter to rest."

A long sigh escaped Constance's lips. "Well, the will will be read next Wednesday. Mother would tell us what she had left, that sort of thing, but I never believed this a hundred percent." She raised her hand. "Not that she was using the will to keep us in line. If that had worked, Ballard would not have blown through drug rehabs, but you know, she could get merry and babble a bit. I didn't discount it, but then again . . ." She waved her hand.

"Wise. She had such an expansive nature." Jerry was good at this.

Constance laughed. "She did. Well, let me allow you two to return to another world."

"That it is," Harry agreed.

Once Constance was out of earshot, Jerry said in a low voice, "There's no telling what Candida wished, but my hunch is she would not want the family papers anywhere but at Lone Pine."

"Well, yes, but who will live at Lone Pine?" Harry couldn't imagine brother and sister co-existing under the vast roof.

"Good point. Constance lives simply for a Ballard. She gave up her big house once she became a widow. Too much to run, she said, but we all know she was in reduced circumstances. It must be a huge money drain and this will be far worse. Then again, her husband had lost much of his money. She kept a stiff upper lip, but given the Ballard vanity it must have been onerous."

"I would expect her mother left ample funds for her."

"Yes, I would, too, so long as the estate stays in the family. And neither sibling has a child."

"Well, Ballard's got a better chance than Constance." Harry stated the obvious.

"She could always adopt." Jerry leaned back in the chair.

"Good Lord," Harry exclaimed. "Never thought of that. Constance is in her sixties."

"Money does strange things to people. That's another thing I learned when I started dealing in rare books, special collections."

"I think it does strange things even if you don't have two nickels to rub together."

They laughed and returned to the task at hand.

Harry grabbed a pile of heavy envelopes, expensive paper. "Out of place."

Jerry took them from her hand. "Italic. Must be envelopes for Candida's Christmas cards. She planned early. Sent out beautiful cards. Paid Ben Wagner to write the names and addresses."

"She thought ahead," Harry said with admiration.

12

October 8, 2019

Tuesday

Every now and then Fair heard a clunk outside.

Mark Catron, standing in the center aisle, also heard the sound. "Karen wants a hardscape. No weeds to pull."

Karen was Mark's wife, who had an eye for decorating, inside and out.

"You know, I expect weeds will wiggle up through the rocks." Fair mused as he took Dee's temperature.

Dee, jet black in winter, faded in summer, stood 16.1 hands and was a Friesian cross. Comfortable, athletic, she displayed strong opinions. She didn't like her temperature being taken but she stood as Mark held the lead shank. She wanted no part of the cross ties today.

"Normal." Fair dipped the thermometer in alcohol, wiping it off with a cloth that hung from his back pants pocket. "Her eyes are good. No muscle spasms. No lameness."

"She's been sluggish."

Fair looked over Dee's back. "Fall's coming. If this continues, let me know. I think she's responding to the change in the seasons. Then again, Mark, do you want her at high energy?"

"Well, no, but half asleep isn't so good, either."

"If she stays lethargic, call me next Tuesday. And if you do hunt her this week, stay in the back. I expect she will find reserves of energy. Dee hates to stay in the back. Let horses move off and she is determined to follow."

The two men occasionally hunted together, glowing in their scarlet coats as both earned their colors. Opening hunt was at the beginning of November so they wouldn't be wearing the scarlet until then. No formal clothing before opening hunt. Fair observed Dee's need to be with the others when out there. On the other hand, she hated going first. Let someone else try the jump. She'd follow.

Mark, as a joint-master, needed a dependable horse.

"All right. Glad you could swing by."

"How's Corey?" Fair inquired about Karen's horse, a made hunter who suited her perfectly.

"Good. Karen's back on a regular riding schedule. They both need it."

"What about you, buddy?"

Mark, a vice president at Wells Fargo, half smiled. "Work is crazy. I'm getting new clients and the market is strong. Makes everyone happy."

"For people who understand it."

Mark nodded then walked the big girl back to her paddock, where she immediately put on a show.

"*Whee.*" She kicked up her heels.

"No lethargy there." Fair smiled, and Mark had to laugh.

As both men walked around to the front of the barn, Ballard Perez, on his knees, looked up. "Can you believe this weather?"

"Indian summer." Mark stepped closer. "That rock has a blue streak in it. It's quite unique."

"Kyanite. Guy Dixon gave me some for special clients."

Fair knelt down to examine the beautiful stone more closely. "This jumps out at you."

Ballard took it back with both hands. "Some people cut it for crystals and say it helps your throat. I guess you put it on your throat or something. I don't know much about stuff like that."

He stood up and all three men studied the progress of his hardscape.

"Karen wants this at the front of the barn," Mark informed Fair.

"Don't you need help?" Fair thought about lifting heavy stones all day. The stones had been hand cut into large squares, the kyanite would be placed between them, for it, too, had been cut into squares.

"No. For a big project I'd hire hands but I enjoy doing this myself. I can think better."

Mark swept his hand along the front of the barn. "She'll put a narrow garden in front, so there goes the argument about weeds. I think she wants white with spots of lavender in the back against the stone. It will smell good."

"Who designed the gardens at Lone Pine?" Fair asked.

"Hugh Gunsten. He'd studied with English designers, especially the Scot Robert Adam. Then he came back to Virginia, hung out his shingle. Thanks to his training and talent, he received many commissions, Lone Pine being one. It's beautiful work."

"That it is. Lone Pine is one of the most stunning estates in Virginia." Fair meant it.

"When I was little I would walk in the gardens with my notebook and draw them. That's when I realized, or perhaps my father realized, I was not going to be a stockbroker, an investment banker, or follow his footsteps in international banking. Really, Constance should have done that, but it was a different time."

"It's still not so easy for women." Mark nodded, for he knew the industry.

"You probably know my wife was over there yesterday helping Jerry Showalter put those two correspondence boxes back in order."

"I didn't know Harry had such an interest in history." Ballard rubbed his hands.

"How many pair of gloves do you wear out?" Mark laughed.

"One a week." Ballard looked to Fair. "Harry did go to Smith. I forget that. So did Mother."

"Which is why my bride agreed to help Jerry. 'Can't let down a Smith girl.' That's one of Harry's phrases. I think all graduates love their alma mater. Well, I love mine." Fair beamed.

"Auburn. Hey, I went to the Harvard of the South." Mark laughed, for he attended East Tennessee State University in Johnson City, Tennessee. "You guys are pikers."

"Oh brother." Ballard punched Mark lightly.

"Yale," Ballard simply replied. "Got as good an education as I could, considering I partied hard. Mostly I was running away from myself. Took me twenty years before I could face a reunion but I'm glad I went and now I go each year. Dad attended the University of Barcelona. If my Spanish had been better, I would have applied." Ballard shrugged. "Dad and I were so different. We finally did reach an accord."

"Pretty common, tension between father and son." Fair liked Ballard and had seen his struggles first with drugs then with being gay. He figured the drugs were part of the escape from himself.

"Constance was the son Dad never had." Ballard laughed. "I don't think I have one thing in common with my sister except our parents. Oh well, let me get back to work here while the light holds."

Fair drove home from Mark Catron's barn, his last call of the day, thinking about how hard it was for older generations to be true to themselves. Being gay was part of it for Ballard but so many boys struggled against fathers who wanted them to be a lawyer, a doctor, a banker, make money. It was always about money and status.

Pulling into the driveway, he saw Tucker flash out from the stable. *"Daddy!"*

Bending down, almost doubling his six-foot-four-inch frame,

Fair scratched Tucker's ears, being rewarded with a rollover to show a white stomach. He scratched that, too.

Pewter, sitting in the open barn doorway, curled her nose. "*Obsequious.*"

However, the minute Fair walked to the barn, next to her, she did rub against his leg. He petted her, too.

Then both cat and dog followed the tall, lean man into the tack room, where Harry had books all over her desk there.

"Hi, honey." She offered a cheek, which he kissed.

Mrs. Murphy sat on one low pile of books.

"What might you be doing?"

"Oh." She turned her swiveled chair to face him. "Sorting those letters yesterday provoked my curiosity. I was aware Candida knew many people but she had letters from Winston Churchill before World War II. They met in England and hit it off. She seems to have known everyone. I would love to read the family papers. Would take years starting with the first Ballard, Percy Ballard. What a life."

"Ran into our Ballard at Mark Catron's. He's building and designing a hardscape. He showed me kyanite. He has some stone that he's cut into squares. Beautiful stuff."

"Jerry and I were talking about what will be World War III once the will is read."

"You don't think Candida cut out Ballard? She adored him," Fair wondered.

"No, but whatever the disposition of her goods, it will be, oh, something to fight over."

"He's cleaned up. Took until his late fifties, but he did it," Fair continued. "Wait and see. About the will, I mean. I kind of think Constance will want to assume her mother's mantle."

Harry put her hands on her knees. "She's a highly intelligent woman but has little of her mother's famous charm. You know, Fair, I'm glad Mom and Dad had enough, worked hard, but we were a long way from rich. So many rich people endure horrible family fights or strained, even abusive childhoods. Abuse isn't just for the poor."

He kissed her again. "I think we were both lucky. By the way, does anyone know when the will is to be read?"

"Next Wednesday," she answered. "Jerry knows everything. He's a bit in the middle, given his expertise with books and family papers."

"They should hire him to go through everything. It's too valuable for all of us, really, to be left unattended."

"You know, honey, that's what I keep coming back to, because Candida knew those papers, starting with the ones from 1640 to now. Her people fled England when Cromwell came to power, or I should say when the Puritan movement was growing. What a mess. Anyway, she knew all of it, I think. So what was she looking for? Something provoked her to sift through 1900 to 1915."

"Probably wanted a reminder or perhaps to reread love letters between her mother and father."

"Maybe." Harry had a funny feeling about those scattered letters.

"What troubles me is not Candida. She lived a long, full life. What needles me is Ben's death. Still not a clue. Not one."

"Yes," Harry replied as Mrs. Murphy moved from a book on the English Civil War to Harry's lap. "Ben took over for Greg Schmidt when he retired. He recommended Ben to Candida as a vet. Then she would hire him to write cards for her, special letters. He was young and needed money. Her hands began to hurt. She had beautiful handwriting and couldn't do it anymore so she hired him because he could do calligraphy. He addressed all her Christmas cards and wrote notes. He started early. We found the envelopes he did for this Christmas."

"You're right. I forgot about that. He'd do any odd job he could. He was kind of artistic, wasn't he?"

"Well, come on. I made some pea soup. Felt like soup."

"Me? I could use bacon. You put bacon in your pea soup." Pewter patted Harry's leg.

"Hey." Tucker loved bacon.

"*Me first.*" The fat gray cat ran toward the house with surprising speed considering her bulk.

Mrs. Murphy, on the other hand, strolled with the humans as they walked toward the house.

"Honey, I'll set the table. Give me one minute. Left my coat in the back of the vet truck."

"Okay."

Five minutes later Fair walked into the kitchen, the aroma enticing. "Honey, my ketamine is gone."

"What?"

"Every bottle."

13

April 3, 1789

Friday

"I ask if it is just even in the century in which we are living, that the two orders, which are not the nation, should dominate the whole nation. We can proclaim until we are hoarse that the power of the nation is invested in us; there are 600,000 voices to contradict us." Ewing stopped, glanced up from Baron Necker's letter from France at his old friend Yancy Grant then continued. "His father responded, 'From his principles, it follows that the only place in which a legal assembly could be held is the Valley of Jehoshaphat.'"

Yancy smiled. "The old marquis has been reading his Bible again. Given his age he is probably considering the Last Judgment."

Ewing carefully put down the letter, the elegant handwriting slightly slanted to the right. "Why would a nobleman, for Mirabeau is his father's son, why would he pander to the people?"

"I suppose that depends on how much he feels he will inherit."

Ewing shook his head. "Not a sou. His father has been ruined by thirty lawsuits. Can you imagine? The French exhibit a love and obsession with suing one another. Well, how else can a lawyer make money? If there are no disagreements, they will all starve."

"I have heard this was one of the worst winters of all time in France." Yancy gazed into the fire, for spring was slow to make an appearance.

"Yes. The baron writes that people are starving and freezing. There is plenty of grain but the mills are frozen, so nothing can be ground into flour. The rivers are frozen, so the log trains can't deliver wood. Fires can't be built. No wonder there is seething unrest."

As a young man Ewing Garth had been sent to Europe for the obligatory tour. He met a young man from Geneva, now the Baron Necker, both being interested in finance and business, a youthful friendship struck up that lasted to today. Ewing, in his late fifties, devoured the baron's letters, filled with political news spiced with tidbits of gossip. It would seem that the nobles drank, danced, and slept with one another. Anything more serious hovered above their enfeebled capacities. However, they dressed to perfection.

"If young men who are ennobled are criticizing their own estate, no good can come of it. And why, my dear Ewing, would any man with a grain of sense think the people, the Third Estate, won't turn on them?"

"I don't know. Perhaps having young men give rousing speeches about voting, political destiny, encourages tradesmen and others to openly gather, to press for more advantages."

"No doubt." Yancy settled even deeper in the wing chair by the fire. "The nobles and the Church will never surrender their tax advantages. Never."

"True, but did not our own struggle with the king start over taxation? That and the fact that he and Lord North would not send more troops or protect us against the tribes. A people must have confidence in their leaders."

"You, as always, are right, but we had not entrenched privileges as do the French. Our former king reached back to 1066 but he was over the ocean. I don't know, Ewing, I believe their situation is quite different; add in this terrible winter and, well, anything is possible."

"Baron Necker sees it but given his position he walks on eggshells. Hates Mirabeau, by the way. These new men in France, I don't know what to make of them. But I don't always know what to make of us." Ewing laughed. "We truly are new men."

"Before it slips my mind, I must remember to congratulate John on his promotion, his vital responsibility."

"He's in Leesburg attending to finding money and muskets now. You know, John is a quiet man, not a lettered man, but he can read and write. When Catherine fell in love with him, love at first sight for both of them, I knew he wouldn't make a penny. He's a soldier. I allowed the match because it truly was a love match, but if Catherine hadn't married how could I allow Rachel to marry?"

"You were wise. Younger sisters can be a burden."

"Well, I thought Catherine would never marry. Despite her beauty, or perhaps because of it, she never so much as had a flicker of interest in young men. And she frightened them."

"She is uncommonly intelligent. She inherited your fine mind."

"Thank you, but if she did she should be silent about it." Ewing threw up his hands. "I gave up and as you know, you are one of the few who know, she has become in many ways my business partner. We discuss everything. She certainly understands profit. But John has surprised me. As you surely have noticed when we gather together for a smoke and brandy after dinner, he rarely says a word. But I tell you, Yancy, he listens. He soaks it all up. He will never have a head for business but the man is a deep well."

"A courageous one. And really, he makes your eldest happy. Both of your girls made suitable marriages, happy ones."

"We are fortunate." Ewing stared into the fire. "Yancy, I have heard that Maureen has moved much of her money out of France to Italy, where she seems to have had good relations with the bankers. She understands money and bears watching."

"What I don't understand about Maureen is her unwillingness to use our bankers. You would think Hamilton would be her best friend."

"Yes. Yes," Ewing said almost absentmindedly.

"What do you think?"

Tapping his fingers on the arm of the chair, Ewing leaned forward. "I think she's waiting to see how this tension between Hamilton and Jefferson is resolved. If Hamilton's view gains the ascendant, she will bring some of her money here. Of course she has some money here now, but I mean bring money in significant amounts. She nurtures a relationship with Sam Udall, the Richmond banker. I find him unimpressive."

"What if she dies soon?"

Ewing raised his eyebrows. "Jeffrey will inherit, I assume."

"He hasn't the mind for money."

"No. He does not. He's a builder. But it is possible they could have children."

"Oh Ewing, she's too old."

"She can adopt."

A look of shock crossed Yancy's face. "I never thought of that."

"The Caesars did it."

"She regards herself as an empress." Yancy laughed.

"Money drives her but so does power. She's up to something."

"But what could she want, I mean apart from more money?"

Ewing shrugged. "I don't know but we had best be wary and tend to our own flock."

14

October 8, 2019

Tuesday

At a long desktop, built into one wall, supported by thick swirling legs, an interesting touch, Fair and Cooper sat side by side. The overhead lighting cast a soft glow while moveable desk lamps, high intensity, could be pulled over to the computer if needed. As it was late afternoon, they did need the brighter light. Fair agreed to meet Cooper after the day's last call. Anyone else would have been exhausted.

Cooper, soft-leaded pencil in hand, checked off a name on the list Fair had printed from the computer.

"No one there but the owner."

"Right. She stayed with her horse. If she had left, I would have known. Simple cut, nothing awful but did need five stitches."

"Is it possible someone could have gone into your truck and you wouldn't know?"

"Not at Fast Run." He named the farm. "I back the truck to the open doors. Jenny has a great setup there. Anyway, unless a ghost haunts Fast Run, no way."

"Isn't every place in Virginia haunted?" Cooper wryly commented.

"Only the old places like yours. You know you'll wind up buying that old Jones place."

"Well." She looked up from her paper to the computer. "Sooner or later Reverend Jones will sell. Now, next."

"The Barracks. Full-blown commercial operation, huge, as you know. Well run. However, I did not lock my truck when I parked down by the indoor arena."

"Do you usually lock it?"

"No. Until Ben's murder, the missing ketamine, I never thought about it. Like any vet, I have all manner of medications. A small animal vet, too. If nothing else, the needles we carry would be worth something to an addict."

"But not much financially." Cooper noticed the client's name, injury. "Hmm."

"Oh, having to tube the mare. She eats paper. How she got into newspapers, who knows, but she had an obstruction. So I tubed her. Passed. Lucky."

"Well, maybe she's learning to read." Cooper couldn't help the comment. "Lots of people?"

"Not lots. It's Tuesday. The owner works at UVA so Claiborne observed." He named the owner of The Barracks, she and her husband owned it. "A young fellow held the mare."

"Okay. I'll call and see who was working today. But when you walked back to your truck you didn't notice anything odd, out of place?"

"No, but in truth, Coop, I wouldn't be looking. Unless the inside of my truck had been disheveled or the X-ray machine taken or the ultrasound, the big-ticket items, I don't really pay that much attention."

"You need things like sedatives, antibiotics. Wouldn't you notice if bottles were missing?"

"Sure. If someone was desperate and clever, they could pull bottles from the back of the rows; I wouldn't notice at first. But that would be desperation, not profit," Fair noted.

"Right. How about criminal records? Do you know of any help at your calls where someone has a criminal record? You know, like from James River Horse Foundation." She cited an organization that continued to train and find jobs for female prisoners who had served their time down in Goochland's prison.

"I don't," he replied. "As far as I know there hasn't been any kind of problems with . . . well, let me back up, there are always problems with workers but that doesn't mean they're drug addicts, would steal for stuff."

"Fair, alcoholics and drug users lie. It's like breathing to them. The smart ones can hide it until finally the stuff takes over their entire life. But for years people can more or less limp along. You wouldn't know."

He thought about this. "I'd know if they were stoned and got on a horse. Or drunk."

"Maybe." She raised an eyebrow. "People pass the flask in the hunt field."

"Coop, that's not being drunk. I mean a flaming alcoholic." He paused. "Although some come close."

"When you've made barn calls, like at number three here, Fox Haven, have you ever smelled alcohol?"

"Once or twice over the years. I'm not saying people don't drink but I don't see it. Then again, most horsemen carry injuries. Maybe a nip now and then, or a snort, kills the pain. I don't know. My left knee sometimes kills me when I ride. Old football injury, but I'm not going to drink. I'll take Motrin."

"Okay, let's get back to this list." She ran her pencil down the left side, at the numbers. "Anything jump out at you?"

"No."

"Well, I will have to question the owners, obviously. Better a drop-in than a call. I learn more. And don't worry, you won't be put on the spot because you're the one robbed. The first thing I will tell them is we are working on Ben Wagner's murder and ketamine was stolen there. No one is going to be upset with you."

"Thank you."

"You've never had problems with thieving? I mean if you did, you didn't mention it?"

"No. Not meds, anyway. I've had, in the beginning of my practice, a camera stolen. Money taken out of my glove compartment. But either I've been lucky or there aren't a lot of thieves in my line of work."

"Have you ever suspected barn help at any of the farms you visit are using or selling drugs?"

"Yes. Over the years there might be someone who has abnormally high energy or becomes irritable. What I do notice is high turnover. Those people rarely last. The owner may tell me why the person was fired but often they don't. Then again, Coop, so much of barn help is a young person dreaming of a show career. That's a hard life. Many can do well at some shows, move up to bigger ones, but a full-time career as a show rider, really really tough, like making it to the NBA. Every hotshot kid at a good basketball school thinks he'll make it. Same with horses."

She leaned back in the chair, folded her hands together. "What I ask myself is, why now? Why ketamine thefts now? Wouldn't this have happened when Special K was at the peak of its popularity?"

Fair also folded his hands. "How do you know it isn't making a comeback or it's one of those tried-and-true drugs, like cocaine? It will always be around."

"Yeah." She breathed in deeply through her nose. "Part of me thinks this is the work of a ring. They steal in upstate New York or Vermont during the summer then here then in Florida or Arizona. I've called other law enforcement departments. The ones around Wellington, Florida, notice a seasonal spike in theft, drug abuse. So maybe someone was on their way to a bigger market."

"I don't know. I'm just a vet." He smiled at her.

"The most likely reason is the university. In a short radius there are enough large and small schools to create a steady market."

He unfolded his hands. "Wouldn't you know?"

"It's possible there have been thefts all along, given the college population. I would suspect the huge drug cartels are supplying them. So, to me, that means this is someone's new idea or someone needs money badly."

"Enough to kill?"

"That's the problem, isn't it? Who would risk getting caught for murder for selling Special K? What was taken from Ben was his supply, which would be small in terms of the market, and the same for you. So where my mind keeps talking back to me is this is something different from just ketamine."

"Either that or the big drug lords are branching out, stealing locally."

"Doesn't make sense. At this moment nothing does." Her eyes lifted up to the opposite wall. "How is it I never noticed your Brown Bess?" She cited a musket used during the Revolutionary War.

He glanced up. "In the family. You don't come into my office."

"As you know I go to the shooting range. Most of us do. We have to keep in shape. There are good shooting ranges in the area. Terrific clay shoots. Well, I got off the track. Anyway, I was chatting with one of the instructors after shooting and we got to talking about the difference between rifles and muskets. He knew more than I. He told me a smoothbore, single-shot, muzzle-loading musket, a trained soldier could fire three shots a minute. For highly trained troops it was twenty seconds per round. At one hundred yards that musket ball could penetrate three inches of steel."

"No kidding."

"I never thought much about muskets being lethal. He also said that by the end of the eighteenth century, rolling over into the nineteenth and the Napoleonic Wars, muskets could be loaded faster than rifles; .640 caliber. The velocity was three thousand nine hundred feet per second. That could certainly kill you. Men stood in squares, fired, and took fire." She shook her head. "What guts."

"My ancestors served in the Virginia militia during the War of Independence. When I look up at the musket I remember not to take my freedoms for granted, then I slide back into the comforts of the twenty-first century and I do."

"So many of the old homes here are from that time." She folded the paper Fair had given her of his stops at clients. "My people didn't get off the boat until the 1880s. Ellis Island."

He grinned at her. "We're lucky."

She laughed at him. "Flatterer."

He clicked off his computer, offered her a co-cola or hot tea, which he could make. She declined.

"Did Ben ever talk to you about women?" she asked as she walked out to the small tidy lobby with him.

"No. I figured he was one of those fellows who wasn't going to look around until he felt secure in his career."

"That's not a bad idea, but somewhat contrary to nature." She smiled, her eyes bright. "That gorgeous babydoll walks in front of you and that's it."

"Seems to work that way. I've known my gorgeous babydoll since grade school. Took going away to Auburn before I realized there's no one like Harry."

"That's the truth." Cooper burst out laughing.

Fair walked her out to the squad car then returned to his office to wrap up the day. Harry had promised her famous fried pork chops so he was eager to get home. He sat for a moment, stared at the musket. He thought to himself, *Am I missing something?*

We all miss something. You just hope it doesn't kill you.

15

October 10, 2019

Thursday

"I know you're not open Thursday but I saw your car parked out front so thought I'd make a quick call." Constance, red alligator handbag on her arm, walked into Country House Antiques.

Nancy smiled at her while she placed a small side table in better light. "Come on in. Getting ready for tomorrow."

"I don't see how you can make money operating only on the weekends."

"I don't make much but I enjoy what I do."

Constance walked over to her, pointed to the wall. "When I was here with Mother I didn't walk over to this part of the store. Mostly I hoped Mother would eventually stop her life story, you know how she could talk. The military prints. I didn't know they were missing until I sorted through Mother's upstairs hallway yesterday. Did Mother bring them in?"

"No. Ballard."

"I knew it." She shifted her expensive bag to the other arm. "He had no right to do that. I'd like them back."

"Oh, Constance." Nancy felt a tempest coming on. "I sold them."

"To whom? I'll pay whatever they paid but I am adamant that nothing of Mother's leaves the house."

"Constance, I can understand your feelings and I had no idea. I think the wisest course would be for me to call the purchaser. It's possible she will be willing to sell. But I can't in good faith say who bought those prints."

Face darkening, Constance got hold of herself. "Of course. But tell them I will pay whatever they ask. I very much want my mother's estate intact." She turned then stopped. "Has my brother brought in other items?"

"Small things. Lamps. A farm table from the dependency. The cradle that you saw." Nancy named the small house for a farm manager correctly.

"I can't believe him. You know he always needs money."

"Don't we all." Nancy smiled slightly. "Should he bring anything to me I will tell him he must talk to you. But Constance, how am I to know what was your mother's and what might be his?"

Now, her expensive Hermes purse hanging in front of her held with both hands, she considered this. "Well, you don't. I know most of Mother's paintings, prints, clothing. She had marvelous clothing. Even some Worth gowns from the early twentieth century. They cost $10,000 then. They're worth a fortune today. She kept them in excellent condition. But the other things in the outlying houses, like a farm table, I took little interest in. I suppose I had better check. Of course, they are now empty, which helps, but still." She moved her feet closer together. "Nancy, I had no idea, no idea, not one tiny thought, that settling Mother's estate would be so, so—volatile."

"Oh, Constance, I fear that's the norm more than not."

"People's emotions flare up. Mine have. I've spent my life watching my brother filch money from Mother. For what?" She took a deep breath. "I don't believe he will ever stop. Once an addict, always an addict."

"I do hope you're wrong. It must be terrible to be in the grip of something you can't control."

"Having seen it up close, I think it must be hell, but the addict drags everyone through it. If it were one person suffering, bad, but no, it's everyone and everything they touch." She caught herself. "I'm sorry. I'm a bit raw from Mother's passing. She seemed so healthy and, well, old though she was, I couldn't imagine her gone."

"None of us could. But what a life." Nancy smiled broadly.

Constance smiled. "There is that."

As Constance left, drove away, Nancy sat behind her desk, took a deep breath, and called Harry.

"Hello."

"Harry, Nancy Parsons."

"What are you doing, girl? I mean apart from talking to me."

"I have a conundrum. You bought those terrific military prints for Fair. Have you given them to him?"

"No. I was going to wait until October 20. Our anniversary."

"Ah. Well, this is a bit odd." Nancy recounted the visit from Constance.

"I . . . well, let me think about it."

"Harry, she will pay more. She's worked up. I can find you something very good between now and then and you will have extra money in your pocket."

"Really?"

"Really. She is burning." Nancy dropped her voice. "I don't see how those two will stay out of court."

"What's the Spanish expression? I think it's Spanish. 'Better to fall into the hands of the Devil than a lawyer.' "

Nancy laughed. "There's a reason they created a great empire."

"And a reason they lost it." Harry knew her history.

"Let me make a suggestion. I will look for Napoleonic prints. So many people are military collectors, whether it's old flintlocks, prints, uniforms, even handwritten battle orders. Virginia is brimming with military history buffs. So would you rather have Napoleonic military uniforms or English?"

"English," came a swift reply. "I like them all. They are so beautiful and elaborate, but if I could choose, it would be English. Why not go with the victors of Waterloo?"

"You have a point there. I'll get back to you and I will hold her off for a day or two. By the way, I did not tell her you bought the prints. Too much emotion and you don't need to deal with it. For Constance, a red face is a lot of emotions. All that WASP restraint retreating."

They both laughed then Harry added, "I am guilty of it myself."

While that phone call unfolded, so did another one.

Constance called Jerry Showalter. "I want you to go through, assess everything in Mother's correspondence files. All the way back to the sixteen hundreds. And give me a possible value."

"Constance, you sound upset." Jerry was thinking fast.

"I am. My brother wants to sell all of Mother's papers. He says we can't properly keep them. Never. Never. Never. Never."

Very calmly, Jerry said, "If I do that, he will want you to buy him out."

"Like hell I will." She swore, rather shocking for Constance.

"I quite understand." He did but he also understood a no-win situation. "I was hired by both you and Ballard to put your mother's two boxes, 1900 to 1915, back in order. I was thrilled to have the job, for I have longed to go through your mother's papers. Centuries of papers even though this is only fifteen years of material." He waited a moment. "But Constance, if you hire me I will be between you and your brother. He will hire someone else. There's no way I can work at Lone Pine with someone hired by Ballard for the express purpose of undermining my assessment. Your value, I should say."

"What can I do?" Her voice wavered.

"Can you talk to Ballard?"

"Jerry, I've been trying to talk to that cokehead, or pothead or whatever he was, all my life. Of course I can't talk to him."

Jerry let that roll over his head then replied, "He may not be as bad as you think but before you fuss at me for taking his part, which I am not, remember he was Momma's boy. Spoiled, weakened in ways. You, Constance, are not. You've got to be logical. However he's dealing with his mother's death will lessen in intensity over time. Why upset yourself and spend money? Really, why spend money for someone to go through all those papers, which will take a year at the least?"

"But if he hires someone, then I must."

"Yes," came the measured reply. "But let him spend his money first. Then you will have to protect yourself, which everyone will understand. Otherwise, Constance, you look as though you are letting him drag you through muck and mire and we all know you are smarter than that."

Bull's-eye.

"Well." A long, long pause followed this. "You are right. Why spend the money if I don't have to?"

"The more irrational he is, the more rational you must be, but you always have been."

This was true.

"I am so glad I called you. I'm more upset than I'd like to admit. After all, she was my mother, too, but she always favored him. I suppose every family has its old wounds, but Jerry, the money she spent on rehab and setting him up in business. Wasted."

"This last rehab . . . what was it, seven years ago . . . seems to have turned the trick. Be glad he never married. If he had a wife or a husband, there would be even more trouble."

A terrific long pause followed this. "Ah."

"You should be the mistress of Lone Pine. You and you alone." Jerry was beyond clever.

Another long pause. "Thank you for thinking so. I would like to continue Mother's traditions."

"You are too modest. You need to be a leader of society, of those people doing good foundation work. Your mother was a stalwart in such things and you, of course, have followed in her footsteps. But now you must lead alone."

Constance hung up the phone consoled, puffed up by Jerry. He was right, why spend money if not necessary? And Ballard had a habit of not staying the course. She could just wait the bastard out.

She really did hate him.

16

April 7, 1789

Tuesday

A clack and a sliding sound, a rhythm kept Bumbee humming. The rhythm of weaving was like breathing to her. Her mother was in charge of the loom and the large weaving cabin at Cloverfields. When her mother passed to ride chariots to freedom in the sky, Bumbee took over. Now in her middle years she couldn't imagine any other work than weaving. The colors of the fabrics, wool, cotton, linen. The feel between her fingertips of the yarns, warp and woof, patterns. Her skills bedazzled many. She took pride in that. Catherine and Rachel would wear her shawls, special aprons never to be truly used, as well as flowing skirts and bodices, all made from the stuff stacked in the weaving cabin.

Bumbee made her husband, whom she called Mr. Percy and with whom she fought regularly, build her squares like bookcases, only squares on shelves, into which she divided up her yarns and fabrics.

Sometimes she would dream of combining cotton with linen.

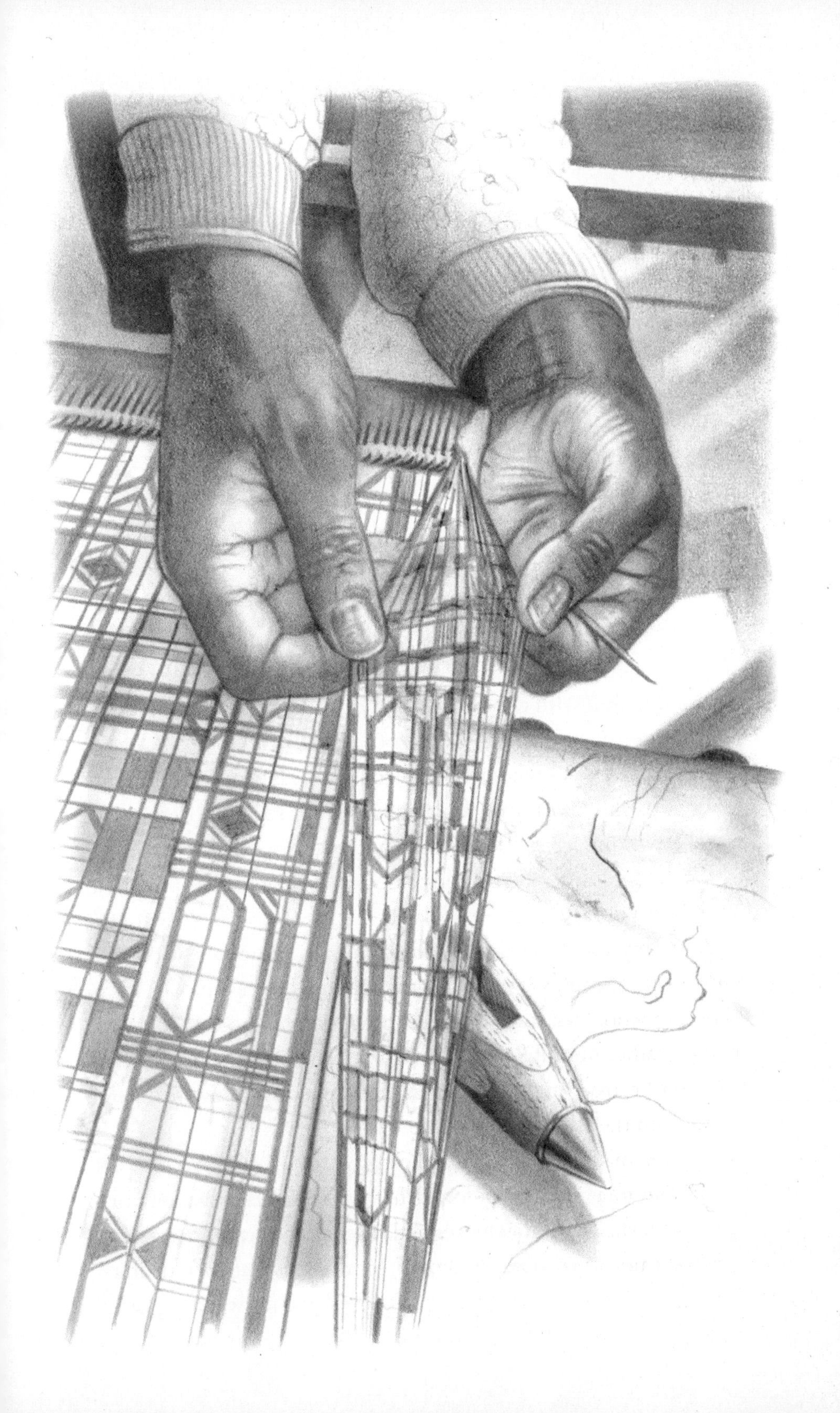

Other times she would awaken with a new idea for a color, a dark peach interlaced with maroon.

This early evening, cold now that the sun set, she stayed to weave a heavy cotton shawl, pulling the threads tight. Soon wool would be too hot but the nights would remain cool, sometimes even into May. A lady needed something over her shoulders.

She rose, tossed a few logs onto the fire in the huge fireplace. The cabin, carefully chinked, roof with a steep slope, kept out the cold. The windows, all the cabins had hand-blown windows, shut tightly and if the night proved viciously cold and she wanted to work late, she would stuff discarded pieces of wool along the edges. If it snowed or winds kicked up, Bumbee often slept in the cabin, next to the fire. Ewing, mindful of her creativity and directed by his late wife, had a sturdy cot built for her, which she could pull over to the fire if she wanted. Many's the night she didn't want to see her husband's lying face so she stayed in the large cabin, complete with stove and a well with clear water outside.

Firewood stacked by the front door, another stacked pile by the back, a small pile rested inside the front door, she was well stocked. Never a good idea to have firewood close to the fire. Even with a screen, an errant spark could escape.

She jumped, for a knock on the door was unexpected.

"Bumbee. It's Bettina."

She stood up, hurried to the door, which she opened, cold air rushing in. "Bettina, get in here, girl. Getting hateful cold."

Bettina stepped through the door, following her old friend to sit in front of the fire. "Brought you some biscuits, and a good chicken pie. You sit down here and forget to eat. If you turn sideways, I won't be able to see you."

"Ha." Bumbee, grateful, took the basket.

"I'll warm it up. You'll forget." Bettina took the basket back, opened the thin towel covering the biscuits, butter, and meat pie. She knew the stove, a good one, might take too long to heat up, so she slid the pie into a square cut into the stone for warming bread.

"Bettina, you're too good to me."

"Won't take long." She pulled up a rocking chair, also built by "the boys," as Ewing called them. "I'm waiting for spring."

"One of these years, I think."

"Well, it was a hard winter. One of the hardest I remember." Bettina felt the fire's warmth. "Seems to me winters are getting colder or I'm getting older. The mistress always said she minded the cold more as she aged."

"DoRe back at Big Rawly?"

"For a few days. Mister Jeffrey asked for him to come and help him with a big coach. Until we are properly married, you know she'll get everything out of my man that she can."

"Hmm. It's a miracle she finally settled the terms with Mr. Ewing."

"A miracle and a lot of money. I wonder. I wonder how she needs more money. She is richer than we can imagine but it's never enough."

"Some people are that way." Bumbee murmured the name *Maureen*. She shrugged.

"Came on down. Heard some loose talk. Actually, I've heard a lot of loose talk. William, still chained at night, been running his mouth over there about Ralston."

"Ralston? They all ran away together." Bumbee knew Bettina heard a great deal, for as the head cook she could eavesdrop on many conversations; also, people would talk to her, hoping she'd spill what beans she knew. She didn't.

"Right, and he says Ralston is at a big place, big with pillars, you know, in Maryland. DoRe has heard him when he's over there with Mr. Jeffrey. William works in the wagon shed. Well, it's a real building, not a shed."

"Ralston's free?"

"According to William he is, but he tells the others at Big Rawly that someone from Cloverfields should get him and bring him back."

"He can stay where he is free or slave. That boy was nothing but trouble." Bumbee grimaced. "Trying to rough up the girls. No sense."

"The story goes that Ralston tore Sulli from William's loving arms." Bettina accentuated *loving*.

"William never loved anyone but William." She brushed back some hair creeping out from her mob cap. "He'll suffer for the rest of his life. He did wrong. He hurt people. Broke Jeddie's shoulder. Stole a horse. But he's chained like a dog. He's crippled. Where's he going to go?"

Bettina nodded. "Never knew a woman so vicious as Maureen. And you know he's chained as an example, which I expect he is."

"She's vicious with everyone. Except with Mr. Jeffrey." She sighed. "Men. He is—"

"Beautiful. A man can be beautiful and he is. Now, my DoRe, no beauty, but what a man. When he's with me I never worry. I can't explain it."

"Well, when Mr. Percy is near me I worry all the time." Bumbee laughed. "If he told the truth, he'd tell a lie just to keep his hand in."

They both laughed.

"Heard that Maureen goes down to Richmond, alone. Supposedly she's considering some kind of business."

"DoRe?"

"He doesn't drive her but he's talked to the man she's hired. She tells Mr. Jeffrey she's going down to see Sam Udall, the banker. I saw Sam Udall once. Looks like a gopher. Teeth sticking out." Bettina laughed. "Must be one of the ugliest white men ever born."

They both giggled like schoolgirls.

"What do you think?"

"Oh, I don't doubt she's visiting moneymen, but the driver swears he saw Georgina, the lady who owns the so-called tavern. Tavern, hell." Bettina rocked faster. "Saw Georgina going in Udall's back door when Maureen was there."

"Isn't that where there were troubles a few years ago? At the tavern? Yancy Grant was caught there. Maureen swore one of her slave girls had run to Richmond and Georgina. These stories change every time I hear one, but more than food is served there."

"True. That is true." Bettina rose on the word *food* and picked out a plate, old but good china, to serve Bumbee, who took it with a smile.

"Well, Bettina, why would a woman of Maureen's standing and wealth do business with such a woman?"

"I can't imagine. If Maureen really is meeting Georgina and Deborah, her so-called best girl, in a banker's office, it would have to be some big profits."

"I can't understand it unless it's illegal."

"The driver told DoRe she gives him money to pick up things, tools for Mr. Jeffrey, and when he comes back she leaves by the front door, naturally. DoRe believes she's setting up some sort of business with Georgina, who is supposed to be very clever. Makes money hand over fist."

"Well." She thought. "Land? Tobacco?" Bumbee strained to think of things.

"Who knows, but whatever they're doing she wants to keep it from Mr. Jeffrey."

Bumbee considered that. "I expect she keeps a lot from Mr. Jeffrey."

Bettina rose, now slid the pie out of the warming square on a wooden paddle with a long handle. She then poured some tea out for Bumbee, as the weaver always kept a pot hanging on an iron rod over the fork in the fireplace. Needed thick hot pads for that task.

"Sit down. You need to eat. Come, pick up your plate and properly sit. I should have made you do that in the first place."

Bumbee did as she was told. They gossiped, talked about fashions, each hoped Catherine and Rachel would have more children, the chatter of old friends.

"Sally's showing some interest in learning more. She's reliable. Not all the young girls here are."

"Bumbee, they're lazy. Luckily I'm not working with lazy girls.

Now, Serena is a good girl. Taught her what I can and she remembers, but she has no ideas of her own. Not one. She's not lazy so much as . . . well, like I said, she has no ideas. I asked her to think of a new sauce for beef. Nothing. She did as I do. Am I expecting too much? I don't know. I couldn't wait to make new sauces, baste a roast with something like raspberry sauce with a touch of thyme."

"The young are different." Bumbee savored the chicken pie. "Jeddie in the stables wants to learn, and that little Tulli does, too. That child isn't growing. I swear he isn't growing at all." She paused. "Doesn't seem sick. But these young ones, looking for the main chance, I say. We looked out for one another."

Pointing to the pie, Bumbee smiled. "You've always looked out for me."

Touching her heavy shawl, Bettina smiled back. "You've taken care of me. Sometimes. Bumbee, I think I'm getting old. Dissatisfied. Then I see shoddy work and it makes me angry. Whoever you are, you can do better than that."

"All the girls here, they weave, they card, they spin. They do as I tell them, but like Serena, no ideas. What they talk about is love. Love. Love. Love. Was I that way? I don't remember it."

Bettina thought a bit on this question. "Oh, there was a time when Mr. Percy turned your head. And the first year of living with him. But I don't recall you ever sitting at the loom with your mother carrying on about boys."

"Maybe we missed something." Bumbee wondered.

"Oh, Bumbee, spring will come and we'll feel better. Always comes, you know. The sun shines. The birds sing and build their nests. The flowers pop up, bright little heads."

"And my man will be out there trying to woo more girls. He'll tell them the sap is rising." She shook her head then smiled. Bumbee nodded in agreement about Bettina's hopes for spring but inside she felt she was getting old. Love would never come again and what she thought was love turned out to be lies, pain, and sorrow.

Why did she ever believe a word that man said? And yet there were times when she still wanted to believe him.

"Bumbee."

"What."

"You drifted off there." Bettina reached over for her hand. "Spring will come. You'll feel young again. It's so short. Life. Spring will come."

17

October 16, 2019

Wednesday

The garage of McGuire Woods, the large law firm in the mid-Atlantic, Charlottesville office, like most garages was too tight, too dark, and built with no regard for how people actually use space. Then again, if you can jam them in, the cost of building is cheaper. Who cares if poles scrape the sides of cars, or bumpers tap other bumpers backing out? Blame the driver.

At this moment, two-thirty on a rainy day, two drivers were blaming each other for far more than bad driving. Constance and Ballard charged down to the basement using the elevator, where she slapped his face hard. To his credit he did not slap back. He did laugh at her, which only made it worse. The will had been read and the moment got colored by relentless pressure on Candida's lawyer from the siblings. Neither sibling was satisfied. Candida either nurtured a rosy picture of her daughter and son or she left knowing they'd kill each other. Or maybe she tired of the constant wrangling, which began when Constance at age three tried to strangle Ballard at the table because she didn't want competition.

While this is not uncommon, the two never truly warmed to each other, rarely played together, and attended different schools. There was little opportunity to know each other and Candida, the belle of the ball, loved them in her own way but kept up her whirlwind schedule with scant regard for the children.

The elevator door opened with a slight creak; they stepped out.

"You liquored her up. That will was signed last year." Constance, hands on hips, squared off against Ballard, much taller than his sister.

"She was in full possession of her mind. And I had no idea what was in that will. You got what you deserved and I suppose I did, too."

"You knew!" Constance exclaimed.

"I did not know. I thought Mom had pots of money."

"She spent it all on you and those hideous rehab bills. Plus, how many sheriff's officers did she pay off or the sheriffs themselves over the years?"

"Oh, Con, she didn't do that. I was hauled in enough as it was. She posted bail every time. You received half the estate. Stop bitching and moaning."

"Half of her debts."

"Okay. I inherited them, too. As well as the lawyer's telling us we should now consider a mortgage if we wish to keep the place."

"A mortgage. I never paid a mortgage in my life and I don't intend to do it now."

"We can keep the place if we go to the bank for a mortgage. If we sell her letters, some of the artwork, Lone Pine will once again be in the black."

"One and a half million dollars of debt? Bullshit. I'm not doing it." She swore, something she rarely did, having attended years of cotillion.

"Well, I will hire Jerry Showalter. He'll put it together and I expect those letters are worth multimillions."

"You are not selling the letters of our family, some of which go back to the mid-seventeenth century, and you know that. Never. Never. Never!"

"What do you have in mind?" He was tired, for the exact nature of his mother's debts shocked him and he knew full well some of that money was spent on him.

"I want to talk to Roy Wheeler." She named a prestigious real estate firm.

"The hell you do. You aren't selling the property when we have a way out."

"I didn't say I would. I would never sell Lone Pine. But they more than anyone will have an idea of what it's worth. And you are not selling anything. Anything. You can't do it without me, anyway."

"I can if I go to the right lawyer."

"Oh, go ahead. Everyone around here knows what a loser you are. All you'll get is an ambulance chaser."

He counted to ten, then again. "I have a growing business."

"For Christ's sake. Landscaping, or hardscaping, or whatever you call it? You can't make that much money."

"I didn't say I would make millions but I work hard. Anyway, I'm not telling you what I think. But I do believe we should end this."

"I will buy you out."

"With what? Kevin didn't leave much or you two wouldn't have sold your big house. You put a good face on it but I know you, sis. You are like Mother in the regard you want to be the queen, the big bug. I don't care about that but you do. Downsizing. Must have killed you."

She bit her lip, finally opening her mouth. "I never said I don't like being important. Kevin and I collected so much stuff it was a relief to weed it out. And yes, at the end, he lost a lot of money in the so-called Great Recession. We never talked about it. I actually think it killed him. The worry."

"He cared about status. I'll bet he worked extra hard, so the move truly did look like downsizing. I'll give you credit, you did a good job of covering the truth."

She let that go. No point in confirming his doubts.

"So?" He pressed.

"I will never agree to selling the family papers. Sue me. Blow what little you have on lawyers. I won't do it."

"You never cared for our history before."

"Mother wasn't dead before!" With that she turned on her mid-height heel, strode to her Lexus, a perfectly respectable car for a well-heeled matron.

He watched her stomp off then turned toward his Dodge Ram. He did not own a smaller vehicle. He could only afford one and it needed to be a work truck. The Ram sufficed. Had some real power, too. Squeezing in the opened door, as there wasn't much room, considering how he was parked, he fired up the motor, listened to the thump, and sat steaming.

Dialing, he heard Jerry's voice. "Jer, Ballard."

"Hello." Jerry knew the will was being read today and decided not to bring it up.

"Mother left us with debt. A lot of debt. I want to sell the family papers. Will you put them in order and market them?"

Patiently, Jerry explained why he couldn't do that, although in different terms than he did with Constance.

"Can you suggest someone?"

"Yes. Give me a day or two to consider a few names that you can trust." What he didn't say was, *Give me a few days to fill them in.*

"Have you any idea what the papers might be worth?"

"Not without going through them, but at least double-digit millions. Perhaps even more. It is an extraordinary trove. Your family took excellent care of those papers. What I read, a few on vellum, could have been written yesterday."

"I see. I don't know if I will trust anyone as much as I trust you."

"Thank you. I do thank you but as I worked for both of you on the tipped-over boxes, you can understand why this could potentially lead to a lawsuit. Your sister won't stand for it."

Ballard sighed. "You know, I hate her. I have always hated her. She is so obstinate about Lone Pine. She believes she can step into Mother's shoes. Obviously I can't."

"Well, if you were into drag you could." Jerry giggled.

This so surprised Ballard that he laughed, too. "Do they make women's heels in a size 15?"

"I don't believe they do. I never noticed your shoe size before."

"Big feet, but at least I don't trip over them."

"Ballard, we have known each other for decades and you know I was devoted to your mother. If you can, don't make a move yet. Think it through. Keep as calm as you can and don't let Constance get under your skin. Grappling with your mother's death and now the will takes a lot out of you. You don't want to be operating with diminished judgment."

"Thank you, Jerry. She'll use everything against me. You've given me good advice, if I can just follow it."

"You can."

"You didn't ask about the will."

"That's not proper."

"Thank you again but I will tell you. Mother must have spent like a drunken sailor. She left us . . . and by the way she left us equal shares, half and half . . . one and a half million dollars in debt."

Jerry immediately replied, "Given the value of your estate, that's surmountable. Even if you don't sell the papers, it is surmountable. She left jewelry, she left artwork. Not all of it has meaning, although all of it is beautiful. Candida had great taste. Sit tight for a time."

"Thanks, buddy." He disconnected, carefully backing out the huge truck, making those tight turns and driving up the ramp into a howling rain.

Seemed prophetic somehow, that driving rain.

18

April 15, 1789

Wednesday

"Unhitch the horses." John, on his knees, knew the plow was broken.

Mr. Percy, Bumbee's wandering husband, along with Cager, a strapping fellow in his mid-twenties, unhooked the traces, put each set over their shoulders, and took hold of the bridles of the horses whose reins they carried.

"Takes a lot of digging." Cager, nickname for Micajah, grumbled.

"No other way." John followed the two men back to the stables, where Tulli eagerly tried to slip off bridles.

"Here." John lifted him up and one bridle came off.

"I can do that," he said to Cager.

"Gotta hurry, little man." Cager smiled at him, as Jeddie came out with lead shanks and halters.

"They all right?"

"Hit a stone," John told him. "Have no idea how big it is so we'll need to dig it up. Might as well do it now. Good light."

"Yes, Sir." Jeddie nodded. "Probably be another light frost tonight. Will just make it harder."

"Percy, two pickaxes, two shovels." John looked at the sun, figuring they had another hour of light.

As the three men walked back to the field, the one closest to the main house, Jeddie watched as Tulli started to wipe down the powerful draft horses; they had some Suffolk Punch in their blood. He picked up a towel and ran it over Billy, withers to hindquarters, then did the same for Bobby, a matched pair.

"Someday I'll be tall like you, Jeddie. I'll wipe everyone down, even their heads."

"Tulli, you will," Jeddie encouraged the little fellow, who didn't seem to grow much.

"I'll pick up Billy's feet." Tulli knelt down. The gentle soul lifted his right forefoot, then his right hind as Tulli worked his way around the horse just beginning to shed his inner coat.

"Do Bobby." Jeddie knew Tulli would fly over to a now drying Bobby.

"Everyone is good."

"That's good news. No hoof, no horse."

"I can lead them both." Tulli reached for Bobby's lead shank.

"Put them in their stalls. Let's give them an extra handful of molasses in their oats. Everyone deserves a treat."

"I will." The boy led the two docile horses to the third stable, which housed the work horses and one newly acquired donkey, which never shut up.

Jeddie watched the kind animals on either side of the slight child. He wouldn't allow Tulli to lead the blooded horses unless he was on the other side. A little too hot for Tulli, but the child so wanted to be useful, Jeddie found ways to work around his small stature and lack of muscle. He shielded his eyes with his hand to watch the three men reach their object, sun low in the sky.

Back in the stable Barker O, the stable manager, repairing a torn headband—he could work with leather better than anyone else at Cloverfields—looked up. "Percy said the damn stone snapped the plow. We have others but we'll need to replace that one. Those mountains left us all kinds of things."

Jeddie nodded. "Kind of like people. You see what's breaking the surface but who knows? Percy is a talker. Then again, what he doesn't know he'll make up."

Barker O laughed. "Maybe you don't want to know."

Jeddie looked around the large tack room. "Anything else?"

"No, just this. Might as well bring the horses in. By the time you're done, sun will have set. Gets cold fast."

"Does." Jeddie left to start bringing in the blooded horses. Tulli was already bringing in the two ponies for the children and the gentle saddle horses for Ewing, John, and Charles. Jeddie whistled for the blooded horses to come to the gate.

"You're doing good work, Tulli. You're ahead of me," Jeddie called to Tulli as he led Ewing's horse into the stable.

Back in the field, the three men worked up a sweat, which would soon turn cold against their skin, shirts soaked.

"Damn, this thing is in there." John swore, something he rarely did.

"Look at this." Cager pointed at the smooth side of the stone as they dug deeper.

"Huh." Percy looked, as did John.

Most people, especially the men, called Percy *Percy*. The women often used *Mr. Percy*, which pleased Bumbee.

"Well, let's get it out of here and then we can look."

"Mr. John, going to take horses to pull this out." Cager kept digging the boulder, which seemed to grow in size.

The area around the enormous dark gray stone had flecks of something shiny in it, quartz? Mica? Not much mica in this part of the world, but the stuff was beautiful. John brushed more dirt off.

"Ever see anything like this?"

"No, Sir," Percy and Cager both said. "Kind of glitters."

"Well, Percy, jump down in here with me, let's see if we can rock it a little."

Percy did, the two men pushed and grunted.

"You're right. We'll need the horses. How we get ropes around this thing?" He shook his head, didn't finish his sentence.

"We'll figure it out and if we don't Tulli will. He can wiggle into all kinds of places." Percy laughed.

John laughed, too.

He started to climb out of the deep dug side, thanks to a leg up from Percy. John turned and leaned down again. He bent over as far as he could, being too large to wedge himself completely down.

"What you got?" Cager leaned over to look in the flaming sunset light.

"Look." Percy pointed to finger bones.

"Damn," Cager exclaimed.

John, flat on his stomach to see better, remarked, "Human?"

"Yes, Sir." Percy felt a chill, hoped it was the beginning of the night air.

"We'll pull it out tomorrow. Maybe it's best to start when the sun comes up. We can talk about it once we know what we've got."

Cager grimaced. "We got a dead person."

"Let's wait until morning," John advised.

19

April 16, 1789

Thursday

"I can't get anything under." Percy winced, hands scraped and bleeding, breathed hard.

John, on the other side of the boulder, agreed. "Me, neither."

Cager, on top of the now large hole in the ground, Jeddie and Tulli standing by the draft horses' heads, holding the bridles lightly, said, "Tie around as low as you can go. Tight. If you can wrap the stone in a couple directions, might could do it."

"Good idea. Hand me your end of the rope," John ordered Percy.

As the two men in the pit fiddled with the heavy rope, the sun climbed in the sky, now shining on the flat surface of the boulder. The surface wasn't natural. It was man-made.

"How you doing?" John asked.

"Give a tug."

John did. "I don't think we can get it any tighter. Come on, let's climb out and give it a try."

The two men, pulled out by Cager, stood on the edge, wiping

sweat from their foreheads, hands dirty, raw. They had been digging since sunup three hours ago. The task proved more difficult than anyone anticipated. The horses walked up a half hour ago when John sent Percy down to tell the boys to bring them up. Even then there was more work than they thought. The horses, never content to stand, ate a treat every now and then offered by Jeddie or Tulli. The two stable boys made treats at home. In Tulli's case it was his mother, but the combination of grains, lightly cooked with diced apples inside, proved irresistible.

"Okay, Jeddie. Slow," John commanded.

"Yes, Sir." Jeddie took a few steps, let go of the bridle, got behind Bobby, and lightly tapped him on his hindquarters.

As the animal walked forward Billy moved with his brother as Tulli now stepped back. "I can ride Billy. I can make him go."

"No," Jeddie simply said. "Come on, Bobby, pull."

The two magnificent beasts strained. Dirt crumbled down into the pit as the boulder lifted upward.

"Don't stop, Jeddie. Keep them moving." John feared a backslide. He could see stone tools next to the skeleton. He didn't want anything destroyed.

Percy grabbed the rope and began pulling as the stone rose. Both John and Cager did the same. Cursing, sweating, straining with all they had, the five creatures managed to bring the stone to the lip.

"Okay, Jeddie. Harder NOW!" John hollered.

Jeddie cracked Bobby across the butt with his crop. The big horse surged forward. Billy surged, too. The boulder at last slid, tearing up earth, away from the hole.

Jeddie reached in his pocket, pulling out a treat. Tulli fumbled for one. Both Billy and Bobby gobbled their reward.

The men untied the boulder throwing the rope to the side. John walked back to the pit, looked down.

"Stones. With stuff cut in. Looks like wiggly lines." He had jumped down carefully, missing the bones.

"Looks like other stuff." Percy, now at the edge, knelt down as John handed him objects. "Arrowheads."

"A little pile and this." John handed up a carved bone, a large bone, carved like a hawk's big claw.

"Can you tell anything from the bones?" Cager felt uneasy unearthing what was left of a human.

"No." John stared at what must have been important tributes. "Haul me up."

Cager, one-handed, yanked up John. "Look at this, Mr. John." The powerful young man led the newly minted colonel to the smooth side of the stone.

All three adults studied it and little Tulli came over as Jeddie held the pair of horses.

"Spirit talk," Tulli said with a shiver.

"Tulli, get over here. No one needs to hear your blab." Jeddie then asked, "Can I take the horses back?"

"Yes. They seem none the worse for wear." John smiled.

People had been watching as they snuck away from their chores. Bettina popped out of the kitchen, flanked by Serena. The men in the fields, plowing with unbroken smaller plows, kept watching, too. Finally, no one could contain themselves. All gathered at the edge, including Father Gabe, an older man well versed in the old arts of his tribe from Africa. He didn't know what that tribe was, he only knew what his mother told him about spirits. He adapted to Christianity without a problem, feeling that all spiritual seeking was one.

The lean, older man, bent now, ran his fingers over the wavy lines on the stone. "Took a heap of work to smooth the face of this boulder."

"Father Gabe, are these holy marks?" Cager wanted to be on the right side of the spirits.

"Yes." He held a stone about the size of a ball that could fit in your hand, a pig's bladder size, that John gave him. "More marks."

"No drawings," Percy flatly stated. "You'd think there'd be drawings."

"There is this." John handed Father Gabe the carved falcon's or hawk's claw.

"Mmm. From a deer bone, I think. This has meaning for the dead. I don't know what it is."

The older man walked to the open pit, a large grave, really, to stare down at old, old bones.

Bettina and Serena now stood in the small group, as did Catherine, Rachel, and even Bumbee and the girls who had come up from the weaving room. Charles, Rachel's husband, was at a building site. He was getting requests now to design buildings, given the beautiful Lutheran church, St. Luke's, he had designed in Wayland's Crossing. As an Englishman he would have been fascinated with this. Rachel would show him everything when he got home.

"Bettina."

"Yes, Father Gabe."

"Come here."

Bettina moved up as people parted for her. Father Gabe pointed to the cut marks and the hawk's claw.

"Conjuring?" he asked.

"Oh, Father Gabe, you know far more about this than I." She took a breath then remarked, "Placating, I think. Seeking solace and entrance to a new world. The flat polished side of that stone with the blue shiny veins took many hands. Many hands."

He nodded. "Too old to be one of our people."

"Yes. One of the people before us."

"Mmm." He nodded his head. "Brothers and sisters. Whoever rests there," he indicated the pit, "has gone to their holy place. We must cover the bones. The dead must be honored."

A murmur of assent arose from the people and all eyes fastened on Catherine. As Ewing was in his office, not grasping the import to others of this discovery, she was the boss.

Rachel reached for her older sister's hand and Catherine spoke in a steady voice. "Father Gabe, you always bring us to God." She waited a moment then added, "To grace and spirit. We will cover this soul and say a prayer that his or her journey was successful."

All looked from her to Father Gabe.

John, not much of a talker but so good in anything requiring instant thinking, echoed his wife's thoughts. "Men, let us cover this soul and place the boulder over the grave so that we can remember and be careful."

Percy, Cager, a few younger men, stepped forward to move the strange boulder as Tulli dashed up from the stable as fast as he could go. Disappointed to have missed what everyone said, he allowed Bettina to put her arm around his shoulders.

"I'll tell you everything. You go on up there and help Mr. John." She called to John. "Another worker. Many hands make light work."

All smiled as Tulli walked up, filled with the importance of his task.

As the small gathering broke up, Bumbee walked Serena back to the kitchen before turning for the lane that led to the weaving room. "I wish Mr. Percy hadn't dug up that boulder."

"I thought you couldn't stand him." Serena just had to tweak Bumbee.

"I can't, but you don't conjure up spirits. You don't conjure up what you can't conjure down. You don't jostle the dead. Anyone's dead."

As if the spirits heard her, there was a rumble and an odd cracking sound, almost a thunderclap. Then another one, followed by shaking underfoot.

The two women looked at each other. Without a word, Bumbee headed for her work cabin, now also her living cabin since she and Mr. Percy had had a knock-down,drag-out.

She thought to herself, as did Serena, that the mountains had spoken.

20

October 17, 2019

Thursday

"Here." Constance slid a check for ten thousand dollars to Nancy Parsons as they sat in the Grill at Keswick Club.

"I can't take that." Nancy agreed to the hurried lunch because Constance was insistent.

"Well, tell me who bought the prints? Ballard has hired a specialist to go through all of Mother's papers, her books, various prints, paintings. He's hired people with expertise in various categories. I'll block all that, trust me, and I'll pay off whoever bought those military prints."

Nancy knew she couldn't expose Harry. The uniform prints were a present for a big day between Harry and Fair. Constance would pressure Harry if she learned it was her. Nancy knew sooner or later Constance would find out. She wasn't the kind of woman to give up.

"How about if we do this? I will personally call upon the purchaser and offer this money. I can write the purchaser a check from my account."

"Well, deposit my check." Constance picked at her poached salmon.

"I will." Nancy stared out the window for a moment at the golf course, recently redesigned by Pete Dye. "You don't play golf, do you?"

"No. It's a lovely game but it never appealed to me."

"I swore when I had enough time I'd learn." She grinned. "Still haven't found the time."

"When you do, give me some." Constance lifted an eyebrow, enjoying herself.

"Isn't that the truth." Nancy put her fork down. "I know you have been undergoing great strain but you look good. Don't let Ballard bring you down. If you have to hire a lawyer, do, but letting him get under your skin isn't worth it."

Piercing fresh asparagus, she said after swallowing it, "He had even suggested we sell some of Mother's furniture. That house has been redecorated many times in its long life. Mother hired Henri Samuelson in 1951. He made it come to life."

"The French really can do anything."

Constance nodded. "So long as it doesn't involve government. They can't do it. Just can't do it."

"I'm beginning to wonder if we can."

"A lot of fuss. Doesn't mean a thing. It's all to divert the attention of the hoi polloi. The same people will run this country who have always run this country."

Nancy grew still for a moment then asked, "Constance, do you really believe that?"

"Of course. It's all smoke and mirrors, Nancy. Don't take a bit of it seriously."

"I'll have to think about that."

"For years I watched Mother beguile powerful men, all of whom wanted my father to do something for them. Usually they wanted a large check. Corrupt, every single one."

"Corruption never goes out of fashion, I guess." Nancy didn't want to believe it but it was hard to turn away from it.

"If you see whoever bought Mother's prints, you will call me immediately, won't you?"

"Of course I will, Constance. You know I would never have taken those marvelous prints if I thought your mother wasn't ready to part with them."

Constance, light nice eyes, stared right at Nancy. "Mother had no idea. Uniforms were a passion of my father's. Dad had a real aesthetic streak. The furniture alone that he bought for Mother is spectacular. Granted, the house had ancient pieces from the seventeenth century that had to be protected and preserved, but what he bought when Samuelson redecorated, I think of it as the daily use stuff, gorgeous."

"Yes, it is. We don't see much of Samuelson around here. People don't know who he was."

"Given that Jefferson was besotted with the French, you'd think we'd see more." She sighed. "Then again, I think the French Revolution took care of that. Mother would talk to me about these things and I wish I had listened more closely. I was going through my Andy Warhol phase." She shuddered.

"You have your mother's eye. Ah, here comes our waiter. Let's be bad girls and order dessert."

"What a good idea."

The two stayed on, Nancy eating a crème brûlée and Constance devouring a moist chocolate cake with a scoop of rich vanilla ice cream. Constance watched her weight but every now and then one must throw caution to the winds.

The Grill, convenient for Constance, had a fireplace usually burning hardwoods as it was today, for the temperature was dropping. Constance, once Kevin died, repaired to Keswick Estates, a well laid out subdivision with expensive homes. She endured it, for her idea of home was, of course, Lone Pine, an impressive pile with brick stables, painted white like the brick house. Originally 6,000 acres, over the years it had been whittled down to 1,500 backed by the Southwest Mountains. Candida made Constance and Ballard swear they would not sell an inch of land. They did promise, but how to keep it going?

Always well dressed, affable, a keen bridge player, Constance fit in at Keswick Estates. She, to herself, thought she belonged back home but she was wise enough to know she couldn't run Lone Pine by herself. The shock of finding Mother's finances in tatters chewed at the edges of her bonhomie. It was all she could think about but she didn't want that to show.

As they walked outside, each to her car, Nancy promised to notify her, hopefully tonight. They each drove out of the parking lot, Nancy turning right and Constance turning left toward her pretty home on Palmer Drive. Most people would be thrilled to live there but Constance always had Lone Pine nagging at her. When her mother was alive it was one thing. Now was quite another.

21

October 18, 2019

Friday

"You see the problem." Nancy Parsons nestled in the sofa facing the fireplace, which emitted a lovely warmth.

On the back of the sofa lounged Mrs. Murphy and Pewter, tails hanging down, flicking a bit. As Nancy was accustomed to animals, the cats did not disturb her but Pewter every now and then patted her shoulder. Vain creature.

The dogs lay on either side of Harry's chair. Head on paws, eyes wide open, they listened to every word.

"I think I do." Harry freshened Nancy's tea using her mother's large teapot, a true Brown Betty.

"I was shocked when she confronted me . . . well, that's not fair, she talked to me at the Keswick Grill. She handed me a check for ten thousand dollars, telling me to give you what you wanted and keep the rest. Actually, Harry, if you do sell them back, I don't want a penny. You paid me fair and square for those prints."

"Ten thousand dollars is a lot of money. I know your prices are more than fair and I know these might bring a few thousand more in New York, Boston, or Philadelphia. Maybe even Atlanta. Men, and it's usually men, who become fascinated by uniforms are all over. Fair loves this stuff."

"It actually is fascinating. The male as a peacock began to change in the nineteenth century, black was considered manly, sober, and one so dressed could be trusted with your funds or be elected to Parliament. As to Congress, I don't know."

They both laughed.

"I like the braid and those hanging tassels. Wouldn't you love to chew on them? 'Course, the material on all the ribbons would be easy to rip up, too." Pewter smacked her lips, imagining the thrills of destruction.

"All those beautiful colors." Mrs. Murphy would consider kneading the dense fabric of a tunic of a pelisse, especially a pelisse with the lamb's fur.

"Fair has a British Hussar's pelisse. He always liked uniforms, military history, even in grade school. His father got him interested. Well, I'm getting off track, but if I give these back to you, can you find other prints, a set? I know you won't find them in time for our anniversary but I can give him something else, then later surprise him with prints. He especially likes the period from the Seven Years War up to 1870. The country doesn't matter so much."

"I will find something and they will be as beautiful as what you bought."

"Give me a minute. I have to get them. Hid them, of course." Harry rose, the dogs rising with her.

"Nancy, there's a chocolate cookie by your tea. There's a dish of them. I like cookies." Pewter purred.

Nancy swiveled around to pet the fatty.

Harry returned in a flash, carrying the carton in which Nancy had packed the prints. "Here you go."

"Thank you. I appreciate this. You know Constance can be formidable. You haven't unwrapped the paper yet. Well, that makes it easy." Nancy continued.

"I suppose I should shut up but Constance, um, she wants to be like her mother. And she can't. She's tremendously bright. She does wonders raising money for any foundation in which she has an interest, but she's not going to be the Duchess of Albemarle, you know?"

"I do." Nancy leaned back after finishing her tea, then held up her hand because Harry was ready to pour more. "Her mother's tenure at the apex of society, she wore it lightly. She never seemed to care because, of course, she never had to do so. She was a warm woman always ready to help. You're too young . . . well, you might remember some of when Patricia Kluge moved here. She began throwing parties as a woman of means does in England. The so-called upper crust of Albemarle was envious. Some even rude. Not all of them, of course, and one woman who welcomed her was Candida. She said to me, 'Do you know how much good this woman can do?' Well, Candida was right. Constance would have been one of the envious."

"Funny how people cling to their little bit of 'I'm better than you.' I hate it."

"You're the First Family of Virginia," Nancy wryly noted.

"Yes. My mother said to me that it didn't matter when anyone came to our country, they were as good as those of us born here or who arrived in 1607. She meant it, too. And we didn't have but so much money. Mother was the Crozet librarian."

"Well do I remember." Nancy smiled.

"Come on. One cookie, one eensy weensy cookie." Pewter tried to look starved.

She was not a success.

"Pewter, stop patting Nancy," Harry chided her. "Let me get some of her fishies. That will keep her busy."

Nancy laughed. "You spoil those cats."

"Well . . ." Harry grinned, walked into the kitchen, and rattled the fishie box, sending both cats launching off the back of the sofa. "Hey, Nancy, would you like a fishie?"

"No, but do you have any mouse tartar?"

Harry walked back and the two laughed, chatted, enjoyed each other's company.

Nancy mentioned, "Today is the birthday of Pierre Choderlos de Laclos, the author of *Les Liaisons Dangereuses.* Born in 1741. He was an artillery officer. Even started an artillery school, which the young Bonaparte attended."

"I love history but you know literary history far better than I. Then again, look at your career."

"I loved running the Sporting Library. Actually, I love any library. To be a good librarian you have to know more than books. You have to deal with local authorities, sometimes state authorities, and even a sporting library can be subject to someone finding offense at a collection. The fundraising took a great deal of time. We are not state funded, as you know."

"I do know. You did a wonderful job. Set the tone." Harry was sincere.

"Thank you. I think so much of what I learned there helps me in my store. I really can recognize fine furniture, or handmade items from decades or centuries back. And I adore finding prints and primitive paintings, for lack of a better word. Occasionally I'll get work from a trained artist but I find so much of the stuff a person painted in, say, 1840 is marvelous. But then again, that's me. When Ballard brought me those uniforms from Wellington's army, the prints, I was overjoyed. He swore his mother was ready to part with them, she was winnowing her holdings down to the very rare and expensive items. These prints aren't on every street corner but they aren't especially rare."

"Do you think Candida was slowing down?"

"No. Not at all. Her memory was as sharp as the day I met her. And that worries me because if this goes to court, Ballard trying to sell the letters, 379 years of letters and family exchanges, as well as stuff from world figures, I swear Constance will be battling him about her mother's mental state. I do not want to be dragged into court to testify. Candida was sharp."

"Seemed so to me." Harry concurred.

"*I ate all my fishies.*" Pewter bellowed from the kitchen.

Tucker called back, "*Shut up.*"

"*Bubblebutt. Brownnoser.*" The gray cat deposited what good manners she had elsewhere.

Seeing her corgi sneer, Harry reached down to rub her glossy head. "Ignore her, Tucker."

"*For you.*" The dog looked up with her large, sweet brown eyes.

"*You know if I stood on my hind legs I could eat every fishie,*" Pirate bragged.

"*Don't,*" Tucker simply said.

"There's no fight like a family fight." Nancy uttered one of the truest statements ever.

"Yeah. If Ballard, who was his mother's favorite, is willing to sell that unique collection, the estate will have money to invest. I mean, she didn't leave as much money as we all thought."

"She left debt. Constance is blabbing that and I so wish she wouldn't."

"Oh dear. Lone Pine has to be saved." Harry believed that historical buildings deserved to be seen by future generations, whether slave quarters or the glories of the big house aping European fashions.

"Yes." Nancy agreed.

"You know from attending the funeral that Constance had her mother cremated. Ballard pitched a fit. He said he wanted his mother to have a proper autopsy. Constance fired back that no one was cutting up her mother, who was two years older than God. Candida was properly buried so at least they agreed on all that. But now the fighting is renewed and redoubled. Nancy, this is awful."

"It is." She slid a check, one of her checks so that Harry's name would not be known; fortunately Constance was fine about that.

Harry stared down at ten thousand dollars written in fine script. "Of course, I can use it. And I am grateful to you for keeping my name from her. But—"

Nancy held up her hand palm outward. "Done."

Harry nodded. "Done. By the way, what happened to de Laclos?"

"Ultimately chewed up by the French Revolution. He was accused of being an Orleaniste. *Thermidor* saved him. Being a smart man he got out of France and died in 1803 in the Two Sicilies . . . Taranto, I think."

"It's a great book. One of the most significant books from the eighteenth century." Harry, thanks to her mother and to Smith College, had read a great deal.

"I'm not sure good behavior makes for good books." Nancy laughed. "Well, I'd better be going. Thank you again."

"I can buy a new manure spreader thanks to you." Harry stood up to walk her to the door.

"Thanks to Constance and I suppose Ballard, unwittingly."

"Let's hope this is the end of it." Harry opened the back door for her, the screened-in porch being now covered, a big job Fair took on every mid-fall.

Nancy shrugged, for as much as she hoped this would settle the issue she knew it would not.

"You've got that look on your face," Harry said.

"I hope they don't kill each other."

22

April 17, 1789

Friday

Jeddie brought the cart around for Charles and Mr. Percy. "Road should be good."

"Dried out." Charles nodded then checked Mr. Percy. "Your chit."

Percy pulled the rectangular chit with the number "11" on it and in script "Cloverfields." As a slave whenever he left the property he needed a chit, a pass. The farm name ensured he would be left alone, not challenged, because Cloverfields was a significant estate. All slaveowners had some type of pass, usually brass, that could withstand bad weather. Since most everyone knew one another between Charlottesville and Wayland's Crossing, the chits might be unnecessary but why take a chance.

Charles drove the pair, accustomed to more refined vehicles, but the cart was well built, painted, and carried a box in the back, perhaps four-by-four and four feet high. Filled with vestments, some prayer books, it was being taken to St. Luke's Lutheran Church. The vestments had been sewn by Bumbee and her girls, lovely jacquard cloth, too. As for the white robes and black robes, they also made those. The high-brass candleholders and heavy candles had been sent from Germany.

"Think it's spring?" Charles asked.

"Sure. Bumbee planted her flowers."

"At your cabin?"

Mr. Percy nodded then added, "Lots at the weaving cabin, too. She puts a store by flowers."

Charles rode along as Mr. Percy commented on farms they passed. Charles never could understand any tempestuous relationship so Bumbee and Mr. Percy's marriage eluded him. Certainly made for theater at Cloverfields.

They covered the eight miles from Cloverfields to St. Luke's in an hour and a half, walking slowly.

"A pleasant ride." Charles stepped out of the wagon.

Mr. Percy did the same on the passenger side. Both men took the reins and tied them loosely to the large hitching post.

"Let me check who's inside. That box is big and heavy."

"Can't be any worse than that stone we all dug up."

"Wasn't that something? Bet there are graves all around but we don't know about them. Had to be an important person, those marked stones. Guess we'll never know. You stay here. See if the horses need water."

Mr. Percy nodded and Charles walked to the church, which dominated the long arcade on either side of it. St. Luke's was a series of descending rectangles at the back of the church itself, with a courtyard on both ends open, terminating at two matching buildings at the end of the arcade, buildings smaller than the church. Simple, elegant—especially with stained glass windows, an enormous expense—the church was the most beautiful structure in Wayland's Crossing. People rode out to see it.

The vestryman, Gunther Rowohlt, looked up, smiled when he saw Charles. "Captain West."

"Need you. Brought the vestments, candleholders, a big box full of things the pastor wants. You, Mr. Percy, and I should be able to do it."

Without comment, the square-built man followed the Englishman . . . or Englisher, as he thought of him.

Reaching the cart, Charles called out, "Percy?"

The horses drank from the trough.

"Percy?"

Examining the box, Gunther, no interest in Percy, said, "We can do it. Let's get this into the vestry and you can find Percy later. If my memory serves me well, Percy has found a woman to impress."

"Oh." Charles's voice trailed off.

The two men slid the box to the end of the cart, dropped the gate, and maneuvered it to the ground. Heavy though it was, two men in the prime of life managed.

"I'll leave you to it and go find Romeo."

Gunther laughed at Charles. "He'd better remember what happened to Romeo."

Charles smiled. "No one ever thinks it will happen to them. One jealous husband too many and sooner or later one will find Percy."

After walking all around St. Luke's, the sun soft and warming, maybe in the high fifties, Charles returned to the cart. He untied the reins from the hitching post.

Flipping the reins over the pair's heads, he climbed up into the cart, standing to see if he could see farther. Percy quietly walked up behind him.

"Didn't hear you at first."

"You managed to miss the heavy work," Charles chided him lightly.

Percy climbed in. "Thought I heard a strange noise," he lied. "Didn't see anything."

The two men started back for Cloverfields. Charles believed Percy was truthful. He didn't see anything. But he thought he heard a muffled scream.

23

October 19, 2019

Saturday

"There's no running thread." Cooper had smoothed out a spreadsheet on Harry's kitchen table, where both Harry and Fair sat.

"Other than a vet stopping to see clients, I can't see anything these calls have in common." Fair slipped a pencil behind his ear.

"Well, aren't some of the calls you and Tiffany Snell have made for the same condition?" Harry hoped to find something they all had in common.

"Well, sure. About eighty percent of what we see are leg injuries. I didn't have one case of colic this week. It's been an easy week." Fair noticed Pewter sitting in the window over the sink.

"Goes in waves?" Cooper asked.

"To some extent. Weather is a big factor. Lots of rain, horses get rain rot even if they have sheets on them. Stuff like that. Nothing serious, just stuff. Abscesses can occur at any time but seem to occur more frequently in the summer, when the soil is hard and the horses are stomping because of flies. These are observations, not hard-and-fast rules."

"Right." Cooper moved down the list. "These were people at the various stops. You know other vets' clients, I assume?"

"I do. I know most everyone at Lynne Beegle Gebhard's barn. I know Big Mim's. People float in and out of barns. You see the list there. Nothing out of order." He smiled. "No felons."

"Actually," Cooper replied, "I'd trust the felons more than some people. He or she has to keep their nose clean or it's all over."

"Let's look at this from another direction?" Harry's mind whirred along. "Has there been a spike in Special K admissions to the hospital? To any of the hospitals?"

Cooper shook her head. "We checked. Have there been some wild spring parties at UVA? Sure. No Special K calls but a few drunk and disorderly ones. However, because the drug has been lifted doesn't mean it will be sold here."

"No, but wouldn't it be easy? A college town?" Harry asked.

"Yes," Cooper simply replied.

Fair leaned back in his chair as Pewter began to chatter, for her nemesis, the blue jay, sat in the large tree outside the kitchen window. "It's one of the big problems for any college administration. Kids are away from home, they have little idea as to their limits. They take a pill or drink half a bottle of bourbon. Boom. Ambulance call . . . or worse, they drive. If anyone was on Special K, you'd know, wouldn't you?"

"Only if reported." Cooper watched as Pewter stood on her hind legs. "That cat is mental."

"You just noticed?" Harry laughed at her.

"That is a dangerous bird. I am protecting you all," Pewter announced as she swatted the window.

Pirate, lifting his bushy eyebrows, asked Tucker, resting next to him, *"Blue jays aren't dangerous, are they?"*

"You have no idea. They dive-bomb you. They'll fly at you, flip around, and show their claws. Terrible birds, the worst."

Mrs. Murphy, curled up in the right side of the big double sink—she liked the porcelain feel—listened. *"If you'd forget the blue jay, maybe you could think about the human problem here."*

"If humans are dumb enough to take drugs, they deserve what they get," came the unsympathetic reply from Pewter.

"What if the thefts have nothing to do with selling drugs?" The tiger cat had been thinking. *"You found Ben. How did he look?"*

"Dead." Tucker dropped her head.

"And you didn't smell anything odd?" Mrs. Murphy asked.

"No. The offices were freshly painted, everything new. No cologne smells or liquor. Nothing. If anything, it was squeaky clean except for the bit of blood." Tucker remembered it all vividly.

"Whoever it was knew where to find the ketamine." Pewter was becoming interested, plus the blue jay had disappointingly flown over to the barn.

"A young vet is murdered. Drugs stolen. No additions to his bank accounts are found, according to Cooper when she first started this. Why kill Ben for a bottle or two? It doesn't make sense." Mrs. Murphy stuck to her guns.

"Mom watches those crime shows. Maybe he had a partner who got greedy?" Pirate was impressionable.

"Over a couple of bottles of ketamine?" Mrs. Murphy stood up, stretched, then stepped out of the big sink. *"We are all being suckered."*

"Because we're focusing on drugs?" Tucker was beginning to think anew. *"There was nothing in that new office to take. Nothing was there. You'd think if something was really valuable, we'd know."*

"Lab coats in the locked closet. The framed pictures against the wall. Mud boots. Station way at the front desk. His computer." Tucker tried to remember everything.

"We are missing something. There has to be more in his office or maybe even more in the other vet trucks."

"Well, we or the humans would have found it by now." Pewter sat by Mrs. Murphy.

They had found it and completely ignored it.

24

October 21, 2019

Monday

"Twenty-five-thousand-dollar salary for one century, the seventeenth. Of course, the volume will swell with succeeding centuries, but I think I can cover the seventeenth in six weeks."

"Clyde, that's quite optimistic." Jerry Showalter walked with the young man through the Lawn at University of Virginia.

"You think?" His auburn eyebrows rose in a youthful face.

"I can't say with authority, but even with that time frame, which as I recall fills about five boxes, starting with the 1650s, you have to catalog and make notes. You also have to note the surface, vellum or parchment? Then you need to read the contents, cite. And don't forget the ink. Some of those old inks were superior."

Clyde agreed. "Quills."

"Goes to prove the tools are not nearly as important as the content." Jerry walked over to the statue of blind Homer at the southern end of the Lawn.

Clyde stared at the representation of the believed author of *The*

Iliad and *The Odyssey*. "I often wonder if we are equal to our ancestors."

"Depends on the ancestors." Jerry smiled then headed toward the amphitheater, the temperature mid-sixties, a light breeze.

Clyde remarked, "I'd heard Ballard is always short of money, but he paid. So I've been starting work at Lone Pine at eight in the morning, leaving at three."

"Has Constance interfered?"

"No. She's walked by the library only once. I thought she'd sue Ballard to stop my work or try to stop me, but she hasn't said a thing."

Jerry murmured, "Constance will wait and drain his money. Then at the last minute, if she feels like it, she'll throw lawyers at him."

"As long as she doesn't question my work."

They walked along then Jerry said, "I don't think she will. In ways, it's to her advantage to have an accurate catalog. But you can't truly catalog, read, refile. You have to check off contents according to the old inventory sheets. As I recall, the last boxes, those from the end of the twentieth century to now, have no inventory sheets. You will have to create them, and that takes so much time."

"How long have you known them?"

"Well, I knew Candida all my life. Constance and Ballard, not being interested in the things I am interested in, rarely crossed my path but it was never unpleasant except when Ballard was drunk or drugged out. He's been clean for some years. Every family has problems."

"The vellum and the parchment have held up. Some of the ink is now lavender but different countries . . . different chemists, for lack of a better word . . . used different mixes for their inks. Ink is like painters mixing pigment," Clyde mentioned. "Some was faded. Some looked almost new."

"You can tell a lot by ink color, pressure on paper or vellum, handwriting. The handwriting of the educated up to about the 1950s was exquisite," Jerry agreed.

"The room is temperature-controlled. Ballard said his mother arranged that before he was born. It's one of the reasons the papers have held up as well as they have."

Jerry turned toward the old main library. "A word of unsolicited advice. If Constance asks you questions, evade. Ballard is paying the bill. And don't be surprised if, say, in a month she hires her own researcher."

"Oh God." Clyde's face fell.

"This isn't going to be easy, no matter how it plays out. Sooner or later they'll wind up in court. You'll be called upon to testify as to the nature of the estate."

"If this were land, you could split it. But you can't really split a family's papers for close to four centuries," Clyde rightly surmised. "Would they be better kept in a university? Yes, but given the care with which they have been tended and the fact that I would expect the estate to be left to Virginia, they could stay where they are."

Jerry cleared his throat. "We hope the estate remains intact. It's too volatile to know. My experience is, if either party cared for the future protection of the papers, of Lone Pine itself, you wouldn't be there."

"So you think some or all of the contents will be sold?"

"I don't know. Ballard needs money. He always does. Even though he has cleaned himself up, who knows what debts are lurking from the past? I hope none, but his willingness to sell those papers is not a good sign. Constance will fight him more for the status of the treasure in her keeping than any genuine interest in the contents."

Clyde paused to gaze at the front of the old library. "You say she is adamant about keeping everything together at Lone Pine? Wouldn't that mean she has to buy him out?"

"Yes, unless they can come to some agreement." Jerry shrugged. "I have to stay out of it. My work was for their mother over the years, and what a delight she was. We would sit and read letters from before our Revolution. Some of the family felt it was pure folly to take on the British army. Others felt they wouldn't be able to adjust to new political conditions. People figured things out as best they could and in retrospect I can understand the Ballard family members who feared the king and the king's men. A mistake and they'd all swing, you know?"

"We forget."

"About everything, but Candida had a passion for her family, for history, for what the Ballards did right and what they did wrong. I'm sorry you didn't truly know her."

"It would appear neither her son nor daughter are much like her," Clyde mused.

"Only in that both are intelligent. The son made more mistakes. It's a curse to have such a successful father, I think. She doted on Ballard, incurring Constance's wrath . . . but then, Constance was her father's pet. The old story." Jerry listened as a light wind rustled the leaves, drying out in fall.

"If nothing else, I'll have money for a down payment for our first house." Clyde had married a year ago.

"True. Be careful. Don't blurt out anything. If something doesn't sit right, keep it to yourself. If you have any doubts or questions, radical as it seems, Clyde, go to a lawyer. It's the old saying: 'Cover your ass.' "

"Okay."

"The anger between those two meant I couldn't do the work, of course. Much as I worked with Candida, and I saw but a fraction of the papers since she was concentrating on her father's time, I had to back out. You can't serve two masters."

Truer words were never spoken.

25

April 18, 1789

Saturday

Sunshine flooded the hay pastures, green shoots peeking through the soil. Daffodils, jonquils, and the first hint of tulips stirred in the late Isabelle Garth's garden, tended by her youngest daughter.

Jeddie, Barker O, and Tulli curried the horses, hair flying everywhere as they began to blow their winter coats. It always seemed as though the hair mostly went up their noses. Spring arrived although the nights remained cold.

Catherine believed one wasn't truly past real cold until the last frost, which often occurred at the end of April. As she walked into the blooded horse stable, the two men quieted while Tulli dutifully picked out hooves.

"All this undercoat will stick to you," she mentioned.

"Itches." Jeddie smiled.

"I am trying to get my father out a bit. He's been sitting in his office all winter, which you know. He needs something." Catherine's voice carried a note of entreaty.

"He walks at sundown." Tulli liked Ewing, who often gave him a coin or some little trinket.

"That he does," Catherine noted. "Jeddie, saddle up Reynaldo. You ride Crown Prince. Barker O, throw your leg over Penny. A simple ride will do her good. She looks more muscled up, by the way." She paused. "Tulli, you ride Sweet Potato."

He dashed off to get the pony from the field.

Barker O nodded at the compliment. "Hill work both under saddle and pulling the gig. All we do is walk and trot."

"No point running any horse through the bridle," she replied. "Hill work, especially slow work, builds those hindquarters. I wish I could get Father more interested in these things, but . . ." She shrugged. "He leaves it to me and perhaps that is easier. Sometimes I worry though. All that reading, the correspondence. The unrest in France. It's too much."

"Mr. Ewing is a wise man." Barker O meant that.

Once the horses were tacked up, a hint of anticipation in their manner, the four rode off. The warmth felt invigorating. An hour's walking and trotting put them all in a good mood. Once back at the stable, Catherine heard a footfall as she fiddled with the girth on the far side of her horse.

"Catherine."

"Rachel, you just missed a ride. Tulli has Sweet Potato behaving."

Rachel smiled at Tulli, his little chest sticking out. "How good of you. Soon Marcia will be able to ride a bit because you've worked so hard on the pony. Of course, you will have to lead her."

Marcia was her adopted daughter. No point in waiting around. Get her on a horse. She had begun to read a bit. That counted as ready to ride.

Thrilled, Tulli boasted, "I'll take care of her."

"I know you will." Rachel beamed at him, while Jeddie laughed.

"To what do I owe this morning pleasure? I thought you were copying Charles's drawings."

Rachel looked down at the ink on her hands. "I was. Catherine, when you're free, come up to the house with me."

A hot pot of tea waited on the small kitchen table. Rachel poured a cup for her sister, one for herself, then sat down.

"You make the best tea." Catherine sipped.

"Marrying an Englishman has helped." Rachel laughed as Piglet, Charles's old corgi, nestled at her feet. "Have you talked to John about asking Jeffrey Holloway for help with the militia?"

"No. I think he's going to ask. Maybe not for money, but he said the state has no sturdy wagons to carry ammunition, artillery shells. Jeffrey makes good wagons and Zachary Thigpen is investigating another source."

"Ah." Rachel thought a moment. "I don't trust Maureen. I wanted to talk to you first."

"Surely you don't think Maureen would refuse to help John. Expanding our militia is critical." Catherine was surprised.

"No. Jeffrey will agree. She gives him what he wants. Then again, this will enhance her. What I worry about is if she will use this in some way to delay DoRe's marriage to Bettina."

"Our father has agreed to her terms. All outrageous."

"No doubt of that." Rachel shook her head. "I don't trust her. She'll declare she needs DoRe to deliver the wagons along with her stable boys and, of course, ours. I just don't trust her."

Catherine sat quietly then said, "You don't think she'll ever let DoRe leave Big Rawly?"

"Yes."

The sisters looked at each other.

Catherine finally spoke. "She'll change the terms?"

"I think so. She won't oppose the marriage but I don't think she will give up DoRe."

"Does Bettina say anything?"

"No. This is a feeling on my part, so I don't want to bring it up. If Maureen drags her feet, she'll either tell Father first or perhaps DoRe."

"Maybe we should talk to Father." Catherine finished her cup. "If the worst does occur, he could negotiate DoRe being here, say, three days a week. The rest at Big Rawly."

"I've thought of that. She'll want Bettina at Big Rawly when DoRe is there. She's been trying to get Bettina's culinary secrets for years."

"Good Lord!" Catherine raised her voice. "I never thought of that." She paused. "Father said he would free Bettina. He has the manumission papers drawn up. She's under no obligation to go anywhere."

"Law is one thing, sister. People are another," said the usually sunny Rachel.

26

October 26, 2019

Saturday

Country House Antiques rested in Keswick Hunt territory. Bull Run, not terribly far, might have members shopping there, as would Farmington Hunt Club, located in the western part of Albemarle County. Oak Ridge Hunt Club from Nelson had members devoted to the store and sometimes people drifted in from Deep Run, Richmond or Bedford, Lynchburg.

Nancy, welcoming as always, was tired from the nonstop day as many of the clubs hosted their Opening Hunt this Saturday. The breakfast, which although it was always in the afternoon was still called breakfast, put most members in a spirited mood. Sometimes that meant money burned a hole in your pocket.

The store was jammed from one in the afternoon on and even though closing was near, Nancy knew enough not to shut the doors, people still poured in.

Parking proved a problem but neighbors helped a bit. All liked

Nancy, personally, and had gotten into the habit of finding unique gifts for birthdays, anniversaries, Christmas, et cetera.

Liz King, one of the Farmington's masters, found a marvelous painting and as she stood at the desk, Constance walked in. Of course, she knew everyone and vice versa, plus she was in her formal hunt attire, having gone out with Keswick.

"Liz." Constance looked around. "Nancy, this place is full of masters."

Nancy smiled. "I don't hold that against them."

Eight people laughed, for they were masters of foxhounds, a title secure since the Middle Ages, when hunting was vital to kings, queens, and those wishing to curry favor with them. Then again, a bold hunter . . . whether for stag, boar, or later fox . . . tended to be someone military people wanted in the field, most especially cavalry.

The buzz raised up. The door opened again and Clyde Mercador walked in, beheld Constance, and started to leave, when she called out, "Clyde, please come in."

He smiled, tightly, shut the door behind him.

Some people knew the younger man, as the county, as well as Orange County, contained quite a few serious book collectors. Many spent more on their libraries' temperature control than regular people spend on their homes. Like any passion, collecting antique books and papers overrides common sense. A good thing, otherwise little would be done, as everyone would sit around counting pennies, nickel-and-diming their lives into tedious oblivion.

No one would ever accuse the late Candida of doing that, nor Constance, who already walked with more deliberation. She would, by God, inherit her mother's standing.

Nancy smiled up at Liz. "You'd better hang this where your Jack Russell can't see it."

Liz smiled, for her dog could be jealous and a bit naughty. If she saw the painting, a barking episode plus leaping straight up in the air would follow.

"Good advice."

As Liz left with her purchase, carefully wrapped, Constance moved over to Clyde. Did everyone notice? They did.

"Look at this." Constance pointed to a framed print of Queen Victoria in hunt attire, riding sidesaddle. This was not the image of Victoria that persevered through the decades.

"What a life." Clyde admired the print.

"Indeed. Having a powerful mother can be an impediment for some. I do think it was for her second son, the first having died, of course." Constance believed Clyde would know his English history, which he did.

"You are one of the few who have flourished." Clyde was not without political intelligence.

"Thank you." She meant that, plus she knew everyone was eavesdropping. "Clyde, I don't want you to think I am angry at you. I am not. I quite understand why you took the job Ballard offered, and in truth, Mother's papers being organized and valued is, well, long overdue. The last time the family tackled this was during my great-grandfather's life. As you know, Ballard and I are at sixes and sevens. We usually are, but I appreciate your efforts and even if my brother and I wind up in court, I rest somewhat easier knowing her papers are in order."

He waited a moment. "Thank you. No one wants to see such a collection undervalued. And so far, even though it has been three generations since this was all codified, things are in good order. Your mother cared greatly about the family history and what it would mean to future historians."

"She did. Mother was a farsighted woman."

Warming to his subject, Clyde again complimented Constance. "Mrs. O'Donnell, I am only now getting into the late nineteenth century. I'm working backwards . . . well, because of the knocked-over boxes. Anyway, you would be surprised at the pristine condition. Some of the papers, the ink remains clear and dark, no edges of papers curling, no vellum besmirched. Remarkable."

Constance smiled. "As I said, Mother truly cared. And you know, I confess I paid little attention. I was wrapped up in horses, parties; history bored me. Poor Mother, she would occasionally read me a letter, say, written by an ancestor in 1730, about a party. She tried to involve me and I half listened. Of course, now I could shoot myself." She put her hands on her hips. "When we're young we think we know everything. Well, time to get back. I need to pull off my boots."

As she left, everyone watched her, then a moment of silence fell over the packed store. Nancy, too smart to tip her hand, rose to help Mark Catron, joint MFH of Oak Ridge, look at the back of a maple wood small chest of drawers.

"Tiger maple," Mark noted. "My grandmother had a tiger maple chest of drawers." He knelt down, checked the small turned feet, then opened drawers, all of which slid easily. "I'll take it."

The buzz picked up as people noted the Constance/Clyde conversation. A few weighed in on either side, Constance versus Ballard. Most wanted no part of that fight. All mourned Candida. She lived so long, there were only a few people in the county who knew her as a young person, for they, too, were pushing a hundred.

Nancy finally closed the store an hour after sundown. Tired, she checked everything, turned off her computer, secured doors and windows, then quietly left, pleased with a good day.

She no sooner drove a mile away from the crossroads than her cell rang.

"Nancy."

"Harry."

"Forgive me for calling you on what I know has been a busy day . . . and how do I know that, because Mark Catron had to drive by and show me the tiger maple chest of drawers."

"Tiger maple and birdseye maple are so special."

"Are. I called to ask you if anyone has mentioned Special K, you know, the thefts out of vet trucks?"

"Well, people have noted it but it more or less has faded. Ben's death shocked everyone but that, too, is fading, as nothing or no one has been found."

"It is a puzzle. Fair hunted today with Farmington, territory out in the Free Union area. Another vet was there. Talk about missing ketamine has people watchful over their medical supplies."

"Why didn't you hunt?"

"I promised Susan I'd put in the spring bulbs at her grandmother's gardens. Big Rawly has such wonderful gardens, essentially eighteenth-century French."

"They are spectacular. And as I recall, over the years, bones keep being found at Big Rawly."

"True, but if you think about it, Albemarle County is full of dead people."

Yes, it was.

27

October 27, 2019

Sunday

A small crowd gathered at Ben Wagner's veterinary clinic, as his parents had hired an auction service to sell off his goods. They specifically requested that an auction not be held but that the X-ray machine and other equipment be displayed with a price.

Fair, like most of the equine vets in the county, attended. He needed little but wanted to see who would attend. In the back of his mind he wondered if whoever killed Ben would show up.

Cynthia Cooper, not acting in an official capacity, also harbored the same thought. She rode over with Fair, Harry, and the animals.

They walked among the equipment, displayed in rows.

"Not much big equipment. There's enough acreage here that Ben would need a tractor, at least to bushhog," Harry noted.

"He wasn't here long enough to purchase that stuff," Fair remarked. "Plus it's expensive."

"Opening a new, big clinic is expensive," Cooper added. "His books didn't reflect huge earnings."

"No, but usually veterinarians, as well as human doctors, have no trouble getting credit. I'm sure you examined that," Fair replied.

"We did. Surprisingly, no debt. Then again, some people have a gift for squirreling away money. He paid cash for everything. I am not one of them," she ruefully admitted.

Reynolds Coles walked over; he was one of the premier vets in the county, and indeed the nation. "Doesn't make any sense, does it?" He shook his head.

Fair, slightly taller than Reynolds, another tall man, shook his head. "The only thing I can think of is selling drugs."

"Yeah." Reynolds paused. "The curse of our time."

Cooper, who of course knew everyone, agreed. "We aren't going to solve it. Not the way we're going about it. Being a law enforcement officer I should shut up, but when people are miserable or desperate or mentally ill, they'll take whatever lifts them up."

"True. Think of the people in history ruined by alcohol." Harry noticed the flower prints piled neatly on a back table.

"*Why don't they take catnip? Better than booze,*" said Pewter, a big fan of that kitty drug.

"*People make tea from catnip.*" Mrs. Murphy started to walk over to some saddle pads, the polo kind, which were colorful.

Ballard came out of the clinic itself, carrying a hoe.

As he paid for it, Mrs. Murphy moved to the framed prints and Tucker followed. The two sat there sniffing while Ballard told Harry, Fair, Cooper, and Reynolds that a few gardening tools rested against the back doors. He broke tools often, so was constantly needing replacements.

Pirate tagged along; being the tallest, he could sniff objects on the tables more easily than Tucker or Mrs. Murphy. Pewter stayed with the human group.

"*Lots of leather smells,*" the big dog said.

"Lead shanks, some girths and bridle. Clients brought their own saddles if needed, but usually if a horse is at a clinic, they aren't needed."

"He didn't have any horses in the layup barn. I mean, he had just opened his doors," Tucker reported. *"But I can smell that faint odor from these prints."*

Mrs. Murphy nimbly leapt onto the table, put her nose down, inhaled. *"Like an old animal smell. But faint. Must have put these prints somewhere near animals before he moved."*

"Murphy, what are you doing?" Harry walked over, noticed the prints, spread them out.

The cat patted them. *"Old stuff."*

A small price tag for the lot rested against a thin gold frame of a pink tea rose: $300.

Harry examined each print, every flower was meticulously drawn whether it be lily of the valley, a snowdrop, a tulip, so many of the common flowers of Virginia, twelve prints. She dug her hands into her pocket, pulling out some bills.

"What's she got?" Cooper walked over as the men talked. "They're pretty."

"I think he drew them. See the initials on the right-hand corner. 'BW,'" Harry noted. "The colors are beautifully done. I can't remember if it was Constance or Ballard who said that Ben would address their mother's Christmas cards in calligraphy. He had a gift. I don't think of vets as being artistic, which is unfair. Well, really, when do they have the time to do anything?"

"When does anyone have the time to do anything?" Cooper mused.

Ballard joined them, stared at the flowers. "Very pretty."

"He wrote out things for your mother, right?" Harry liked to get her facts straight.

"Did. They got along so well because both liked art, design. Mother was shocked when he was killed, and all for a damned drug."

"Maybe." Cooper looked at Ballard.

"Sorry. I jumped to conclusions."

"Think we all did," Harry soothingly said. "How's business?"

"Good, but once winter hits that's the end of that. I guess it's one thing landscape architects, hardscape learn. Your business is seasonal." He inclined his head to one side. "But I can still keep designing on paper. I enjoy it and think I've finally found what I'm supposed to do."

"Always a happy moment." Harry grinned.

As the little group broke up, Fair, a head taller than most, looked over the crowd. "Honey?"

The prints were in a large shopping bag. "The flower prints."

"Ah."

"I'm going to hang them in the tack room so I can look at them in the winter."

"Sounds good."

Pewter paid little attention to the shopping bag. *"No food."*

"No," Tucker confirmed her dolorous assessment of the shopping bag. *"These prints. Smell old but they aren't old. Very odd."*

Ballard stopped by to chat. "Harry, you bought them."

"Did."

"Good for you." He smiled then lowered his voice, conspiratorially. "Don't tell my sister. She'll say they were for Mother. She has gone through the Christmas cards for this year, as he already started them. So Constance will believe he drew the flowers for Mother. He often gave her some small gift."

"I won't breathe a word," Harry agreed.

28

October 31, 2019

Thursday

"Wouldn't hurt to refresh the croci." Constance stood over her mother's spring garden with the gardener, still on payroll. "And snowdrops."

"Yes, Miss O'Donnell." The grizzled wiry gardener nodded. "Your mother loved her spring flowers."

"She was so clever to divide her gardens into seasons and colors." Constance walked and he followed her to the fall gardens, still in bloom, as the hard frosts had not yet covered the land. "It's been a long, warm fall. Look at those zinnias. When they're done, plant some more; cover the beds, of course."

"Mulch or leaves?"

"You know what, Seth? How about if you buy some of that good mulch from out on 250," she named the state road, "then mix it with our leaves. You can chop them up."

"I can and I will. If you will permit me, I'd like to mix in a little straw, your mother and I had been experimenting. Of course, this brings more weeds, but that's my job. I'll snatch them quickly. Straw has such good insulating properties."

She crossed her arms over her bosom, a thick olive green cashmere sweater keeping her warm; a long-wearing wraparound skirt also kept her warm. "Did she leave notes?"

"No, but I have some. She was satisfied with the spring and fall gardens, more of the same, but she wanted to shift the summer gardens."

"Summer is rough."

"If we didn't have a watering system, it would be really rough."

"The lilies and crepe myrtles save us." Constance laughed.

"She read everything, as you know. Well, she found new colors of petunias that will be available for 2020. Rich colors, some with polka dots, true polka dots, and others with a stripe on each petal. The colors are intense. She was leaning toward magenta," he pointed to a spot, "pure white with a hint of pink, almost a dusting, and then over here, purple. She said, 'Caesar's purple.' She would think of that." He missed her already, as they so loved horticulture.

"Go ahead. I'll start researching stuff, too. Mother didn't use a computer but I know where she kept her gardening books. The colors sound wonderful." She looked at the sky, intense blue. "Marvelous weather."

His gaze followed hers. "'Tis. You never know in Virginia."

She smiled at him. "These days I don't think you know anywhere. When I was little there might have been a snow by now. Here, right here in Albemarle County. And what is it today? Mid-fifties?"

"Close."

"Seth, while I have you, we haven't really had time to talk: Did Mother mention what she was looking for when she was going through those boxes?"

"No. She did say sometime before her passing that she wanted to reacquaint herself with the family. Her word, *reacquaint*. Between the gardening, the horses, and furniture . . . I don't even know what the furniture is except that it's centuries old . . . she knew so much."

"Mother spoke five languages: Greek, Latin, French, Italian, and German. I speak two, and the second one is French, which I do badly. She had an ear, plus she had curiosity. I am learning how much she did know. We both liked gardening, as you know, but her other interests not so much. I was social, loved fashion and the theater. I must have driven her crazy as a child."

He smiled, for he wasn't as old as her mother but older than Constance. "I was in eighth grade when I started here. You must have given more parties than any little girl in Virginia."

Constance smiled. "Once all this is settled I intend to renew my party life. You know, it's the best way to get people together, differing people. They learn to cooperate. I watched Mother and Father do that. Well, let me get back in there. I left my coat in the kitchen. Not as warm as I thought. Clyde was busy in the library. He barely makes a sound. I don't mind him, really."

Seth nodded. "A big job."

"If I had my wits about me, I would have initiated this. Instead, I let Ballard steal a march on me. I couldn't think clearly after Mother left us. Didn't seem to affect my brother." She turned to head to the house.

Seth watched; like most people, he wished brother and sister would settle their differences. No one would win if they didn't, and friends would be forced to pick sides.

Clyde, bent over a stack of envelopes from the 1880s, a time of incredible corruption in various cities as well as in Washington, scribbled notes.

He flipped up a large Rhodia tablet with a graph pattern. He didn't know why, but those little squares kept him organized.

He wrote under *Payoffs* the name *William E. Cameron*, governor from January 1, 1882 to January 1, 1886, followed by one word, *Failure*. He thought this a succinct and damning conclusion.

Joshua Ballard was in his fifties then, on the edge of politics. Cameron had written a letter begging for money.

Hearing the door open in the kitchen, he looked up. A jacket hung on a chair in the library, Ballard's.

Constance walked in, saw her brother's jacket, said, "Is he keeping tabs?"

Ignoring the jab, Clyde smiled. "He checked in. I don't think he had any idea of your family's friendships or achievements."

"Mmm." She looked at the jacket, an expensive leather one. "He always has the best. Always."

Not wishing to comment, Clyde returned to his notes, carefully moving the envelopes from the left pile to the right when he finished reading the contents, which his curiosity led him to do for quite a few.

Constance lifted the jacket off the chair, took her own off and slipped her arms through the slim, buttery soft leather.

"Fits." Clyde couldn't resist.

"Does. Usually I can't wear men's clothing but this is very slim; Ballard isn't a big man." She put her hands in the pockets.

Her face froze for a moment, Clyde could see her fingers rolling something around. She pulled out a vial of ketamine, quickly returning it.

Again he said nothing but obviously saw it was a vial, although he didn't know of what. She put the jacket back, walked out with a shrug.

When Clyde heard the back kitchen door close—well, slam—he rose, walked to the chair. He touched the soft leather, wonderful stuff. Couldn't help himself. He picked out the vial. Ketamine. Standing there for a moment. He knew, of course, about the ketamine thefts and Ben Wagner's death; he didn't know what to do. He dropped the vial back in the coat pocket, returned to work. Better to do nothing.

Harry, keeping a back pasture in corn, silage, which she wasn't going to cut, walked back to the barn. Overhead, a flock of blackbirds babbled noisily. They whirled about then headed for the trees along the creek dividing Harry's property from the land Cooper rented, the old Jones home place.

"*Big mouths,*" Pewter complained.

Mrs. Murphy, happy to be outside, ran through the corn rows then out again to join Pewter, Harry, Tucker, and Pirate.

"*They're getting ready for tonight.*" Mrs. Murphy knew it was Halloween because Harry had put a broom on the stable door.

"*Bother.*" Pewter padded toward the barn.

"*Do you think the dead really appear tonight?*" Tucker wondered.

Pirate's considerable mustache twitched. "*What?*"

"*Pay them no mind.*" Pewter's tone was imperious. "*Humans believe this is a night when the dead can roam. It's an old belief. So kids dress up and go trick or treating. It's a party now.*"

"*And tomorrow is All Saints' Day.*" Tucker sidestepped a sunning copperhead still not in hibernation.

The snake wiggled away, only Tucker and Pewter seeing her. Not that they liked copperheads but she meant no harm and the sunshine must have felt good to a cold-blooded creature.

"*What's that mean?*" Pirate tried hard to understand humans.

"*After all the ghosts and witches go back to sleep, or whatever they do when the sun comes up, this day humans celebrate the saints who have gone before and all departed souls. Kind of a day of remembering the good.*"

Pirate looked at Tucker after this explanation and said with admiration, "*You know everything.*"

"*O la.*" Pewter pranced ahead.

29

November 1, 2019

Friday

Country House Antiques was only open on the weekends. Harry called Nancy to see if she would meet her there early in the morning, before Nancy drove to her regular job, so she could pick up the prints Nancy had found for Fair. Harry's weekend was looking packed.

After the fall equinox, the sun rose later, setting earlier, but by the time Harry arrived, Nancy, with pale light coming from the east, pulled in at the same time.

The two women got out of their cars.

The dogs shot out of Harry's.

"Get back in there." She opened the door to the now ageing station wagon, a Volvo, hanging in there.

"*Oh please. We won't make a sound.*" Tucker looked up with large begging brown eyes.

"Harry, they won't do anything." Nancy smiled as they both heard the click of the key opening the simple lock.

The humans stepped through the door, Nancy flicked on the lights. The dogs stopped in their tracks.

"Breathe," Tucker commanded.

Pirate did as he was told. *"Uh-oh."*

Nancy started for her desk, then she, too, stopped cold, as did Harry.

"My God," Nancy exclaimed.

Clyde sat in her chair. His eyes were wide open. He was dead.

30

November 1, 2019

Friday—One hour later

"Turn that off," Sheriff Shaw told Dwayne, his young officer.

Deputy Cynthia Cooper was already in Country House Antiques, responding to the call first, as she had been in the area.

Tucker and Pirate sat by a child's table in the front, watching the law enforcement people. First came Cooper, whom they knew. Then came a forensic team, super fast. Then came the ambulance and finally the sheriff himself with Dwayne, young, learning the ropes.

As Sheriff Shaw walked through the door, both Harry and Nancy looked up.

"Ladies." He walked right to the corpse. "You boys get what you need?"

The forensic team nodded, as they had carefully examined Clyde in situ.

"We did."

"Okay, take him out." The sheriff noted the small muscles were going into rigor.

As Clyde was wheeled out, covered with a body bag, people drove by slowly. No one dared to stop but it was obvious something had happened at Country House Antiques. A body being wheeled out confirmed that. People reached for their cellphones.

Within minutes, half of Keswick had heard about an unidentified corpse being hauled off from Nancy's store.

People badgered Susan, the concierge at Keswick Club.

The personable blonde, who herself had received a phone call, wisely said she knew very little, which was the truth.

Constance O'Donnell, meeting a friend for breakfast, took a call on her cell. "What? Well, who is it?"

With no further information forthcoming, she clicked off her phone, looked at her friend. "I don't know whether to believe this or not."

Cindy Chandler, across the table from her, asked, "What's going on?"

Constance told her what she knew.

Cindy, quiet for a moment, replied, "Whoever it is or was, it can't be good news."

Back at the store, Cooper studied the floor as the dogs watched her.

"He wasn't dragged."

Sheriff Shaw stood next to her. "He walked in or someone very strong carried him." Turning to Nancy, he asked, "Back door?"

She showed him. It was a simple back door to an old building but it did have a security system attached to it.

The sheriff followed the wire to where it was inserted into the wall through a drilled hole. "How many people knew you had a security system?"

"Part-time workers. It's not a very expensive system." Nancy looked up as she stood next to the sheriff. "And any of my neighbors here who come in the back door might have noticed over time. Most times friends knock but sometimes they don't."

"Cut." He looked down at the ground. "Not a damn footprint." Then he corrected himself. "I'm sorry, Nancy. I shouldn't swear in front of a lady but there's something about this, something odd like at Ben Wagner's. No marks, at least the team hasn't found anything yet. No footprints. No dragging. And someone knew your security system or was smart enough to figure out where it might be."

"He worked for Ballard Perez."

"Yes, I know. Constance called to complain to me that he was trespassing but we worked that out. What surprised me is that it wasn't Constance or Ballard who was killed, given how that's going. I guess I shouldn't say that, either."

"He was a nice young man thrilled to be working on such important papers. Ballard hired him."

"Ah."

As the humans pieced together what information they had, the two dogs, who had sniffed the body before Harry shooed them off and the sheriff's people arrived, watched the humans.

Tucker checked everything. She fished for a small bottle under an end table.

Harry got down next to her. "I can push it a little. Pocketknife." She opened her pocketknife, which she usually carried in her jacket.

The sound of a rolling small bottle rewarded her efforts.

"Tucker, get out of the way now."

"*I found it*," the corgi insisted.

Pirate, learning how huge he was, remained still as the bottle rolled out and Harry grabbed it, giving it to Cooper.

"Boss." Her voice carried an edge.

The sheriff came through the back door, which he was still studying, walked to the center section of the smallish building. "I'll be."

She handed him a bottle while Harry read the label. "Ketamine."

"Harry, don't jump to conclusions."

"No, Sir," Harry agreed. "But it is interesting."

"Yes," was all Sheriff Shaw uttered.

Tucker, now leaning on Pirate, said, *"When we sniffed Clyde did you smell that old skin smell?"*

"What we smelled at the vet's office?"

"Yes. The same faint odor on the military prints Mother bought then gave back. Same on the flower prints she bought. It's an animal odor but I can't place it."

"Maybe it's too old," Pirate logically answered.

"I don't know," the intrepid little dog replied. *"I have never smelled it before and now on Clyde. Faint on his hands, but there."*

"He could have played with an old dog or cat toy." Pirate lifted the tip of his long tail. *"That would be old skin, wouldn't it?"*

"Would have been stronger. Plus this doesn't smell like a toy. This is different. If only I knew what it was." Tucker took a deep breath. *"If only we could get Harry to leave this alone. These murders have to be connected. That scent isn't turning up by coincidence. It's too rare."* Tucker frowned. *"Too rare."*

31

November 2, 2019

Saturday

Upset by yesterday's events, Harry focused on the tack room in the barn. She'd been meaning for months to reorganize it. Perhaps this would take her focus off the subject of murder in general and the murders in particular.

The saddle racks in a line against the back wall, the big tack trunk underneath couldn't be improved upon. However, the pile of washed saddle pads resting on a box could be moved.

Placing the pads on her large old desk she studied the area. For a tack room it was spacious, the size of two stalls and her stalls were ten feet by twelve feet.

Rarely did she make use of the old sofa and two chairs at the opposite end of the tidy room. If anyone came to see her, it was an old friend who pulled up a chair, because Harry was usually at her desk or cleaning tack.

"All right." She picked up the saddle pads to take them outside to

one of the tack trunks in the center aisle. Once there she flipped open a trunk. It wasn't as empty as she'd thought.

"Drat."

Tucker, following her every step, sat down.

She left the saddle pads there, walking back into the tack room. She brought the flower drawings to the room, along with her small hammer and picture-hanging nails and semi-triangular hangers, as opposed to a single nail driven in the wall.

"Go sit down." Pewter moaned as she rested on a lower saddle, liking the feel of the leather under her.

"She's in a mood. She'll calm down eventually," Mrs. Murphy said.

Pewter peered over the side of her perch, as Mrs. Murphy was similarly placed on the saddle underneath the one she sat on. All the racks were in a row. A cat could easily jump from one to the other. The lower ones pleased them the most and sometimes Harry even threw a saddle pad over the seat of the saddle. The best.

Harry lined up the framed flowers on the sofa and the two chairs, then moved them about according to the color of the drawn flower.

Picking up a pink tea rose drawing, Harry ran her fingers around the outside of the frame. "These look from another century but his name is on the bottom. I had no idea Ben was so talented." She then put the pink tea rose back in place, which was next to a purple morning glory, sensuous.

After an hour she had hung the drawings on the wall behind the sofa but not so low that someone's head would bump them. Having a very tall husband made her aware of needing to put hanging items higher. Stepping back she looked.

Pirate, sprawled on the sofa, opened one eye then closed it.

Tucker, at Harry's feet, cooed, *"Very pretty."*

Pirate, giving up on sleep, said, *"She can't smell that faint odor, can she?"*

"No. It won't bother us. It's not strong enough to fill the room," the corgi replied.

Pewter, eyes wide open, called to the dogs. *"Maybe it's an old perfume, or cologne, since Ben drew the flowers. Maybe that's why it's not clear."*

"Why wouldn't cologne be clear?" Pirate asked a sensible question.

"Blends," Tucker succinctly responded. *"Perfumes and colognes aren't one scent. They are a medley. Some even used tobacco."*

"Oh." Pirate was surprised as it seemed like a great deal of work to produce a perfume or cologne.

"Humans like to disguise their scent," Pewter offered.

Mrs. Murphy added, *"Many think it attracts other humans, and given their poor noses they often overdo. You can smell them coming."*

"Harry always smells like, I don't know, something outside." Pirate puzzled over this. *"It's never strong. And Fair smells like horses."*

The animals laughed as Harry walked back to the center aisle, picked up the white sheepskin saddle pads, expensive, walked back in. The pads were driving her crazy. She put them on the desktop.

"Pirate, you usually aren't in the bedroom and you're too big for the bathroom. Every morning Harry takes her shower just as she takes one at night, but in the morning she grabs her bottle of Green Irish Tweed, sprays it in the air, and walks through it." Mrs. Murphy smiled at the thought of Harry's morning routine.

"That's strange." The big fellow lifted his eyebrows.

Pewter dropped her tail over the side of the saddle, it gently swayed. *"Someone once told her if she did that she wouldn't overload on the perfume. Who knows who told her that? Maybe her mother. Of course, humans have no idea how they smell. Walking through spray doesn't do a thing. She might as well just do the usual, pat the inside of her wrists, behind her ears, and some women even put a dab between their bosoms."*

"Gross," the young wolfhound blurted out.

Hearing the yip, Harry turned to Pirate. "What's the matter with you?"

Tucker grinned. *"Don't ask, Mom."*

Pewter asked the big dog, *"What's gross, the perfume or the bosoms?"*

They all laughed.

Mrs. Murphy looked down at Tucker. *"Well, it may be the bosoms. Tucker, if you did this you'd have to spray three times."*

They howled and Harry said to herself, "I will never understand them. What could possibly have their attention?"

She did make a decision about the saddle pads. She got on the small stepladder to place a pad on every saddle. When she reached the bottom two she didn't have the heart to move the cats, so she put the pads back on her desk.

The old phone rang. Harry moved to her desk.

"Harry."

Hearing Susan's voice, she sat down. "What's up?"

"I just heard that the sheriff closed off the library at Lone Pine. No one can go in or come out except Constance or Ballard, if necessary."

"No kidding." Harry rubbed her forehead, which now smelled like sheepskin, although she couldn't smell it.

"If Sheriff Shaw thinks the library is key to the murder, he has to hire someone who understands what's in there."

"Jerry Showalter," Harry instantly replied.

At that very moment Sheriff Shaw and Deputy Cooper sat in Jerry's living room.

"We'll have a guard with you." The sheriff sounded reassuring.

"With all due respect, one man alone can't possibly examine the contents of that library. It would take me one year and I would be lucky to get anywhere in that time. The holdings are enormous."

"We've thought of that." Cooper leaned forward. "Can you bring in other experts? We know, the contents are worth millions. Double-digit millions. Is the library the key to Clyde's murder? And what about Candida? We don't know, but we have to consider that both Ballard and Constance agreed to cremate her without an autopsy."

Jerry quietly stated, "That may have been a hard-won agreement. However, given her age, it isn't unreasonable."

"No," Sheriff Shaw agreed. "But we have to consider that Candida, too, may have been murdered."

A long silence followed this, for it had occurred to Jerry, just as it occurred to him that being in that library could be dangerous even with a guard. "What is it exactly that you want me to do?"

"The first thing would be to review all of Clyde Mercador's notes."

Jerry nodded to Cooper in agreement. "If the department can pay, there are two librarians I would trust to give us an overview. One is head of special collections at Washington University in St. Louis, the other is the head librarian at Lafayette College. Whether they will be allowed a leave of absence, I don't know, but I do know these two women are at the top of their fields." He hesitated. "I also know they can't be cajoled. Or bribed."

At this both Sheriff Shaw and Cooper straightened in their seats.

Then Jerry without fanfare added, "I believe you are on the right track. Whatever this is about is in the library. I don't think any volumes are missing. That would be quickly obvious."

"Surely the Ballards had them put in order." Cooper thought someone must have realized the value of same.

"They did. Over the centuries there was always a Ballard with a great interest in the family's history and history in general. In the nineteenth century an inventory was carried out at least once a generation. They were meticulous. As the twentieth dawned, the interest waned, so the inventories stopped about 1980. Granted, the family had dropped back from elected office, high military command, et cetera, but they remained involved in politics if for nothing else than their money. Everyone running for office in this state stopped by and most presidential candidates made a call. However, the recent materials may not be as well arranged as one would wish. I don't know that Candida carefully put them in her leather boxes. She wasn't as interested in them as the older papers and letters, but she was interested."

"I see." Sheriff Shaw was beginning to realize what an enormous task this was. "I know you can't carry out an inventory. Perhaps after reviewing Clyde's notes, if you and the ladies you suggested could go through the boxes. I would imagine there are lists of what should be in there, given the prior inventories."

"There are, Sheriff. I know where they are, assuming they haven't been disturbed. Again, at some point even though there have been prior inventories, everything should again be painstakingly reviewed; preserved, if there are signs of damage; that sort of thing."

"Yes. But can you do what we've asked?"

"With the help of Marge and Tammy, I can."

"Do you mind telling us why you aren't using anyone from your old library, UVA?" Cooper wondered.

"Given what has transpired it is possible those few who could do this work already have been contacted to not do it, if you will." He held up his hand. "I've been years out of the library. I don't know many of the newer people, but given the money that may be at stake if papers or books have been stolen, I wouldn't discount payment for silence or refusing to work on this project."

Both the sheriff and Cooper exhaled at the same time. "Let us know when you're ready to go to Lone Pine. We'll have security arranged."

"I know you have Ben Wagner's murder to solve as well," Jerry mentioned. "This is a lot of pressure on you all. Small town. Shocking events. I can imagine people are pressing you."

"We're used to it," the sheriff said honestly.

"I don't mean to pressure you and I will take on this work. If for no other reason than I adored Candida and she was good to me over the years, but . . ." He took a moment. "I don't want to be the next victim. You might give me security at home, too."

"Of course." Sheriff Shaw readily agreed, for the thought had occurred to him as well.

He kept silent, as he didn't want to spook Jerry. Then again, a car sitting opposite your house on a twisting road is pretty obvious.

Security would be necessary. Very necessary.

32

April 27, 1789

Monday

Peach trees at Big Rawly, in full bloom, filled the air with fragrance. Soon the apple blooms would follow. Spring had triumphantly arrived. The last frost was over.

A soft rain four days ago encouraged growth and the roads were now serviceable. Hard rains, especially in spring, turned roads into a quagmire. Winter frosts meant one could travel if careful, but spring was anyone's guess.

Shank and Martin rode to the wagon shed. Hearing hoofbeats, Jeffrey walked out of his larger carriage shed to see the two men ride to the wagon shed.

"Tips, I'll be back soon."

His second-in-command nodded and the tall well-built man strode over to the wagon shed, where William slunk away at the sight of the two men who'd captured him and returned him to Maureen. They ignored him.

Caleb, pulled over to the wagon shed to work there today, smiled when Jeffrey came in.

"Caleb, the wagon looks ready." Jeffrey smiled back.

"You could put a house on this wagon. Look at those axles." Caleb pointed to the axles forged at Big Rawly.

"Red," Martin remarked. "No one will miss it."

Jeffrey nodded. "Perhaps a bit showy. Cardinal red. Well—"

The two men grimaced slightly then Shank said, "Well, best be going. We can reach the river by sundown if all goes well."

"Good." Jeffrey nodded. "Everyone in Maysville will see the wagon. Might get more orders." He smiled.

The two hitched up the horses they'd been riding, soon driving out of Big Rawly.

Sulli, watching from the distant small house, pursed her lips as they drove off. Captured with William, she prudently did as she was told. William did not. She so hated William she wished Martin had cut behind his left knee so he would be so crippled he would need crutches just to drag around.

Olivia watched her observing. "Hard men."

Sulli nodded. "We have people that could deliver wagons. I don't know why Mr. Jeffrey has to use them."

"He wouldn't be using them if Maureen didn't wish it. Having them come to Big Rawly to pick up wagons frightens people. Everyone knows what they did to William."

"And everyone knows that William lied, stole, and—"

Olivia interrupted. "He's not worth your hate."

Crying, the blind baby furled and unfurled her fingers. Sulli picked her up, she was getting heavier. The spring air warmed all creatures today, so the tiny little thing gurgled with pleasure. Sulli wondered how to teach the girl to walk. She'd never had an interest in children, and resented being stuck with the simpleminded, the physically harmed, but the sightless child somehow snuck into her heart.

Olivia, maybe thirty feet away, was trying to get Gaston, ancient, childlike, to help fold the blankets for the house.

Maureen, cruel, nonetheless made sure all her people, as she thought of them, had good blankets, decent clothing, and most importantly, good shoes. If anyone came to Big Rawly, they would assume the slaves were well treated. It was a mark of power to do so and Maureen wanted more power, more money. Having grown up in the Caribbean and being educated in France, she couldn't believe that these people actually thought all were equal. She kept that to herself.

Gaston would half fold a blanket then open it and wrap it around himself. Olivia, who had tended to him for decades, they weren't far apart in age, finally took the blankets from him, placing them on an outside bench. She'd do it herself later.

"Blossoms. Blossoms. Blossoms." The harmless fellow babbled then sang the word, a big word for him.

Sulli stared at him and Olivia, the soul of patience. "We should name the baby."

"We should," Olivia agreed. "She is sturdy, which is a help."

"I was thinking if we had a harness, it would be easier to teach her to walk."

"Ask Mr. Jeffrey. Don't ask anyone else."

Sulli nodded as she watched the red wagon slowly approach the big house, modeled after a French chateau, somewhat medieval in appearance. The Selisses, Maureen's first husband's name, determined not to look like the English, as they called them among themselves. Maureen, in particular, found English ways aesthetically displeasing. She dumped this at Cromwell's door, wondering how anyone could believe in Puritanism.

It wasn't so much that she was a devout Catholic but she enjoyed the ritual. She also enjoyed being publicly seen at her chapel. To which she invited other Catholics. There were few, very few.

The kitchen door opened. From the vantage point of the hill on which the house, called a haven by some, was perched, Sulli could see everything.

Maureen, holding a basket, walked out, the wagon stopped, and she handed up the basket to the two men. Maureen would give that task to her main woman, a lady-in-waiting in essence. Why would she come out and hand a basket to two white men, former slave catchers and now wagon delivery boys?

Transfixed, Sulli half closed her eyes to see better. Olivia, observing her, watched also. As was her wont, she kept her thoughts to herself.

Sulli knew she was seeing something unusual. Why would Maureen ever have direct contact with such men without someone else with her? Shank thanked her, picked up the pace, and Maureen returned to the house.

The baby pulled at her hair. Sulli removed the grasping fingers. She knew she had seen something important but she had no idea why. Then she turned to Olivia.

"Sophia. I'll name the baby Sophia."

The loom shuttle clicked, a soothing rhythm. Bumbee sat there with her three assistants, quietly unfolding a medium-weight wool that Yolanda showed to Bumbee.

"Too dark. Get me a lighter color."

"Yes, Ma'am."

All her girls called Bumbee Ma'am.

Two girls sat in chairs, repairing torn garments, a full-time job on a big estate like Cloverfields.

Felice threw down the torn heavy jacket she struggled with. "It can't be fixed."

"Let me see it." Bumbee stopped her work as Felice brought over the heavy short jacket lined with thick wool. Bumbee herself had lined that jacket eleven years ago. She remembered things like that.

Turning it inside out, then back right again, she placed it crossways on her lap. "Felice, you're right. I think digging out that stone finally destroyed it. You take this, make a new one."

"Oh, I can't do that."

"Why not?"

"It's too . . ." She thought. "Hard. All the cutting, getting the sleeves on right and lining them before putting them on."

"You'll learn. Lining the sleeves is easy if you know how. Now get to work and don't complain."

Grimacing, Felice passed Yolanda, a new fabric in hand. Rolling her eyes, Felice shrugged, while Yolanda only lifted her eyebrows.

Bumbee, a hard taskmaster, worked especially hard and expected her girls to work hard, too. And to whom could the girls complain? They were thought lucky to be learning such a valuable trade. Better than sweeping floors.

"This will do." Bumbee handed the beige-colored fabric back to Yolanda. "Help Felice. She has no patience."

Felice wanted to defend herself but didn't because Bettina and Serena walked through the door after a light knock.

"Girls," Bettina acknowledged them. "Bumbee, come with us to Rachel's house. She and Catherine want you to look at an old dress of their mother's that Rachel has kept."

"I don't think Rachel parts with anything." Bumbee sighed, not that she thought it was wrong to keep old clothing if you had room to store things.

The women left the less-than-happy girls to take apart the coat, to study every seam.

Once inside Rachel's clapboard house, the women sat.

"Bumbee, we can't trade with France anymore. I need fabric like this." Rachel held her hand under a sheer fabric, gauze-like.

Bumbee felt the fabric. "Only the French can do this. The Italians make beautiful fabrics, but only the French get it this sheer."

Bumbee had loved fabrics since childhood. Her knowledge was extraordinary.

"Oh dear." Rachel sat down, still holding the dress.

"That takes care of that," Catherine, always sensible, said.

"Your mother had such beautiful clothing." Bettina had loved Isabelle, and vice versa.

"Is there any way to make this more fashionable?"

Bumbee took the dress handed to her, testing the seams. "If I make alterations, especially at the bust, raise it up a bit. Lace could do that, white lace, and I'd raise the hem. Not much. This style will never go out of fashion as long as women want to look like women," she said with authority. "You will look wonderful. Of course, I'll do what you wish, but I can't make you a new dress."

Rachel studied the garment. "All right. I don't think Mother will mind."

"How can the French afford to lose so much business?" Bettina shrewdly observed.

"They can't," Catherine matter-of-factly answered.

"Funny how many things get set aside when profits falter," Rachel mused.

"I think more than profits will falter over there. The Baron Necker's letters to Father paint a grim picture." Catherine stopped then smiled. "Nothing we can do about it."

Logs on the fire, for the night proved once again cold, Bumbee stood in the middle of the large room, right hand under her chin, studying the bolts of cloth and wool in the square cases built to contain them. In many ways summer and winter were easier to face than the changing seasons. A spring day could start cool, move to luxurious afternoon warmth and sunshine, then sink with the sun to a night's hard frost. Fall tested one, as did spring. For summer, combining cotton and linen or using each separately was easy. Spring, well, if you started with a heavy shawl or coat, you would need to discard it, then pick it up again later.

Mumbling to herself, Bumbee fingered a rich wool imported from England. "Hmm, fine, light. Unusual." Then she touched cotton. Could she find a way to twist these fibers together and then weave them? She felt certain the answer to a changing-season fabric, as she thought of it, would be twisting the two fibers into one before working at the loom.

A light knock on the door sent her to it. "Yes."

"Let me in, honey."

"Why?"

"I need to talk to you."

"You need to lie to me. That's all you do."

"Bumbee, this is different. I need you to help me think."

That was a new one. She opened the door. He stepped through it, didn't kiss or hug her, walked to the wooden chair before the fire, took off his coat, made by her, and dropped down. She sat in the accompanying chair.

"I saw something."

"What?"

"Mr. Charles and I delivered church stuff to St. Luke's. Before I helped him take the box off the wagon, he went into the church to find help. I thought I heard something so I sprinted over to the work shed off to the side of the church."

"The one Charles is going to take down?" Bumbee had paid close attention to the construction of the Lutheran church. Seeing Charles so excited provoked most everyone's interest.

"Yes." He felt the fire's warmth for a moment. "Two white men behind the building were dragging a white girl. You know Livia Taylor?"

Her eyebrows raised. "Young. All that flaming red hair."

"One had his hand over her mouth, dragging her. The other ran ahead. I didn't see a wagon or horses but the ground rises up behind that and the one man was having to drag her up the rise there."

"Any blood?"

"No. One arm was pinned behind her back. I figure she had no chance to fight."

"Did you tell Mr. Charles?"

"No."

"Livia, well, I don't know, but I figure she might have been on her way to the church because her mother helps plant stuff there. I don't think they are members."

"No. Pauline," Percy named Livia's mother, "is a good gardener. She helps out."

"You would know." She always admired his skill, as had Isabelle Ewing, who designed her gardens when he was a young fellow. She liked his talent and he soaked up what he could, then over time his own thoughts crystallized. He had a way with color, seasonal blooming, what looks good as a backdrop, what should be in front.

"I didn't know what to do."

"Given that it would have been two against one, there wasn't much you could do. Let us pray they don't abuse her and kill her."

Grimacing, he shook his head. "People are crazy cruel, Bumbee. Cruel like Maureen Selisse. I didn't recognize the men; Livia was easy to recognize because of her hair."

"You'd know if you knew them. People move different. You can spot them far away and know who they are by their way of walking."

"I didn't know them."

"You didn't tell Mr. Charles?"

He shook his head. "He would believe me but when he might tell other white men, you know, if they would search for her, I don't think they would believe me or him if he said I was the one who told him. Bumbee, I feel bad. I feel really bad."

She folded her hands together. "If she isn't found, alive or dead, she might have been stolen."

"Someone would buy her like a slave?"

She nodded. "There's always money in women's bodies."

"She's white. She could run away."

"Not if she's kept in locked rooms or if she was put on a ship to go to the Barbary Coast. Heard Mr. Charles once talking about pirates there stealing everything and everybody on ships they boarded." She thought a moment. "He said there are sultans over there that own thousands of women. Keep them locked up in glamorous quarters but no one can see them or visit them except the sultan." She paused. "You would have liked that."

He sighed. "Bumbee, I make mistakes. Something comes over me. I don't mean to hurt you."

"You know, I believe you, but I don't want to be hurt anymore. You go your way and I'll go mine."

"Ah, Bumbee." He stopped before he started pleading. "About Livia. What should I do?"

"Nothing you can do. Let white people take care of white people."

33

November 6, 2019

Wednesday

"All we need is the list confirmed." Constance reposed in the brown leather club chair by the library fire.

Ballard, seated in the companion chair, gripped the arms. "Every letter, every piece of paper should be examined and photographed."

"That can be done after whoever simply determines if all the materials are in the boxes. The only reason you want a drawn-out and expensive process is to establish value. A general idea could be figured from just a catalog of the contents, which we have, by the way. For much of the earlier generations of Ballards inventoried their materials."

Burrowing farther down in the chair, Ballard mumbled, "So you can cheat me. A general idea of value lets you off the hook."

"What I will do is fight you tooth and nail not to sell the family papers. Establishing value even if not to the penny lets me know how protracted this fight will be or what I can bargain with, assuming I have anything of equivalent value."

"Well, you don't. You're not on food stamps but you can't possibly keep half of the papers. Your husband lost more money than you care to admit."

"I will keep all of the papers." Her voice rose. "Furthermore, it's not my fault that the special-collections experts from Washington University and Lafayette College can't work on this project until the end of the semester. I mean the spring semester. No temporary replacement can be found. That's what Sheriff Shaw told me."

"He told me, too," Ballard snapped. "We can't wait that long. For all I know, you'll kill me."

"Don't flatter yourself. You're not worth a bullet."

Silently, Ballard stared into the fire, which he started to lessen the evening's chill.

Living in what is called a dependency on the estate, Ballard kept an eye on things. His mother gave him the house for his use because he had bellied up once again before starting the hardscaping business. Then again, it was a huge property. Having someone relatively close was an advantage. Although Constance wasn't that far away at Keswick Estates, Ballard was close enough to Lone Pine in case of emergency. Then again, Candida doted on her son.

He finally spoke. "Will your lawyer accept an estimate?"

"He will. I've told him I don't want this to drag out. I'll have enough bills to pay without years-long legal fees, and so will you, unless of course your rock business can do it."

"And should we settle on the papers, what about the estate itself?"

"Nothing is being broken up. Nothing."

He shifted in his seat. "If we sell the papers, there will be enough to keep this place going for centuries, I don't doubt. You can't pay for it any more than I can."

"Lone Pine must stay intact, just as the papers need to be kept intact."

"For God's sake, Constance. Nobody lives like this anymore."

"Ah, but they do. New money. A few of the old families are left, the money not squandered over the centuries or decades, but in the main, it's new money which means it's vulgar."

"Oh, for Christ's sake." He groaned. "Do you want to live like Mother?"

"No. No one could ever live like Mother. She exercised just the right balance between social blowouts and giving. And when you think about it, her parties were ways to get people together to give more. She never let down her foundation for homeless children. Nor did she forget the arts. I don't have Mother's mind. Lone Pine has great historic value. We owe it to her to keep it going as best we can."

She spoke in a composed voice, which took effort. "We can't wait for experts. We can't. If Sheriff Shaw will allow it, then I say we hire, or the county hires, as I don't know if Jerry Showalter would be working for us or the sheriff's department, but I say let him come in here, with assistants if he chooses, and go through every box, checking off the contents according to the lists we have from prior, what would you call it, certifications? A kind of Dewey Decimal System?"

"There is no more Dewey Decimal System."

"I know that. I actually miss the old system, but through the centuries the cataloging of our papers used it—that and chronology. All Jerry would need to do is go through each list and each box to see if the inventory contents are in the boxes."

He ruminated. "And we leave him alone?"

"Well, we can be civil. I like him very much and he was good to Mother."

"I don't mean that. I mean no money under the table to sway things your way."

"How can I sway things my way? I don't know the possible value."

"You can do so to lower the value so you need not pay me the sum, as close as it can be to attested value."

"But I'm not paying you." She purred. "We're going to court over this."

"Constance, this is so wasteful."

"Protecting our family is not wasteful. Those papers are of incredible value to historians, biographers, you name it. Mother knew that. It wasn't just family pride. She cared about the future. She cared about future generations reading from first-person correspondence. Oh, how things get twisted today to suit political ends. It's hard to twist a heartfelt letter your way."

"Bullshit. People have been re-editing events, lying about history for millennia. Think of the Triumvirate."

He mentioned the period in Rome immediately after Caesar's murder, where Octavian, Mark Antony, and Lepidus in 43 B.C. formed a power-sharing triumvirate. As all three were well educated, this made sense. The struggle for power, untruths, half truths, and bald lies were no different then than today, with the exception that the earlier practitioners may have been more intelligent.

"I concede your point."

"My God. This day goes down in history," Ballard crowed.

"If we allow Jerry here, it will take time, but nothing like assigning a monetary value to each scrap of paper in every box. All he has to do is use the prior lists, ascertain that each document exists, as I said."

"And you will stay out of it?"

"Ballard, the sheriff's department will be here. We have no choice but to stay out of it. But even so, let the man do his job, and if he has assistants, fine. I'm not saying I won't pop my head in and say hello."

"Shall you call Sheriff Shaw or shall I?" he asked.

"We both should. You call tomorrow and I will, too."

"This doesn't mean I am agreeing to anything." Ballard suffered a moment of cold feet.

"No. But we can't wait for half a year. If nothing else, who will run Lone Pine?"

"There's enough for that. She left a sum for that, for Margaret's salary and the horses."

"That's not the same as running Lone Pine." Constance correctly understood the situation.

"We can hire someone." Ballard had no head for money.

"No, we can't. Do you want a stranger in this house? The silver alone means it has to be one of us or someone who is bonded, and that someone won't be cheap."

"God." He nearly wailed.

"I will do it. It comes naturally to me. I am not asking for money."

"Well, how do I know you won't steal the silver?" He threw that in her face.

Rising, she looked down at her brother. "Ballard, get a grip."

34

November 7, 2019

Thursday

"It'd make a good small animal vet clinic." Fair walked from the layup barn at Ben Wagner's equine vet clinic to the main building, unlocked.

Cooper, walking with him, agreed. "It's a good location right between Crozet and White Hall. Roads aren't bad, a little twisty, but it's pleasant and there's so much room. Boarding would bring in money, too."

"Would. The Wileys have the listing."

"That's a wide client base. I'd be surprised if this stayed on the market longer than four months, if that. Of course, winter is around the corner, always harder to sell in cold weather and snow."

Fair pushed open the door for Cooper, who nodded her thanks. Not for her a fuss about a man opening a door. Given what she often faced in her workday, anything anybody did to make the day a bit better, she was for it.

Fair quietly pulled up chairs for them then said, "He gave this place so much thought."

"What preys on my mind is we've had two murders. Neither of which makes any sense. Why would anyone kill a young vet, well liked, for a couple of bottles of ketamine? I can't think that's the sole reason."

"You're probably right. Then the bottles taken out of my truck, it's not enough to make money, is it?"

"No. Would be plenty for personal use. Well, I guess it would."

"Not if whoever took it was having a huge party. You know, one of those sexathons."

She half smiled. "Where do people get the time?"

He laughed. "Weekends, or they don't work." He looked around. "He built for so much natural light."

"That bothers me, too. You'd think there would be one fingerprint or a footprint or even tire treads. One locked door where his lab coats hung, the flower drawings. No damage to the lock or door. A kick on that door and his supply room. A smudge. No print. When this initially happened, the team was here, of course, I went out to the layup barn thinking what if whoever it was hid in here and then snuck out the back? They'd go up over the ridge. If they had a car with four-wheel drive, the farm road would be easy. We asked around, drove to the other side. Nothing. I'm thinking whoever killed him came in with him."

"Ah." Fair's brow wrinkled. "Then how did they get out?"

"I don't know." Her voice raised. "But remember the day. If someone walked on the grass by the drive, the grass, fall, color fading, would still spring back up. What if a car was parked or hidden along the Crozet Road? There are plenty of places. Might be a long walk, but then again, maybe he or she was picked up or the killer drove him, promised he'd drive him back."

"Back to what you said earlier. I, too, am beginning to think ketamine wasn't the only reason. Ben was clean as a whistle. You and the team investigated everybody and everything. He was squeaky clean."

"Well, we think he was." She shook her head. "People can fool you."

"Right." He nodded.

"Thanks for coming by. Thought maybe something would occur to us or we'd see something missed before. Doesn't seem to be the case." She changed the subject. "Your wife grabbed those flower portraits at the sale. Another loss, Ben was an artistic guy."

"You know, Coop, someone or something will drop into your lap. Sooner or later even the best and the smartest make a mistake."

"So long as the mistakes aren't more murders."

35

November 8, 2019

Friday

The potbellied stove in the old schoolhouse kept the large room warm even with the huge long-paned windows. Harry, Tazio, Nancy, and Susan hung the photos of the presidents, which Nancy had found, matted and framed.

"Can you imagine grooming those whiskers?" Harry noted Taft's mustache and sideburns.

"Well, the sideburns are manageable; that mustache, I don't know." Nancy laughed as she held up the photograph for Susan to place.

"Up about an inch," Susan directed.

Tazio, standing behind her, walked over, slightly touched the bottom of the frame. "There?"

President Taft between two attractive women might have smiled had he been there.

"Good," Susan said, then added, "Taft and Roosevelt. What a story."

"Not exactly as emotional as Jefferson and Adams, but they had worked closely, and then pfft." Harry loved history.

"Roosevelt would have been a handful for anyone." Tazio smiled. "All that energy."

"Do you think he ever got over the death of his first wife?" Nancy asked.

"No," came a chorus.

"Mmm." Nancy nodded. "Well, Mrs. Taft supported the arts. Cincinnati still owes her a debt. Isn't it something the number of leaders who have come from Ohio? We like to think Virginia leads in the number of presidents but Ohio gave us Grant, Taft, the Longworth family, they were so powerful in Congress."

"Nancy, don't forget Ohio also gave us Rutherford B. Hayes, who was pretty awful."

"Harry, the economy shot back up." Susan's voice sounded matter-of-fact. "He undid all that Grant had done to assist the former slaves, to help them learn to navigate the political system."

"You know, I never once thought about Rutherford B. Hayes." Tazio shrugged. "We did think about Sherman, though, because he moved to St. Louis. Had a real belief in the future of my hometown. But Hayes?"

Susan added the bad bits. "Cotton had been our first or second industry, export industry, depending on the year. The war ruined it. Well, no president wants the economy to tank on his watch, so Hayes withdrew the troops, turned a blind eye to suppression of voting, and worse, really turned a blind eye to pushing the newly freed back out into the cotton fields. They were the jobs mostly available. He wasn't such a good guy, but like most people he thought he was, and indeed, our economy shot back up."

"Well, what happened to forty acres and a mule?" Tazio wondered.

"That's just it. That program ended in a hurry. It always comes down to money. And money soon turns into greed." Harry uncharacteristically raised her voice. "I hate it. I really do hate it."

"All right, back to more presidents. How about Woodrow Wilson."

Nancy laughed. "He always looks as though he's sucking on a pickle."

They all agreed that he never looked like a fun guy.

As the photos began to fill the wall, they all liked what they saw.

"Can you imagine anyone putting up the presidents today?" Harry asked.

"No. Every one had flaws, as do we all, but someone would holler about the dead. Well, they can't fix it now, can they? And they were our presidents. Would we rather have photographs and paintings of the Tsars?" Harry raised her shoulders.

"Well, the clothing would be more exciting." Nancy laughed.

"True."

As the task neared completion, Tazio pulled some chairs closer to the stove. Once finished they all sat down and she poured hot tea from a thermos while Harry offered co-cola.

"Wasn't it great? Jerry getting those schoolbooks for all the grades. He can root out anything," Susan admiringly noted.

"He's at Lone Pine." Nancy filled her in. "Checking the papers against the inventory sheets from centuries back. Some of those sheets start before the Revolutionary War."

"Coop said the department put him to work and there's a guard," Susan added to the news. "Actually, it's Dwayne, with both a gun and a computer."

"What's even worse is that Ballard has hired someone to inventory the silver." Nancy threw up her hands. "He called me and said he'd be at the store tomorrow. Wanted to talk about odd pieces. Nothing from the actual silverware but something like a small silver box that had been on Candida's nightstand."

"Is he that broke?" Harry wondered.

"Who knows? He and Constance are fighting over the will," Susan again informed them, as Sheriff Shaw often kept Ned abreast of developments, given that he was their representative to the House of Delegates. One never knew when something would spill over into the larger political forum.

"No good will come of it." Tazio spoke the truth. "Never does."

"Well, this seems especially contentious." Nancy sipped her hot tea. "It's a vast estate, a huge house, many outbuildings. Can you imagine the annual upkeep expense? Has to be a couple of hundred thousand dollars. Just overseeding the fields will run way up. I can see both sides of the issue but I doubt either of them wants to find a way without snatching the other's half."

"If they worked together, maybe it could be easier. You know, like historical tours. Even a historical bed-and-breakfast. That isn't the best example but I don't think they are helpless." Harry was ever the optimist.

"They will never agree. It's at the point where finding a middle way looks like one is losing. If they go to court, then everyone loses, really, plus the paper will have a field day with it." Susan was realistic.

"Is he truly having the silver inventoried?" Harry asked.

Nancy replied, "That's what he said."

"Ballard is not the sharpest tool in the shed," Tazio, who had occasionally done odd architectural drawings for him, said. "He's a nice man, but like so many people who inherit great wealth or have grown up with it, he's never had to learn the basics, so to speak."

"Well, some do. Look at the Rockefellers," Susan remarked. "But I agree, it must be very difficult. And people think money solves every problem. If your father is beating the tar out of you or your mother or both, money isn't going to solve anything. What it will do is cover up the damage," Nancy shrewdly observed.

The door opened and cold air rushed in. "Hey, girls." Fair stepped through quickly, shutting the door as Tucker ran in as well as Pirate.

"An early day for you?" Harry smiled at her tall husband, his hands in warm gloves she had given him last Christmas.

"Slow day. Two brief calls then spent most of the day in the clinic. You know, I can perform difficult operations. What I can't do is keep up with the paperwork."

"Isn't that the truth." Tazio agreed, for she, too, was swamped.

The building codes alone could make your hair fall out from stress. Fortunately, Tazio's did not.

"Want a co-cola, or Tazio has tea?" Harry offered him.

"No thank you."

"Honey, before you sit down, do you have that laser measure in the truck?"

He looked at Harry. "Do."

"Would you mind getting it?"

He left, the door opened, more cold air. He was away a bit longer than seemed timely, so Harry figured he was rummaging through the back of his specially outfitted truck, which all equine vets have to have.

Finally the door opened, more cold air, Fair walked in, closed the door. He looked troubled.

"Couldn't find it?" Harry asked as Tucker looked up.

Neither dog wanted to leave the stove, so they didn't.

"Here." He handed it to her. "No, as I walked into the back, I easily found it. I also found two bottles of ketamine on my shelf."

All stared at him.

Finally Harry exclaimed, "What?"

Tazio asked the obvious question. "How many bottles do you usually carry in the truck?"

"Two to four. I keep anything like ketamine in the safe at the clinic. I carry bottles with me in case I get an emergency call. Sometimes it takes two shots to put down a horse. It's one of the things every vet has to learn. Ending misery is a blessing, really, and fortunately a lot of horses aren't miserable. They grow old, their hind end becomes weak, and one day they can't get up."

"Call Cooper," Harry told him.

"I will."

"How odd." Nancy then said what wasn't privileged information, but what no one had said anything about since Clyde Mercador was found: "Tucker located the bottle of ketamine on my floor. Maybe this gets back to Ben Wagner after all."

"But what did Clyde and Ben have in common?" Susan was puzzled. "Did they even know each other?"

"Cooper might know." Fair pulled his cellphone out of his coat pocket and dialed her.

As he was talking, the others remained silent.

Clicking off, Fair said, "She has no evidence that Clyde knew Ben."

"What the hell is going on?" Tazio blurted out.

36

May 13, 1789

Wednesday

A weary John Schuyler, walking, reins in his hand, led his mare up from the river warehouses to Richmond's Grace Street. The rapids burbled behind him.

The James River, moving along but restrained on this spring day, could turn into a formidable enemy. Navigating the rapids took skill on those days, and finding a decent ferry below the rapids took patience. The city needed bridges, good wide bridges, but Richmond needed money.

So much called for attention after the war that the bridges, which would aid commerce, still had not moved up to number one. The Haxall Canal provided passage for goods from the west; although short, it did help to avoid river traffic. The cost of such public works—or private, if one dreamed of owning a toll road—shot past the moon.

Even John, a born soldier not a banker, realized recovering from war debt would take time and building a city on a wide, wide river would also take time. Fortunes would be made and fortunes lost.

The sun setting cast an almost lavender glow over the waters, the buildings. Once away from the slip, as the wharf area was called, the noise died down.

Fortunately, he hadn't far to walk to the pleasant inn on Grace Street.

A stable boy rushed out to greet him.

"Are you Colonel Schuyler?" The kid's eyes shone.

"I am, and this is Miss Renata. She needs a rubdown, two handfuls of grain, and the best hay you've got."

John reached in his pocket, taking out a fifty-cent piece, a very fine tip for a young fellow, maybe fourteen if a day.

"I can't take that, Sir. You are the hero of Yorktown."

John smiled softly at the skinny young man. "What's your name?"

"Ferlin, Sir."

John reached in and this time pulled out a bill, which he folded longwise and stuck between Ferlin's collar and neck. "Ferlin, you take this money. If you can, save your funds and buy a good musket. Nothing that will rattle in your hands. That will set you back between twenty-five and forty dollars. A lot of money."

Ferlin whistled. "I'll say."

"But when you have the money, you buy the musket and you find me. I live at Cloverfields in Albemarle County. Cloverfields. Because I want you to join the militia. I need men like you. Virginia needs men like you."

Speechless, for no one ever called him a man, Ferlin finally managed to gulp out, "I will, Colonel. You can count on me."

John handed him Miss Renata's reins, patting him on the back.

"I know I can."

Ferlin, in a daze of feeling he now had a true purpose, clucked to Miss Renata, who readily followed.

Opening the door to the simple, large inn, John heard a loud greeting.

"Into the breach!" Percy Ballard rushed forward to greet John, as he'd been sitting in the front room sipping a refreshing cold drink splashed with uplifting gin.

"Turning into a Limey, are you?" John teased him.

"Well, I'm ginning up. We must admit our English, Irish, Scot, and Welsh cousins do know how to enjoy fine spirits." Percy motioned to a woman of indeterminate years. "My friend could use some spirits." Turning to John. "You look tuckered out."

"I am." John followed him to a padded chair, halfway between a wing chair and a high-backed chair.

"How was Chelsea and the Moores?"

"Much improved. When General Lafayette had his headquarters there before Yorktown, it was overrun. Now it's all put back to rights. Beautiful, even the outbuildings glisten."

"Well, Mr. Moore dreams money, wakes up, and there it is." Percy laughed.

"Some people have the knack. My father-in-law."

"Yes, indeed. I often think of how someone like Bernard Moore and Ewing Garth, Yancy Grant, many men, risked every penny and their necks should we lose. They never get credit, you know."

The hostess of the inn returned with John's drink. "Here you are, Colonel. I'd know you anywhere. You look like the pictures of you, the drawings." She curtsied lightly. "When you are ready, your room is next to Captain Ballard's."

"Thank you, Madam." John sipped his drink then leaned over toward Percy. "Thank the Lord I don't have to bunk with you. Percy, you snore."

"I do not. You thrash around in bed. You wonder why I slept on the floor even in the cold." He paused. "I look back and wonder how we did it. Half the time we didn't eat. Sleep was a blessing. I would dream about taking a bath."

"I would dream about you taking a bath, too." John, those long arms, reached over to give Percy a punch.

They loved each other, risked death together. Had they been

women, they would have hugged and kissed and sat tightly together. Of course, they couldn't do that, but the love wrapped around them, easy to feel.

"Well . . ." John paused. "I had success, what about you?"

"Met with delegates. Everyone promises help, good drilling land in their district. A few promised to introduce me to rich landowners in their district. A few promised money. I'd say I was moderately successful. Governor Randolph had prior meetings. Give me time. He'll come around when he sees it is to his advantage. He's afraid we'll push for a tax to pay for the militia. Eventually, we'll need to do something, but we can sidestep that for now."

"Good. You are the right person to deal with our politicians. I fear I'd punch them in the face." John ruefully smiled.

"Of course, one has to hear how brave they were when the British burned Richmond in 1781. Mind you, John, most of them were not here. Many were not even holding public office yet. Public office became more desirable after we won." He sighed. "Well, we know who risked themselves and we know who is working to protect us now. You know Colonel Ulrich is right. The European powers are already fomenting trouble on our western borders. The last thing we can do is think we are safe. To some extent, we are here, but I wouldn't want to be trying to build a life on the Ohio River banks."

"No, me, neither." John shook his head.

"How did Chelsea go?"

"As you would expect. Everything we need. Alexander bent over backwards to help. He was an outstanding aide-de-camp to General Lafayette. His father, Bernard, dying was a loss. Then again, Alexander possesses all of his father's drive and intelligence. He has also agreed to purchase one hundred muskets. That's a large sum to help us. I hope his example encourages others."

"I think it will. Didn't Bernard pass in 1775?" Percy inquired.

"Think so."

"The Spotswoods, the Todds, well, all the old families that fought for freedom, we can always turn to them for aid and advice. I often think men who have made money have special insights."

"Percy, you're on your way to those special insights."

"Mother Nature is my business partner. We'll see, but I am betting America needs good apples, plus apples can keep for a time. Easier to transport than other crops."

"My father-in-law had put up one hundred acres and Maureen Selisse Holloway also has started an orchard, based on Ewing's saplings." John smiled, reinforcing Percy's thoughts.

"Hmm. Well, I need to find other sources of income. I've been thinking of building a forge. We don't have many, you know."

"We don't. You mentioned Maureen Selisse. Have you seen any of her husband's coaches?"

"Have. An impressive four-in-hand was delivered at Castle Hill and I happened to be there visiting Dr. Walker. He's a most interesting man. Had the carriage made for his wife so she could travel in style. He also showed me a wagon that Jeffrey Holloway also built. Looks like Big Rawly is branching out."

"Yes." John finished his drink, feeling a bit revitalized. "At this point I don't know how many people work for her. She has orchard people, her hay and so forth are managed by her own people. She pays drivers to deliver the wagons; more workers, free men. That's what DoRe tells us and he still works each week at Big Rawly. Comes to us on Saturday and Sunday sometimes. No one can drive the carriage like he can. DoRe is critical to the carriage trade. Of course, I think our Barker O remarkable."

"Ah. With the peace comes profit, we hope and pray."

"Richmond is growing," John remarked. "Will need more workers."

"It is, John, it is but it will never be Williamsburg," Percy said with finality.

The next morning the comrades walked to the stable, Ferlin ran to get their horses, which he then tacked up as each gentleman held his horse. The inn could have used more staff in the stable.

"Ferlin, this is Captain Ballard. We both served under General Lafayette together."

Ferlin looked over the horse's back. "Pleased to meet you, Captain Ballard."

"Percy, Ferlin has taken such good care of your horse and mine. I think we should take care of him."

He handed Ferlin a dollar in coins, a fortune to the boy.

Percy smiled and dug out a dollar's worth of coin.

"Thank you, Sir. Thank you."

"I told Ferlin that he should save his money. When he has enough for a musket or perhaps a rifle, he should find me and I'll put him in a militia. Cloverfields. Right, Ferlin?"

"Yes, Sir."

"Here." Percy gave the boy an envelope with his address on it. Lone Pine. Then he took the envelope back and wrote out "Cloverfields, Albemarle County." "Let either of us know. You'll work hard in the militia."

"I want to work hard." Ferlin's face glowed with such honesty.

The two men rode off. None could have known that Ferlin would keep his promise to John that he could count on him. That promise would be kept dramatically twenty-three years later.

37

November 9, 2019

Saturday

"Can you think of when you weren't by your truck?" Harry looked over her husband's listing of where he had been on Friday, quite a few barns before coming to the school, but they were short visits.

"Honey, I'm in the barn or with the horse. I'm not looking at my truck."

"So anyone could walk into the back, put in the ketamine?"

"Yes."

"Cooper has called everyone on your list to check if the owners of the stable or of a horse saw anyone. Then she asked who was in the barn or working on the property. Okay. Let me go through the list. The first place you stopped was at Kenny's." She named Kenny Wheeler, Jr.

"Right. No equine problem. He wanted me to check the Keswick winter fixture card before he and the other masters, club officers signed off on it."

"Can't believe they work that far ahead. If I were doing a fixture card, I'd probably start December 15 for the new year."

"Well, they have a folder over two inches thick with landowners. I swear, I've never seen anything like it. The Wheelers have been such faithful supporters of Keswick Hunt Club.

"Everyone should be so lucky," he added. "So who was there? No one, really. The truck sat in the drive in front of the main house. I suppose someone could have opened my side door, put the bottles in there. Do I think anyone did? No. What would someone from Kenny and Ceil's want with Special K, especially giving me more?"

"Well, honey, that's the question, no matter who it was. Why give you more? Okay, so I'll put a check by the Wheelers. Next, Cismont Manor."

"Dropped off a bottle of the glucosamine for Cindy."

Cismont Manor was the home of Kenny's father, Kenny Wheeler, Sr., and Cindy was his partner. She'd been using the glucosamine.

"I hasten to add," Fair said, "that I gave her the human pills not the equine. Since I ordered a big batch it was easy to throw in a human. Constance was visiting. So was the Episcopal priest and Kenny's beagle huntsman."

"How about some glucosamine for me next time?"

"*Could we use this?*" Tucker asked Mrs. Murphy.

The two sat under the kitchen table, where Fair spread his papers.

"*I don't have any aches and pains, do you?*" the tiger cat replied.

"*Well, sometimes I feel a little stiff,*" the corgi confessed.

Pewter, laid out flat on the kitchen counter, gloated. "*You're getting old, Tucker.*"

"*I'd rather be old than fat,*" the tough dog fired back.

Normally the gray cat would instantly retaliate but she was comfortable, so she warned, "*I'll get you for that.*"

Before more unpleasantries could be uttered, Tucker ran to the back door. "*Car.*"

Pirate, sound asleep, didn't stir. So much for guarding duties.

The porch door opened then there was a knock on the kitchen door as Cooper pulled her scarf tighter around her neck.

"Come on in." Harry motioned to her neighbor and friend.

"Bites out there."

"Well, it is November. We've had Novembers that stayed in the fifties and sixties and those that stayed in the twenties." Fair rose to greet her, and as she took off her coat, he helped.

"You never know, especially being by the mountains. Coop, want anything to eat or drink?"

"No thanks. Stopped by as I'm on my way to Country House Antiques, then a quick stopover at Lone Pine. Wanted to get in the store before Nancy opens. I want to check the back door again. The security wire had been cut when we found Clyde. Dwayne and the crew who were there said popping the lock was easy as well, since it's really old. But I didn't see any marks or footprints then. Of course there won't be any there now but I want to have another look inside." She threw up her hands. "All dusted, photographed, I know, but I like to look over things and think. It's easy to miss something. And you know, it's always the little things. Oh, Fair." She sat down as Harry pointed to a chair. "Have gone over your calls yesterday. Could have been any of them. You said you didn't lock your truck. By the way, your 'office,' for lack of a better word, how come you never bought a box truck?"

"Don't like the way they handle. My setup isn't perfect but it works for me."

Cooper folded her hands on the table. "The other reason I am stopping by is Jerry Showalter is digging through an avalanche of work. He called Sheriff Shaw to say he could finish this in one month or two, checking the inventory lists against the articles, if he had an assistant. He also said he brought this up to both Constance and Ballard, which gave them an opportunity to fight in front of him."

"Poor Jerry," Harry said.

"Both agreed Jerry needed more help because they want to settle this. A court battle still seems in the offing." Cooper grimaced.

"Why can't he find someone local? Surely there's someone at the University of Virginia Library." Fair stated what seemed a simple solution.

"Neither one will agree to having a stranger in the house. They completely backtracked from their earlier position. I guess the woman from St. Louis University and the other from Lafayette College passed muster, because they didn't have time to think about it. Jerry knows both of them and each feels he will be evenhanded."

"He will. But how long before one or the other tries to buy him off?" Fair picked up his pencil, a Rhodia pencil.

He couldn't resist buying different pencils and notebooks.

"I'm coming to you because I'm aware you know both Constance and Ballard, not as best friends but as longtime acquaintances. And Harry, as I recall, you got along famously with Candida."

"Cooper, everyone got along famously with Candida."

Cooper smiled. "If you're willing to help, the department will pay you fifteen dollars an hour. I know Jerry would be relieved. But I have to run this by Constance and Ballard. If they agree, no sure thing, could you start Monday?"

Dumbfounded, Harry sat silent for a moment. "Tell me exactly what I would have to do."

"Jerry can better answer that, but each box has an inventory sheet. Those sheets were in a locked drawer in Candida's desk; copies, I should say. The originals remain in the box. So you check off items in the box if they are on the sheet. It's simple but time consuming. Lots of boxes, but with two of you it would move along. Clyde went through the seventeenth century before he was killed. Then again, fewer materials from that time. Still, it doesn't appear to be complicated."

"Fair, what do you think?"

"You should do what you want to do. My question to Cooper is, can Harry carry a gun?"

"I was coming to that. Sheriff Shaw and I think if you are armed, that could set one or both siblings off. We all believe the problem, or the answer, is in that library. Whatever is there will lead us to maybe a murderer, but if not at least clarify what is at stake. For instance, why kill Clyde?"

Fair leaned toward her. "She needs a gun."

"We have Dwayne there with his computer. He is armed. Whatever you and Jerry do, he puts on the computer, which goes to the department. We are taking no chances on losing material. And no chances on losing your wife."

"If you leave the work there, maybe it will be lost," Harry cited.

"We've thought of that, too. Ballard just taking it because Constance won't budge. That's another reason Dwayne is there. We also are bringing in a large temporary safe on Monday. Once a box is studied, it goes into the safe. Only Dwayne will have the key."

"Ah," was all Harry said.

"*If she goes, we go.*" Tucker was resolute.

"I'll go. It sounds interesting, and if Dwayne is there, what could go wrong?" Harry grinned.

38

November 11, 2019

Monday

It was still dark at six in the morning when Harry broke eggs into a large bowl, put in a little milk, and stirred. Then she cut up small cubes of cheese, stirred some more. Her mother's old cast-iron skillet warmed on the stove. Tossing in a big chunk of real butter, she poured the scrambled egg batch into it.

"Love that sound." Fair made coffee for himself, tea for Harry.

The animals, faces in their bowls, were too busy eating to speak. Harry had poured some chicken broth on the mixture of kibble, some canned food. She liked to entice her friends with more than just kibble. But in a pinch, kibble served its purpose.

Flipping over the fluffy eggs, Harry looked out the window. "I always notice the dying of the light. Then we reach December 21 and I feel better because we'll get about an extra minute of daylight per day. Don't you love the solstices and equinoxes?"

"Do. Good way to keep time." He poured English Breakfast tea into a heavy mug, poured himself stout coffee. Fair took longer to awaken than his wife. Her eyes popped open and she was ready for life. His eyes popped open and he was ready for coffee then life.

"Okay. Fresh parsley on top." She crumbled parsley on the eggs.

They sat down, happy to be with each other. Croissants sat in the middle of the kitchen table, along with butter and strawberry jam that Susan's mother made.

"Fair, is it worth putting a surveillance camera in your vet truck? And how about one at the clinic?"

"I've thought of it. They aren't that expensive. The clinic is worth it. Don't know about the truck. Yes, ketamine has been stolen then replaced with extra bottles. But this can't go on. It's too weird."

"I've thought about that, too. If it were just you, I'd think it was a prank, but a few other vets have lost bottles."

"So far none has been replaced but mine."

Harry tasted the fresh parsley in her mouth, a clean bright taste.

"I'm finished. I'll have what you're having." Pewter meowed from her bowl, a big bowl, too.

Harry pinched off a bit of croissant, dropping it for the cat, then realized Tucker, Pirate, and lastly Mrs. Murphy would follow. Well, there went one croissant.

"Fair, I don't think the ketamine is the issue and I don't think Ben was killed over it. If he were, why would bottles be showing up again? The drug is a red herring."

"I don't know. I wish I did."

"Why was a bottle on the floor at Nancy's store? Clyde, at least according to the research on him by the department, could drink, but no drugs. I swear, honey, this is meant to divert our attention."

He felt the hot coffee roll down his throat, the bittersweet taste waking him right up. "Two men are dead. One had ketamine stolen. The other may have been carrying a bottle. That can't be proven, but why was it there? Ketamine may be diversionary, but for what? I can't see what Ben and Clyde had in common."

"That doesn't mean there isn't a thread. It's too coincidental in some way. I feel this in my bones but I can't articulate it."

"What would Ben have worth killing him over?"

"If we knew that, Fair, we'd have our killer or be close to it."

He scraped up the eggs; although he shouldn't have made a noise on his plate, he didn't care. "No one makes scrambled eggs like you do."

"Thank you. Anything else? I'm feeling a slight burst of culinary creativity." She smiled at him, still the handsomest man she'd ever seen.

"I counted through the barns I visited, the people I saw. Little Kenny, Big Kenny." He cited the Wheeler men by their nicknames. "Lone Pine. I was there all of five minutes and it was Margaret who called. She wondered if she should say anything about the gelding and the mare being turned out together . . . to me, that is. Ballard has been letting them mingle. I said fine. They were lonely, they know each other, and the old boy isn't studdish, never was. Then I drove over to Glenmore's barn, sat with Mary Shriver for maybe twenty minutes. Told you she wants to ride again but has to be careful. Said I would keep my eye out for a calm citizen, but her physical type. Truck was wide open. Before I drove to the school I swung by The Barracks to check on that mare, the flashy flea-bitten gray, the Thoroughbred. The owner wants to breed her. I was there maybe half an hour. Claiborne said nothing about the breeding, which means she thinks it's not a good idea. It's not like it would be hard to put two bottles back in."

"Not a good horse?"

"The reverse. If the mare is to be bred, then cough up the money for a stud with bloodlines that will nick into hers. You don't take an animal like that to old Sam down the road, because he, too, is gray."

Harry forced a tight smile. "I see."

"People really need to be careful about breeding. You're bringing an animal into the world so you want it to be the strongest, healthiest animal it can be. Otherwise what kind of life will the horse have? How many people will he be bounced to? You know, honey, the older I get, the more I think people who have dogs, horses should take bloodline classes and health classes before breeding. Look at pugs. Fabulous little buggers but one health issue after another."

"I do adore them."

"I don't," Pewter forcibly stated her opinion.

"I'm sure you are descended from the best Russian Blues in the country," Tucker snidely remarked.

"Cur." The rotund kitty turned up her nose.

Both humans looked down, Harry finally saying, "That didn't sound good."

Pirate, sensitive, uneasy with arguments, came over and put his large head under Harry's hand. *"They fight all the time."*

Mrs. Murphy rubbed against the Irish wolfhound, who was still a bit of a puppy. *"Be glad of it. This way they ignore you."*

Harry picked up the dishes, quickly washing them in the sink.

"You off to Lone Pine?"

"To be there at nine. If a timber truck gets on our road or Route 22, boy, that slows you down. This way I leave in time. Then again, I go east on 64 for a bit, and have you noticed how many accidents there are?"

"People are fiddling with their phones, looking at the screen on their dash, switching channels on the radio. Who's paying attention to the road?" He kissed her, threw on his worn but still serviceable work jacket, and opened the door, blowing her another kiss.

"You know, kids, I'll get him another jacket for Christmas. His work is hard and the longest any jacket has ever lasted, you know, not been torn up, has been three years. Okay, let me put that in my notebook." She leaned over the counter, pulled out a catch-everything drawer, retrieved a Moleskin, and wrote down "coat." She'd know what that meant.

Arriving fifteen minutes early, Harry let her animals out of her beat-up Volvo station wagon, old and beloved. Being at Lone Pine enlivened her. She'd look around at the buildings, the architectural signature of the place, the fabulous garden and trees, impressive even in early November, and a sense of Virginia, the history both good and bad, would dazzle her.

She had asked Jerry about the animals, all of whom he knew, so he agreed. If nothing else, Jerry felt that Pirate might be an additional deterrent should there be trouble. Between the wolfhound and Dwayne, all should be well. He wasn't particularly anxious but he did feel that the library was the key, but the key to what? The fighting siblings would only settle down when the papers, and even some of the first edition books, worth thousands, were cataloged, confirmed, tidied up.

"Good morning." Harry smiled as she walked through the door.

Jerry stood up to greet her, ever the Virginia gentleman.

Dwayne, pecking at his computer, didn't until Jerry squeezed his shoulder. Then he, too, stood up. Learning to be a gentleman takes time and a tutor.

"How wonderful to be greeted by two handsome men." She acknowledged their good manners in her own fashion. "All right, boys, put me to work."

"Are those animals okay? I know you love them, Harry." Dwayne knew Harry mostly because of Cooper.

"They'll be a big help and quiet." She stared at her brood. "Quiet."

"Bother," Pewter grumbled.

A long table, highly polished, had been carried into the library so the three people could sit abreast as they worked. If a paper needed to be double-checked, all you would require would be to carefully hand it to either Jerry for verification or Dwayne to double register.

The temporary safe, on the floor, bolstered one end of the table.

Jerry sat her down, putting a lustrous, dark green Morocco leather box in front of her. "You have the box." He stepped back to check the brass number. "It's 22. So this is the early nineteenth century, up to Monroe's presidency. We're moving along here. The eighteenth century, between both Dwayne and myself, sped along. The inventory sheets are impeccable so far."

"So all I do is basically check the contents off using the inventory sheet or sheets?"

"Right. Here's your big notepad. I'm using yellow paper so we won't misplace it. You'll be tempted to read the letters. Don't. You'll never finish."

"Jerry, do you have to authenticate the contents?"

"No. Candida kept this library and her papers close to her heart. She maintained everything in good order, amazing. And were I called upon to go over every scrap, you know, carbon dating the vellum and that sort of thing, the ink, too, this would take years. Really years, and," he lowered his voice, "I don't know that either one, Constance or Ballard, can afford that long a wait or afford the research."

"Right." Harry sat down, carefully lifted up the box cover.

Mrs. Murphy jumped on the table, followed by Pewter; large as she was, she could jump.

Mrs. Murphy, next to the box, inhaled deeply, as did Pewter.

"Tucker, Pirate, come over here," the tiger cat commanded.

The two dogs walked over. Pirate could put his head on the desk.

Harry apologized to Jerry and Dwayne. "They'll settle down. New place. I promise. If not, I'll put them in the Volvo."

"Sniff." Mrs. Murphy's voice rose.

The other three animals inhaled as deeply as they could. Fortunately those great canine noses didn't need to be up on the table.

"The animal smell, but this is fresh." Tucker sniffed again.

"What can it be?" Pewter, curious, wondered, and tried to stick her head in the box, so Harry lifted her up, putting her on the floor.

"That same smell. The smell from the military uniform prints and then Ben's drawings." Mrs. Murphy paced.

"It is the same odor. And so fresh." Pirate also had an excellent nose. *"What can it mean?"*

Mrs. Murphy stopped pacing. *"I don't know but I do know we have to take apart one of those flower prints. Maybe we'll have part of the answer, but I know this, we can't let Harry out of our sight. Whatever that smell is, the old skin smell is dangerous."*

"*Why?*" Pirate asked, his sweet brown eyes worried.

"*I don't know. When we tear apart one of those prints we might be closer to the answer.*"

"*Leave it to me.*" Pewter puffed out her chest, unleashing one claw from her forepaw. "*I can open the frame with this. Just leave it to me.*"

39

November 11, 2019

Monday 6:00 P.M.

"Good I have great eyes," Pewter bragged as she perched on a saddle, reaching for one of Ben's prints.

Pirate, too big to go through the dog door, sat outside. *"What's happening?"*

"Nothing yet," Tucker answered, sitting under the hung prints.

"Pewter, if you push the top of the frame, I can push the bottom a little bit out. Maybe it will slide off the hanging wire," Mrs. Murphy suggested.

"Okay." The gray cat maneuvered her left paw as she gripped the side of the saddle, claws deep in the leather, for balance. *"Getting it."*

Mrs. Murphy reached as far as she could, for she was sitting on the saddle underneath Pewter, all the saddles on racks in a line, per most tack rooms. *"Got my paw under. Let's see if we can dislodge it at the same time."*

This took more time than either cat expected, each trying to balance as they wiggled the frame forward. The wire now hung on the edge of the nail head.

"What's happening?" Pirate anxiously asked again.

"They've almost got it," Tucker encouraged the cats as she answered Pirate.

"Flip on one, two, three," Pewter ordered then counted. *"One, two, three."*

Both cats pushed outward simultaneously and the flower picture, the lily, slid off the hook, falling to the floor.

"Watch out." Tucker jumped sideways, for the glass covering had broken.

The cats looked down.

"Stay where you are. Our night vision is better than yours," Pewter commanded.

Tucker didn't really believe that but was smart enough to know this was not the time to get into an argument. She could already smell the old skin smell.

The cats dexterously jumped on the side away from the wall and then gingerly walked to the lovely drawing, which had fallen faceup but the jolt had been enough to crack the glass.

"I'll get on the other side." Mrs. Murphy carefully walked around the lily drawing to the opposite side.

"Tucker, can you see glass bits?" Pewter asked.

"Yes," the corgi replied.

"Okay. We're going to turn this over. I can smell that smell, faint. Do you think you can see what it is in this fading light? The sun set about forty-five minutes ago," Pewter said.

"There's enough light coming from the window in the door," Tucker answered.

"Ready, Murphy?" Pewter had claws out under the frame.

"Ready."

The two cats, claws sunken into the frame's side away from the glass front of the flower drawing, cautiously turned it over with a little thump.

"What's happening?" Pirate wailed.

"Shut up," Pewter yelled at the big dog, which made him whine a little. *"Baby."*

The three animals stared at the back of the frame. A paper rested behind the lily drawing.

Tucker, inhaling deeply, said, "*It's exactly the same smell. Faint. Sort of old.*"

Pewter touched the paper with her nose, as did Mrs. Murphy.

The tiger cat sniffed again, looked hard at the back of the paper, which was blank. "*It's animal skin. Like what humans call parchment or vellum. I think they're different, but both are skins.*"

"*I don't see anything on it.*" Pewter was puzzled.

"*Has to be on the other side. Whatever this is, it's been used for these flower drawings and was probably used for the military uniform prints.*" The tiger cat, like Pewter, was baffled. "*Maybe used is the wrong word.*"

"*Can't see. We'll have to come back in the morning. Harry won't leave until after breakfast. Will be plenty of light.*"

"*Right.*" Mrs. Murphy sat down, hearing Pirate whine again, this time a real cry.

"*God, what a big baby,*" Pewter fussed.

"*Cut him a break. He's not even full grown yet. He's left out. Hurts his feelings.*" Tucker stood up for the youngster.

"*Well, nothing more we can do. Let's go to the house.*" Mrs. Murphy popped through the dog door.

Tucker followed, then Pewter, who ignored Pirate on the other side. Tucker filled in the big boy.

Fair had built a new winter door for the porch, which Pirate could enter. It swung to the side and next to that was a standard animal door, easier for the smaller animals to open. He also built a new door from the porch to the kitchen.

As all four animals burst into the kitchen, Harry, testing her casserole, looked up. "You all let in cold air."

"*We were on a mission,*" Pewter self-importantly announced.

Fair, reading the evening paper, looked from it to the four friends. "Out there in the dark. Bet it was a varmint. Something captured your attention."

"*Did,*" Tucker matter-of-factly replied.

Pewter, face already in her filled bowl, which contained some fresh small beef scraps, was too busy eating to talk.

The other three followed suit, the aroma enticing.

Fair folded his paper in half, longwise. "Armistice Day. My grandfather and father always celebrated it."

"Mine, too. My great-grandfathers on both sides of the family were in World War I. They were gone before I was born but it was a big day for us. My grandfather was with the 11th Airborne Division. Didn't talk about it."

"They rarely do." Fair noticed the animals, stuffed, now looking up at him.

"*How do we get them into the tack room?*" Tucker wondered.

"*I can pull them in. I'm stronger than they are,*" Pirate volunteered.

"*That's not a good idea.*" Tucker squelched it.

"*How about if we trick them into it? Pirate, you can be the trickster,*" Mrs. Murphy placated the dog.

"*Sure.*" The long tail smacked the floor.

Pewter observed the thumping. "*Better wait until you hear what she has in mind first.*"

"*I'm ready for anything,*" the enthusiastic youngster proclaimed.

"*Well, here it is. Harry will go to the old Volvo station wagon maybe fifteen to ten minutes before she leaves. She hates to be late. We all go out with her, of course. Then Pirate, you run into the barn and start screaming.*" The tiger cat laid out her plan.

"*Want to hear me now?*"

"*No, sweetie. Save yourself.*" Mrs. Murphy had to remind herself that no matter how big he was, he really was still a puppy.

"*Okay.*" Pirate remained very bright-eyed.

"*She'll run into the barn. You have to be very convincing. You have your front leg stuck through the dog door of the tack room. Howl, act as though you can't extricate yourself.*"

Noting Pirate's confusion, Tucker explained. "*Pull out. You can't pull out your leg. I know* extricate *is a big word.*"

"Now, that means the rest of us blow through the tack room door and we start screaming from the inside. She'll come in."

"Murph, she can't smell the old skin smell. She can't even smell the fresh skin smell in the library at Lone Pine."

"I know, but her curiosity will get the better of her. She'll kneel down, pick up the paper, and turn it over. It's what's on the other side of that parchment, or whatever it really is, that's important." Mrs. Murphy was very confident.

Tucker thought for a moment. "She will. But here's what I'm wondering about: We have picked up that scent on two sets of drawings. Right?" They all nodded so the dog continued. "That means there's more of whatever it is."

All quieted, then Pewter swept her whiskers forward. "It must be big."

40

May 15, 1789

Friday

Ewing and Yancy leaned against a fence behind the stables, watching Catherine and Jeddie lay out a steeplechase course.

"Tricky, that slope," Yancy drawled.

Ewing agreed then added, "We don't really know how this is done in Ireland, but Catherine thinks she can create interest in something other than flat racing."

"Mmm." Yancy watched intently. "Lost my taste for flat racing when that William stole my horse."

"And broke Jeddie's shoulder," Ewing remarked. "He's paying for that and more now."

"No one can accuse Maureen of not being revengeful. Ah well, I think women can be crueler than men when they have a mind to do so."

"Oh, I don't know," Ewing carefully responded. "Maureen is in a class by herself, but she said she will support this new type of race.

Catherine has been diligent in promoting it. In wooing her. Then again, Yancy, many people need to sell horses. Can be good money."

"Indeed. Is it because Maureen is dragging her feet over the wedding of Bettina and DoRe? What else does she want?"

"I don't know. Her latest impediment is, she doesn't want DoRe to leave Big Rawly until he trains a competent coachman. With Maureen, there's always more." Ewing inhaled. "Perhaps her happiness comes from denying it to others."

"Ha." Yancy laughed then noted, "You know, that slope really is tricky and I wonder if she'll have horses cross the creek down below."

"We can wait until she's laid it all out. She says she will have Charles draw a map plus will allow people to walk the territory before the race. Of course, it will be a few miles. I doubt anyone will walk it, all of it. She is nothing if not organized."

"True." He changed the subject. "Like you, I wait for news from Europe from old friends. I have heard from my friend who is a member of Parliament in England that the Duke of Orleans walked as a commoner in the procession to the Estates General in France. Tawdry."

"Yes, Baron Necker wrote me the same in his last letter. Each letter he includes more information. He is discreet. You know the mail is read. Being director of finance, he is in a perilous position."

"Ewing, I suspect everyone is in a perilous position in France. If a prince of the blood wants to be seen as an ordinary citizen, well, he is playing a very dangerous game trying to ride the tide. France will never be as we are. Never. Even though they have freemasons who talk of equality and democracy, it's not going to happen."

"Given that the money has run out, something is going to happen."

"We have our own money problems. What do you think of Hamilton's ideas?"

Ewing pondered this. "We can't survive as a nation if the war debt, the states' debts, are not assumed by Washington's government."

"If the states agree, if Congress agrees, then are we not back in the same pot we were in with the king? Being told what to do by government."

"Yes. But at least it's not a king. My dear Yancy, you and I will go under if these old obligations are not retired."

"Well, where are we going to borrow money at a lower interest rate? We can't pay them as they are," Yancy wisely noted.

"We need foreign investment. We don't really have the money to invest in ourselves and you and I spent heavily during the war to finance artillery, muskets . . . well, I'm not telling you anything you don't know. If this plan goes into effect, if it is agreed upon, then we will be attractive to foreign investors who can buy our debt at a low interest rate. We will be seen as a worthy credit risk, and, really, those people are more sophisticated investors than most of us. I wonder if this isn't part of why Maureen keeps going to Richmond. Is she helping to pull in money from the Caribbean, from her father's old banking associates?"

"Possibly, and she'll take a big cut for herself."

"Human nature, I fear, but if she attracts investors, she deserves profit." Yancy climbed up to see better, hard for him due to his shattered knee. "As you know, Jefferson will fight it tooth and nail. He fears tyranny."

"He fears not being the center of attention." Ewing half smiled. "Brilliant man, but he'll never get over not being a Tidewater man."

"Is the alternative anarchy? We simply must have order or all our risks and those who died, it will all have been in vain." A hint of passion infiltrated Ewing's voice.

Yancy sighed. "Who thought this would be so hard?"

"Well, how do you start a new nation? And I do wish some of our leaders would stop quoting Cicero. He played both ends against the middle. At least that's what I think."

"First we need good schools. What happens if our young people don't know history? Don't know Cicero or why Caesar was killed? It has happened throughout time, those struggles, and will happen again."

Ewing listened closely to his old friend, whom he deeply admired in many ways. "Yes. I fear it is happening in France."

"Well, whatever is going on over there is their problem. I don't see a parallel, which I hear from others, especially the young."

"The young are usually idealistic. Think how we were and then life knocks you down a few times and the world takes on a new hue. Not necessarily bad, but better not to assume everyone shares your moral values."

Yancy laughed. "True. I'd settle for a uniform currency, which I believe we will have."

"Ah, there goes Jeddie over that high fence. She wants to build fences, by the way, stone fences. Tree trunks, water jumps. Again, we don't really know how they are doing this in Ireland, so my dearest daughter is more or less making it up."

"Making it up as she goes along." Yancy grinned. "A bit like our government after the Constitutional Convention."

Ewing grinned back. "We have no choice. To change the subject, have you heard that Livia Taylor, the Taylors' daughter, disappeared?"

"No."

"Not a trace. Never appeared to be unhappy there. Just disappeared."

"She's a pretty thing. I hope she is found or didn't run off with some love-spouting fool." Yancy slid down, a bit wobbly in doing so, then Ewing handed him his cane.

"Yes. You know how you get signs when there's dissatisfaction? I certainly never noticed any, but I confess I noticed Livia."

Ewing laughed. "No harm in appreciating a pretty girl. The Taylors are offering a reward for information. Two hundred dollars."

"Quite a sum." Yancy pursed his lips. "I do hope she is found safe somewhere."

Catherine rode up, Jeddie alongside. "We've got half of it done, Father; hello, Yancy. So good to see you."

Yancy touched his brow in deference.

"Jeddie, what do you think?" Ewing asked.

"One won't just need to be a good rider. One will have to be smart, and we haven't finished yet."

"We're done for the day." Catherine turned toward the barn as Jeddie fell in behind her.

"She has a gift." Yancy smiled.

"Yes. And that is why we have to settle our war debts, issue a stable currency, and look to private investors. I have grandchildren, Yancy. I go to sleep thinking of them. What am I leaving them?"

"Ah, I do not have that happiness but I would hope any man would feel the same."

"I often think the gods are kind not showing us the future." Ewing started to walk toward the house.

Neither man could know how true those words were, for the problems that plagued them, be it national or Livia Taylor's disappearance, would come to light in good time. And the steeplechase race would prove a big success.

41

November 12, 2019

Tuesday

"My leg is broken. Ow!" Pirate hollered.

"More drama." Pewter, sitting beside the Irish wolfhound, who had his paw in the dog door of the tack room, coached.

"Royal Academy of Dramatic Art," Tucker whispered with glee to Mrs. Murphy, who had to agree that no one could out-dramatize Pewter.

"I'm in horrible pain." The good dog tried to add more feeling to the barking.

Harry, walking to her beat-up station wagon, stopped then hurried into the stable.

"He's dying." Pewter ran up to her, fur puffed out.

"Help me." Pirate looked as miserable as he could.

Harry ran to him, knelt down, lifting the dog door. "Pirate, what have you done?"

As she started to inspect a perfectly fine front leg, the other three animals blew through the dog door, the flap slapping against the wood three times.

"Come in here!" Tucker barked.

"Harry, we need you." Pewter added to the moment by rushing out of the tack room, door smacking again, then turning around and running right in. A thap, thap.

"Open the door." Mrs. Murphy meowed as loudly as she could.

Pirate licked Harry's face then stuck his paw back through the dog door then out again.

Wishing her husband had not left for work early, Harry carefully opened the door, not knowing what was going on.

The ruckus intensified as she stepped through the door. "Oh no."

"It's important." Pewter patted the flower print on the floor, the frame broken on one side at the corner and a bit of glass on the floor.

Harry walked over then knelt down. "Well, a frame is easy to replace."

"Mother, look." Even Mrs. Murphy lost her patience.

As her gloves were in the station wagon, Harry carefully picked up the framed drawing using her fingernails more than the pads of her fingers. She turned the pretty lily over then over again, finally noticing the vellum paper.

"What in the world?"

"Tell us." Pewter evidenced rare enthusiasm for somehing other than food.

Again using her fingernails, Harry lifted the page from the back of the drawing.

She read out loud, "'May 20, 1789. Dear Colonel, I still want to call you major, but well, anyway. I have pressed Sam Udall for more assistance in raising money for the Richmond militia. His enthusiasm quickened when I provided him with a list of current contributors, including those who have promised land for drills. He especially noted your father-in-law, Yancy Grant, and Maureen Holloway.

"'He has promised significant assistance, quoting one thousand dollars. Yes. One thousand. When I come to the Cloverfields steeplechase we can discuss this further. Tempted though I am to ride in it,

I think not. But back to the monies. He has also volunteered to be the bank for whatever is raised. Another discussion and Colonel Ulrich, Brigadier General Daniel Slipka, and Major Horace Moses need to join us in a discussion. We did not anticipate protecting funds. Sam Udall declares he can enhance the funds through investments. That, too, we must discuss, but I am very grateful we have something to discuss and monies to bank, given we have not been working on this for long. It does mean our civic and political leaders appear to be waking up to potential dangers without a militia. On another subject, Livia Taylor: A young woman is missing from Orange County. She disappeared from a small farm near Somerset. I pass that along and do hope that no more women disappear. It may be best to be alert. It is strange. Well, I leave you with happier thoughts. My extraordinary, beautiful, and sweet wife will present me with our firstborn next February, God willing. Until the races. Your obedient captain and lifelong friend, Percy Ballard.' "

"*You can smell it.*" Pirate nudged Tucker.

"*A little stronger than when it was in the frame but not by much. What is it?*" Tucker wedged tightly next to Harry, now sitting on the floor.

The two cats, immobile, watched Harry.

"I don't know what to think," Harry confessed then checked her watch. "I'll take this to Jerry. He'll know."

She then looked at the flower drawings on the wall, stood up, and lifted a sunflower drawing off the wall. "Come on."

The four animals piled into the station wagon, Pirate taking up the entire back, Tucker in the second-row seat, while Mrs. Murphy and Pewter commanded the passenger seat.

"*She doesn't know what it is?*" Pewter had been certain Harry would know.

"*Well, she knows it's an old letter,*" Mrs. Murphy noted. "*But what is it doing behind a flower drawing? You know, she's pretty good at figuring things out.*"

Tucker spoke up from the backseat. "*She is, but often a day late and a dollar short. Then she's in deep doo.*"

They all laughed at that, as it was more often true than not.

Driving into Lone Pine, which took forty minutes, as traffic on I-64 proved heavy this Tuesday, Harry cut the motor; opened the doors for Mrs. Murphy, Pewter, and Tucker; closed them; then opened the large back wagon door so Pirate could step out. As she closed it again, she heard loud voices from Lone Pine. She had parked next to Jerry's car and Dwayne's police car at the side of the house, the kitchen side, a small overhang protecting the door. Constance's car was also parked there.

Looking around, Harry held the drawings, the one with the damaged frame had a piece jutting out, as she walked with some apprehension toward the kitchen door. The voices grew louder.

Carefully, she opened the door. Ballard's voice and his sister's filled the hall right outside the kitchen. Actually, they faced each other in the cavernous pantry. Not wishing to be drawn into whatever they were fighting about, she slipped into the library, where both Jerry and Dwayne readied their spots for the day.

Before anyone would say anything, a crash sent all into the hall. Ballard and Constance were still in the pantry.

"You liar!" Constance screamed.

"I didn't steal that ketamine."

"Then what's a bottle doing on the morning china shelf? Did it walk in here?"

"I don't know, but I didn't steal any of it."

"You always lie when you're on drugs, you know that, and you must be on them again," Constance bellowed.

"There's an officer from the sheriff's department in the library. Why don't I go have a blood test? I am not on drugs. I am not drinking and I have no idea how ketamine wound up in Mom's pantry."

A short silence followed this. "Did you give Mother ketamine? She was in some pain."

"Of course I didn't." Ballard's voice returned to a normal level but the three humans plus the animals now silently standing outside the pantry could hear everything. "I would never give Mom anything that wasn't prescribed."

"Your idea about a blood test is a good one. Let's go to the library right now."

"Constance, Dwayne isn't going to pull my blood."

"On a first-name basis, are we? Well, he can call in one."

"I'll go if you go. You have to have a blood test, too."

"I'm not the one under a cloud," she snapped.

"You're clever enough to hide it, Constance. Women are better at these things."

"You know what?" She glowered at him as the humans and animals started for the library. "I will agree to it." She looked at the floor. "Clean up this mess."

"I didn't throw the glasses."

A venomous impasse followed this, then Constance pushed open the heavy swinging door. "Margaret can clean it. Let's go."

Harry jumped back as the door nearly hit her. Constance didn't see her because she turned on her heel as the door swung shut, nearly smacking her in the behind.

"Where is Mother's sable?"

Ballard, on his hands and knees, sweeping up the glass with a dish towel, looked up. "Where it always is."

"And?"

"In cold storage."

"It's November. Did you sell that coat? It's worth thousands. Thousands," she repeated for emphasis, while Harry, Jerry, Dwayne, and the animals hurried to the library, feeling lucky they weren't caught eavesdropping.

"She died before she took it out. She always took it out for Thanksgiving. Call them yourself, Constance."

"Then again, how do I know you aren't wearing it?"

Folding the towel, glass inside, he placed it on the shelf, the glass cabinet doors above it closed. The glass allowed the help to quickly grab whatever was needed from the pantry. No matter how often one used the pantry, it was easy to forget where everything was, hence the glass cabinet doors.

"I don't wear women's furs."

"The Baron von Thyssen did. I remember Mother telling me that when she was at a dinner party in New York, he swept in wearing a full-length sable. She said it was perfect . . . but then, so was hers."

"Why do you want the sable?"

Their voices carried, loud, into the library, which made it difficult for the three to concentrate. Harry, the two framed prints at her space, hadn't even gotten to show them to Jerry yet.

"What woman wouldn't? You can't sell anything without talking to me."

"I am talking to you, and our lawyers can talk in court. You can't keep everything. You haven't the money to run Lone Pine and you'll drag me down with you."

"I've put my house in Keswick on the market. That will bring me a decent sum. What have you got? Money from ketamine?"

"There isn't enough of the stuff to make money. Furthermore, I don't sell drugs. I took enough of them but I never sold."

"You didn't have to." Her voice dripped with disgust. "Mother always bailed you out."

"What are you going to do with the ketamine?"

"No, what are you going to do with the ketamine?"

"It's not mine. How it got here I don't know. And I don't care."

"Well, Ben Wagner was murdered, his ketamine stolen."

"Since when have you cared about Ben Wagner?"

"Ballard, Mother adored him and he addressed her envelopes for Christmas and other occasions. He drew little things for her."

"Maybe Mother took the drugs. Maybe she thought it would be a peaceful way to die."

"Are you suggesting our mother killed herself?" Constance reached for another glass.

Ballard quickly grabbed her wrist, wrenching the glass from her hand. "No. But Mom never wanted to be a burden. You fought over an autopsy. Did she die of a stroke? A heart attack? I was a fool, I should have fought harder."

"Oh bull. The only reason you wanted an autopsy was to see if whatever took her away might get you. Not soon enough, I fear."

"You'll die first." He smiled maliciously.

She stopped, took a step toward him, then stopped again. "Only if you kill me. I'll long outlive you. The damage you did to your body. I can't imagine what organ will go first. And as for an autopsy, ghoulish. Let the woman rest in peace. She was in her nineties. She lived a good, long life."

"I need to go to my house. I have a business call to make."

"It's not your house. It's part of the estate. You live there due to my forbearance."

"I live there because Mother gave me the house."

"You have no paperwork."

This shut him up for a minute. "I believe her lawyer does. And you aren't moving me out of the house."

"I will be moving here when my house sells."

"Not until the estate is truly settled."

Back in the library, dogs flanking the fireplace, cats on the sofa, Harry handed the two framed prints to Jerry.

"What could this mean?"

Jerry read Percy Ballard's letter, concentration intense. "Let me get box 15. Letters from 1789 are in there."

He rose, went to the end of the large table, opened the safe as Dwayne handed him the key. Found 15 and carried it over. As he leafed through the papers, letters, he found May 20, 1789, pulled it out, and laid it next to the letter behind the lily. Jerry's face turned white.

"Jerry?" Harry moved closer, for it appeared he would fall over.

"Harry, give me the other drawing."

She handed him the sunflower drawing. Pulling a penknife, the kind used to cut pages, still popular in Europe, Jerry expertly slit the brown paper on the back of the sunflower drawing. He lifted it off. Using the tip of the penknife, he lifted up the paper. Careful about fingerprints, the grease from fingers, he turned it over. Harry and Dwayne both now stood next to him.

"It's the same," Harry exclaimed.

Jerry, face still shocked white, whispered, "I credited Candida's care with the excellent condition of the papers, even the inks. My God, what a fool I was."

Harry staring at the two May 20, 1789 letters, side by side, said, "The vellum looks old. The ink in the box papers looks newer. How could you or anyone tell?"

Intently examining the two letters, Jerry shook his head in disbelief. "Harry, the original letter is in great condition, but see, the ink is a bit faded compared to the letter that was in the box." He pointed to the first sentence of each letter.

"So what is in the box is a forgery?" Harry asked.

"Yes. A very, very good forgery. We may never know, but putting the original materials behind a print, thin cardboard covering it, then flicking down the small holders on the back of each frame, it's incredible. First off, the letter will be protected. Secondly, you can deliver the framed prints or mail them carefully boxed. Who would ever suspect such a thing?"

"I sure wouldn't," she admitted.

Jerry practically dropped in his chair. "Clyde must have figured it out." He then looked up at his two assistants. "Someone has been forging these letters and selling the originals, and whoever has been selling the Ballard papers killed him. I've been blind." Jerry, overcome with despair, put his head in his hands.

"You couldn't have known. They look identical. Even the handwriting is almost the same." Dwayne tried to comfort him.

"A skillful forger or artist could have duplicated the different handwritings. Especially if he used a quill for the earlier papers. You can buy a quill today, a good one, for about twenty dollars. This May 20 letter was written with a quill, one with a sharp point. My God, a man is dead."

"Two men are dead, Jerry. Ben Wagner. Calligraphy. Who else could it be and who knew? Candida? She wouldn't be selling her papers. I can't believe she would." Harry then paused. "The ketamine on the floor at Nancy Parson's. To throw us all off."

Just then Constance strode into the library followed by Ballard.

"Don't give him one paper!"

"I don't want one paper. I want to sell all the papers. Constance, this place will fall apart or be sold and to whom? A dot-com billionaire? Would such a person care about our history?"

As Ballard protested, Constance looked down at the two papers. "What's this?"

"We've found an irregularity." Jerry sounded normal.

The two dogs came to sit behind Harry, still standing. The cats jumped on the end of the long table, not near the papers.

Mrs. Murphy alerted Pirate, who had the best chance of protecting Harry thanks to his size. *"One of these two is a killer."*

"What do you mean you've found an irregularity?" Ballard bent over to look at the two letters. "They're the same. Hey?"

"As I said, we've found an irregularity. We'll have to carbon date the vellum and the parchment, as well as the inks. As you can see from this paper, the one in box 15, the ink is brighter, slightly, than what was behind the lily drawing."

"What do you mean behind the drawing?" Ballard was shocked.

As Jerry began to explain, Constance stepped over to examine. "They look identical."

"One is a forgery and I think it's the one in the box," Jerry calmly stated.

Harry should have shut up but her curiosity always got the better of her. "Could your mother have been selling the originals to make money?"

"Mother would never do that. Ballard would." Constance turned on him. "I'll hand it to you, brother, damnably clever."

"I'm not that clever, but you are, sister dear. Now it makes sense to me. The new car. Angling to get back into the house, putting yours on the market."

"Idiot," Constance spat at him.

"You fooled Mother, you fooled me. Did you use ketamine to kill her? Was she getting close to figuring out what you were up to?" Ballard moved toward her.

That fast Constance grabbed Jerry's penknife, swooped behind her brother, pulling his arm up behind him as she pointed the penknife, small but sharp, at his throat. Cool, brilliant, arrogant, Ballard was the one person who could shake her.

"Constance, put the knife down." Dwayne pulled his Glock handgun.

"You use that and I'll slit his throat. I can do it, you know."

Harry, stunned, stood still.

"You all stay where you are. I am taking this worthless oxygen thief to a better place." As she slowly hauled him back, he nearly tripped.

Harry, heedless of danger, came around the table to walk in front of Ballard.

"Harry, get back here," the sheriff's officer commanded.

"She'll slit his throat."

"If she does, she has no protection. She won't kill him now. Get back."

Constance swept the knife toward Harry but kept Ballard's arm up behind him.

That fast Harry dodged it. Pirate leapt for the woman, hitting her with his weight as Tucker grabbed her ankle. Mrs. Murphy bit the other ankle and Pewter clawed the back of Constance's leg, drawing blood.

Dwayne, gun in hand, came alongside Constance, still dragging her brother, whose throat was bleeding from the sharp knife even though she hadn't plunged it into him.

"You can't get away with this," Dwayne counseled her as he told Jerry, "Call 911, Jerry. Now."

As Jerry picked up his cellphone, Harry and Dwayne followed Constance at a distance, the cats doing as much damage as they could and Tucker hanging on to her ankle. The Irish wolfhound kept slamming into her. She tried to stab the big animal then returned the knife to Ballard, who was terrified.

Harry said, "Constance, let him go. Give yourself up. If you explain everything, maybe your sentence will be lightened. If you kill him, it's all over."

"It's all over, anyway." Constance, rage overflowing, was beyond reason. "He got away with everything. Everything. She bailed him out over and over. The money she wasted on him. All I ever got was a wedding present. Mother said my husband would take care of me. Ballard had no one."

Ballard, silent, kept stepping back.

Tucker released Constance's ankle, stood behind her, and she tripped a bit backwards over the dog, the knife sliding across her brother's neck, cutting him but not killing him. Ballard fell forward clutching his throat.

Constance scrambled to her feet as Pirate joined Tucker in trying to push her over from behind.

"She'll hurt Harry. We've got to stop her," Tucker shouted.

As Constance felt the dogs behind her she did right herself and lunged for Harry. She wanted to hurt anyone she could. Harry jumped sideways as Dwayne fired the gun in the air. Didn't stop Constance, who moved to kick her brother while he was down.

Dwayne shot her in the leg. She kept going. He fired again, she lurched over, but kept moving toward Ballard.

"I'll kill you, Ballard. If it's the last thing I do, I'll kill you." She crawled for him and he, on his knees, moved away, blood running through his fingers on his throat.

The front door opened. "Dwayne!"

"In the library."

Cooper and Sheriff Shaw reached them. Coop tried to handcuff a fighting Constance. Sheriff Shaw had to help her.

"I'll never talk," was the last thing Constance said as they led her to the squad car.

Harry knelt down to inspect Ballard. "Don't worry. We'll get help."

"I never knew. I never even dreamed," he gasped before he sobbed, "she killed Mother."

42

November 22, 2019

Friday

Winter arrived this day. A hard frost greeted everyone in the morning and lowering skies promised snowflakes or more. Harry, Susan, Tazio, Jerry, Fair, Nancy, and Cooper had fired up the large potbelly stove in the primary school building. Both the building for grades nine through twelve and the primary building had been outfitted for electrical heat at hideous expense. Running it would cost less than a furnace and far less than baseboard heat, but at $7,000 each installation for two buildings with high ceilings, that was a big hit. The pumps sat outside, under shade trees in summer, and the air flowed into the buildings and out the carefully placed vents. Tazio especially didn't want the modern technology visible. To save on the electric bill, the group used the stove, which proved effective if one didn't have a desk in the back of the room. As most students sat according to alphabetical order that meant M's to Z's shivered without extra sweaters. Those closer to the front sweated. Still, it was pretty good if one wanted to keep warm.

Note—
We hold these
self-evident,
are created eq
endowed by th
certain unalien
these are Life,
rights
Living

Tazio didn't even want to turn on the electric lights, but given the gloominess of the day, she did. She was focused on experience as close to the former students as possible.

Jerry had brought more books. They now had a cache of reading books and arithmetic books from grades one through eight. There were some frayed edges and some marked pages, but in the main the books were serviceable.

"Thank the Lord a lot of this wasn't tossed out." Tazio held a seventh-grade arithmetic book.

Nancy flipped open a page. "They didn't fool around, did they? The beginnings of algebra are here, seventh grade."

Harry opened to the same page. "You're right."

"It was a different day in many ways. Parents expected their children to study, to be guided by teachers who knew them and knew the families. No excuses."

"Tazio, there had to be children with learning disabilities then," Susan said.

"They were called slow," Nancy offered. "Some were, but I expect most were dyslexic in some fashion. Others couldn't concentrate."

"That will never change." Fair smiled, as he'd always had trouble concentrating until he discovered he wanted to be a veterinarian and then he knuckled down.

"Isn't it sad that we now expect so little of our children? We're telling them they're dumb. Think about it." Jerry leaned back in the chair seat attached to his desk. "Those children were encouraged, maybe pushed, but they were told they were capable. Without education life would be hard. You earned that grade and if you fooled around, you were held back. Try doing that now."

"Hell, the lawyers would have a heyday with it." Tazio believed ardently in education, as she did not come from money but her parents were adamant she learn.

"Tazio, you're too young to have gone to segregated schools," Nancy observed.

"For which I am thankful but I grew up with many people, in my own family, too, who had gone to segregated schools. And you know what, no one believed more in education than they did. If I had sassed back or not done my homework, I would have been grounded." She smiled shyly. "A fate worse than death."

They all laughed, remembering how much they had liked to meet with their school friends, play on various school teams, and generally believe you were smarter than any adult around you.

"*Why do humans go to school?*" Pirate asked.

"*Because they're stupid.*" Pewter was ever ungenerous.

"*Some are.*" Mrs. Murphy swept her whiskers forward. "*But mostly it's because they don't use their senses. They don't trust them. If it isn't written out, they think it can't be true.*"

"*Well, they'll learn the hard way.*" Tucker put her head on her paws. "*Mother Nature always gets even.*"

"*That's the truth.*" Pewter felt vindicated.

As the small gathering had finished their placing books in desks, seeing to old-fashioned pencils and pencil sharpeners, they sat together recalling the dramatic events of the month.

"Coop, does anyone know how Constance jumped bail?" Nancy asked.

"She posted the three hundred thousand bail without a hitch. So being a woman, of course, not only was she let go, she was severely underestimated. We're pretty sure she had really good false documents in another name, like a passport and a driver's license. She thought ahead just in case."

"But they found her car at the Charlottesville airport." Nancy had read the papers.

"She had so much money . . . cash, I think . . . that she had to have paid someone to drive her wherever she was headed. The airport was a ruse. We wasted time there once her car was identified. Mexico. One can get over the border undetected to Mexico, just as one can get in here," Cooper filled them in. "She didn't fly from anywhere. Obviously the first thing we did once we knew she was gone was call the aviation department. Also Canadian border patrol, as well as our southwestern border. She had cash. Solves myriad problems, cash."

"Out of the bank? How could she make a huge withdrawal without people knowing?" Susan wondered.

"She didn't touch her money here except for bail. That reduced her account a lot. We can't prove anything, but both Sheriff Shaw and I, as well as most of the department, feel she had a few million in cash, if not much more. She had a safe at her home. She'd really thought of most possibilities. She believed she could get away with selling the papers, the fakes replacing the real stuff, but just in case she had a backup plan. The woman was brilliant."

Harry nodded. "She had her mother's brains."

"And hid them well enough." Jerry held a book in his hands but didn't open it. "The difference being, Candida wasn't a thief and a murderess."

"Jerry, I like that. *Murderess*. You don't hear that anymore." Harry smiled at him.

"Oh dear." He wrinkled his brow.

"We don't care," Susan consoled him. "We all know one another too well. Even if you say *actress*, we don't care."

"You know," Jerry's voice sounded soft, "I don't know what to say anymore. I guess some people feel *ess* is diminishing or too gender specific."

"You always say the right thing. Tell us how she did it." Fair liked Jerry a great deal, respecting his acumen, and wished to ease his discomfort.

"Let me start with the vellum and the parchment." His voice rose a bit. "Parchment was used for the very earliest correspondence in the library, the mid-seventeenth-century papers. Parchment, if cared for, can last more than a thousand years. So something from the 1600s is relatively modern if you think of it. Vellum was used more, it's a bit lighter. Vellum can last millennia also, if properly stored. Many people used the two words as indistinguishable. They really aren't. Parchment is often goatskin, whereas vellum can be calfskin. Well, when I pulled the two boxes that Candida had knocked over as she died, I was dealing mostly with paper, wood fibers. It was of excellent heavy quality and stored to preserve it. I didn't notice anything amiss, although the ink was dark." He held up his hand. "It could be the original, as inks, expensive inks, do hold their hue. We won't know until everything is carbon-dated. Absolutely everything. Armored trucks took the papers away to the lab. A true lab, and all must be guarded, put into temperature-controlled safes; a big safe, big as a bank. You won't believe what must be done."

"Carbon-dated?" Cooper repeated the term. "I am a deputy, not a forensic law officer, but I remember from college that a carbon half life is 5,730 years. After that only half the original amount of carbon remains in original material. Parchment, vellum, and paper are organic."

Fair—after all, a veterinarian is a scientist—remarked, "The process has become so sophisticated. They will be able to determine when those papers were written. I guess what is really at issue is how much did she manage to sell?"

"My hunch is, knowing a bit about value, that she sold the papers around the Revolutionary War and the Civil War first. Carefully, over the last two years, I suspect. Usually I hear a collector bias, but not this time. She didn't have time to do all the papers, which would take her years. Then again, as she believed she would wind up with Lone Pine, she figured she had years. Who would ever suspect her of stealing from herself?" Jerry rubbed his finger over the old clothbound schoolbook. "As to the ink, a recent ink, say from the last two centuries, would be water-based and contain solvents. Earlier inks were also usually made from organic materials ground into a fine powder, the same as Michelangelo's paints. So they, too, should be able to be dated with a fair degree of accuracy. Same with the line of the writing. Quill writing is almost like italicized writing in a way, the nibs being so versatile and having to be sharpened. This changes letter thickness as the nib wears down. Hence the sharpening. Some quills had metal nibs, but that fell by the wayside after

1827, when pens as we now know them were invented, a wood base or some material and a metal nib, gold being the most useful. Think of a Diplomat, a Montblanc 149. They've had incredible gold nibs since 1906. Of course, other brands also use a gold nib, like Pelican, but Montblanc remains the pinnacle if one likes to write with ink, real ink. The Germans make the best pens. Japan and Italy also produce good instruments. We are far behind."

"I take it you want the best." Tazio smiled at him.

"Am I being a snob?" He laughed at himself.

"No, just a man with a strong aesthetic component." Harry meant that. "My mother used to say, 'Buy the best then you only cry once.'"

"Wish I had known your mother." Tazio returned to pens. "Mostly I have to use Rapidographs. Yes, I know, I can draft on the computer and I do, but for me, when I'm working a design out or struggling with a difficult site, Rapidographs, then when I figure it out, I go to the computer. Well, got off the track. The real question is, where did she go and did she kill her mother?"

"We have no idea where she fled to. She either was driven down into South America, say Argentina or Chile, or she hired an ocean-going yacht to take her to Europe," Cooper answered.

"Won't those countries send her back if they find her?" Harry asked.

"Well, Harry, the Italians have been handling money since before France was France. Who is to say where she will go? She'll have a great fake passport, possibly one from where she intends to land. Obviously she has been sending the money from the sales offshore. Where? Could be Switzerland, although they would have to report it to the United States." Cooper shrugged. "Or maybe she bought a fabulous dacha in Russia and will live like a queen. She'll be safe there."

Nancy, having come upon Clyde Mercador, returned to murder. "Do you think she killed Clyde?"

"Yes." Cooper nodded. "And Ben. Obviously we can't prove anything, but once Ben realized how much these papers were worth, and him doing such a great job on the fakes, he probably wanted more money. A lot more. She had to have worn-thin rubber surgical gloves and probably some form of footwear with a smooth bottom. No prints. She got out the back way. That we do know, as there were some almost vanished tire tracks behind the barn. I had to sync up with her car once we knew where that was and knew she'd escaped. We missed a lot. I hate to admit it. No one suspected her. No one."

"Ben seemed like such a nice guy." Fair was puzzled.

"Nice guys can be crooks." Susan sighed. "Add in money, a lot of money, few people can stick to higher ethics."

"Money cleanses all sins, right?" Tazio shook her head. "Well, what I wonder is, did she kill her mother? She certainly had the way to do it and make it seem natural."

"Ketamine. Easy to administer, put it in a drink. Obviously, Candida wouldn't be snorting it, nor would Constance have given her a shot with a needle. But putting a lethal dose in a drink, removing the glass or cup. Pretty easy. And Candida was cremated. Constance can justify it by saying Candida had lived a long, long life and she always favored Ballard. Constance needed money, a great deal of money, to take over Lone Pine."

"Yes, but that means Candida realized some of the papers were forged. She had to. Why kill her otherwise?" Harry believed this.

"True. But how long could Constance hang on, whether Candida realized the theft or not? That's another fact we'll probably never know. I don't believe Constance will be caught. What is a couple of hundred thousand dollars now? Bail was chicken feed." Cooper accepted that crime really does pay, despite protestations to the opposite.

"How is Ballard, by the way?" Harry asked.

"Can you imagine? On top of everything else he has to get the papers authenticated. I wonder if he'll sell the rest?" Tazio felt badly for him.

"Depends on the insurance policy on Lone Pine. Does it cover the archives?" Jerry had thought of this. "If it does, Ballard can keep it all going. If not, I expect he will have to sell what is legitimate if he wants to hold on to the estate."

"I hope he doesn't sell Lone Pine." Harry loved the estate.

"We all hope that," Susan agreed. "Now that he knows what has happened, I can't imagine he would sell the papers that are legitimate."

"Well, here we are. Oh, Jerry, can you fake parchment or vellum?" Nancy wondered.

"Not with carbon-dating, but you can fool the naked eye. One can make the skins look older, say if you bought fresh vellum or parchment, which you can. Same with paper. Fairly easy to age. You can heat parchment a bit or even put it in direct sunlight. Ben had to have done all that work. I can't imagine Constance doing it."

"Did she steal the ketamine?" Fair still felt upset over the stuff being taken from his truck.

"Easy to take from Ben's new clinic. Pretty easy to take from a vet truck parked with the vet inside a building. She had opportunities to get what she wanted, to confuse us by putting some back and eventually to frame her brother. Who would even think to consider her?" Cooper knew now that Constance was unrestrained in exploiting an opportunity. She was a bold person.

"Well, she got away with it, with millions." Harry closed the seventh-grade book. "Since justice can't be served, do we hope for karma?"

"The only difference I can see between justice and revenge is justice is legal revenge. Society needs that, otherwise anger and uprising is always possible," Susan answered her old friends. "That's why people say 'karma.' They don't believe the culprit will ever serve, and if rich will almost always get off, so we delude ourselves into thinking they will suffer at the hands of a higher force. They don't suffer. They have no conscience. I ought to know. My husband serves in the House of Delegates."

"An awful thought, but I expect it's true," Tazio rejoined. "So if there is ever justice, true justice, we take it into our own hands."

"Yes." Susan looked to Harry. "You're the Smith graduate. What does history tell you? I know you couldn't slide away from that when you were there."

"Well, not so much history as the Greek tragedies. Think of the Furies, the Eumenides. They torment and punish Orestes for killing his mother, so I figure that's a form of vengeance that goes back to matriarchy. Athena comes down and saves him, essentially saying that people must now live by laws not blood revenge, et cetera. So she gives the Furies or Eumenides a high place in the firmament of Athenian honor and they agree, so they become the 'Beloved Ones.' If you think about it, it's not a bad beginning for the rule of law; patriarchal, of course, but still an improvement over blood law. We all know that laws can be corrupted, unequally applied, and so forth, but we still believe in something higher than blood law." She held up her hands. "Nothing changes, you know that, only the clothes."

Pirate, hearing that, asked Tucker, a more reliable source than Pewter, although Mrs. Murphy was pretty good: *"Why do people wear clothes?"*

"No fur," came the terse reply. *"We are always well dressed."*

Pewter popped off, *"Our parts don't sag. They need clothing."*

"Horses get swaybacked," Mrs. Murphy said.

"We aren't horses." She changed the subject. *"Here they are jabbering about Constance and the murders. Well, who figured it out? I did,"* Pewter boasted.

Careful not to start a fight because Harry would reprimand them in front of the others, Mrs. Murphy replied, *"You knocked the painting off the tack room wall. That's what set them off. Of course, she couldn't smell the old animal skin. You, however, have an excellent nose."*

"Smelled it on the military uniform prints, too." Pewter puffed out her gray chest.

"Bet she took that with her," Tucker thought out loud. *"She wouldn't have had time to sell the stuff, I don't think."*

"Unless this has been going on for some time. Whoever or however many people she sold to sent money to a foreign account. She was clever, very clever." Mrs. Murphy got up to rub against Harry's leg. *"Also, the buyers don't want to be*

caught even if they didn't know Constance stole the stuff. They had to have known something was off. Clearly she swore everyone to secrecy. Using Ballard as her foil, of course."

"So people will be upset? I mean, the killer doesn't pay." Pirate was getting it.

"They will," Mrs. Murphy agreed with him. "They need to believe their laws work. And the laws of one country are usually different than the laws of another. So who is right? Makes them crazy."

"Ah," was all Pirate could say.

"Don't worry about it, Pirate. Go along with whatever Harry says. She's relatively smart for a human . . . but never forget she is human." Pewter moved a little closer to the stove. "She's not so bad, but humans think they can control Nature."

"To some extent they can," Tucker said.

"No they can't," Pewter snapped back. "All they can do is pervert it."

"Ah well." Mrs. Murphy pondered this. "The human animal doesn't change, but the times do."

"Is that why they have face-lifts? Because they don't want to change? They can't change? Gravity will get them." Pirate really was growing up.

"Oh, I don't think they need plastic surgery." Pewter smiled seraphically. "They need taxidermy."

Harry listened to this chatter then said, "I wonder what they're saying?"

"No, you don't." Tucker, who loved Harry, laughed with the rest of them.

ACKNOWLEDGMENTS

Anne Bonda Hartman, DVM, showed me the bill for her new portable X-ray machine. Costs as much as a new Toyota. Factor in ultrasound equipment, computer setups, medications, operating rooms, layup stalls, and on and on, well, the next time you see your equine vet, be impressed.

Her time spent with me was a big help in understanding clinic costs and setups.

Jerry Showalter really does know everything about collections, book values, and even ephemera. He delights me as he does so many. Just had to put him in the book.

Nancy Parsons, owner of Country House Antiques, sparked the idea for this volume. We engaged in a wonderful chat about the National Sporting Library, and the lightbulb turned on. Then again, Nancy is so engaging she could get anyone thinking.

I thank them all.

I do not thank my house cats and dogs. The cats, in particular, nosed around my pages, getting things out of order. The last thing any writer needs in the house is a critic.

P.S. Jenn Dungan did a great job typing this manuscript. My cats would like to visit her office to desecrate same.

Dear Reader,

Well, the animals led the way. Mrs. Murphy, Pewter, Tucker, and Pirate are smarter than the humans. I readily confess my animals are smarter than I am.

Usually I tie the eighteenth-century storyline to the twenty-first. Percy Ballard is ancestor to the twenty-first-century Ballards, but that's it for a tie-in.

Given that Bastille Day is on the horizon, I decided not to include July. The prelude to the mass death in Europe was a time of uncertainty here. Also, what was about to happen was incomprehensible. We severed our ties with Great Britain. France severed heads, only to descend into Hell. Jefferson and others believing democracy would be established in France is understandable. They underestimated the difference between a former colony and a nation entrenched in monarchy for centuries.

Our economic life, our military preparedness, focused our attention until the news arrived after July 14. Our economic life took a blow but we quickly recovered.

Better I start the next Mrs. Murphy mystery with that moment than try to address it here. The book would be huge.

While I am not writing historical fiction or history proper, I can't ignore it. Just can't. I promise that in the next volume our Cloverfields characters and others will be swept up in ways surprising to them, in terms of both politics and personal life.

May you all be in good health and your four-footed friends also.

Yours,

Rita Mae Brown

Dear Reader,
Me. Me. Me. I solved everything.

Your star,

Dear Reader,

Pewter thinks the world started when she came into it. Take it with a grain of salt.

Yours truly,

Dear Reader,
I could throw up.

In truth,

Dear Reader,

I am learning to write. I am not good at this. All I really want is a cookie.

A big woof,

ABOUT THE AUTHORS

Rita Mae Brown has written many bestsellers and received two Emmy nominations. In addition to the Mrs. Murphy series, she has authored a dog series comprised of *A Nose for Justice* and *Murder Unleashed*, and the Sister Jane foxhunting series, among many other acclaimed books. She and Sneaky Pie live with several other rescued animals.

ritamaebrownbooks.com

To inquire about booking Rita Mae Brown for a speaking engagement, please contact the Penguin Random House Speakers Bureau at speakers@penguinrandomhouse.com.

Sneaky Pie Brown, a tiger cat rescue, has written many mysteries—witness the list at the front of the novel. Having to share credit with the above-named human is a small irritant, but she manages it. Anything is better than typing, which is what "Big Brown" does for the series. Sneaky calls her human that name behind her back, after the wonderful Thoroughbred racehorse. As her human is rather small, it brings giggles among the other animals. Sneaky's main character—Mrs. Murphy, a tiger cat—is a bit sweeter than Miss Pie, who can be caustic.

ABOUT THE TYPE

This book was set in Joanna, a typeface designed in 1930 by Eric Gill (1882–1940). Named for his daughter, this face is based on designs originally cut by the sixteenth-century typefounder Robert Granjon (1513–1589). With small, straight serifs and its simple elegance, this face is notably distinguished and versatile.